About the Author

David Clarkson grew up in the North East of England, where he studied English Literature at the University of Sunderland. One day, following a drunken challenge from a friend, he bought a one-way ticket to Australia and spent the following three years travelling the world. Upon his return, he struggled to adapt to a normal life and sought solace in his own overactive imagination, where he remains to this day.

To learn more about his writing and what inspires him, you can visit his website at:

www.davidclarksonwriter.com

THE OUTBACK

This book is dedicated to Katie, without whose patience, love and support it would never have been possible.

The author would like to thank Andrew Park for looking at an early draft and for providing invaluable feedback, which has helped make this novel what it is today.

Prologue

The game had ended only hours earlier. His teammates were seated around a table at the back of the tavern rejoicing in their triumph. Not one of them looked over. They were each too self-absorbed to notice that their star player had quietly slipped away. So far as she could tell, she had his undivided attention.

'What time do you finish work tonight?' he asked; the intimate implication of the question bringing colour to her cheeks.

Working at the bar, she had been privy to much gossip about girls going with footballers. The rumours were not at all flattering for the young ladies in question, but this was different. She was different. The girls people spoke of were easy, but he would be able to tell she was not like that. She did not have one night stands. She had never even had a serious boyfriend.

'The bar closes at eleven sharp,' she told him. 'But with the time it takes to clean up and put everything away for the night it can be close to midnight by the time I get away.'

He took another sip from his drink. Every action that he

performed was precise, controlled and calculated. Those intense, dark eyes of his, penetrated deep into her being.

'That gives us plenty of time.' he assured her. 'The summer nights are long. Maybe you could come back to a party at my place after you finish work. By midnight things should be warming up just nicely.'

A shudder ran through her body as if he had reached out and tickled her spine. Despite going over this conversation in her head a dozen times it was proceeding more quickly than she ever imagined. The last thing she wanted was to come across as too eager, too keen. It was important that he respected her. She was not sure if it would be considered acceptable to go back to his place so soon.

'Are you sure that you want me there? I mean, I wouldn't want to come between you and your friends.'

He addressed her concern with his most reassuring smile.

'Lots of the guys have girlfriends,' he said. 'Trust me. You won't be intruding at all.'

To be mentioned in the same breath as his teammate's girlfriends was all the encouragement she needed. She took it as proof beyond doubt that his intentions toward her were noble.

'I guess I could maybe drop by for a short while,' she said. 'Would you be able to pick me up?'

'It's a date,' he replied.

After finishing his drink, he bought a replacement and joined his friends at their table. They all stayed until last orders and collectively consumed more beer than the bar would normally sell in a week. Glasses were raised, songs were sung and everybody had a great time.

Despite the rowdiness of the group, there was one, however, who kept his composure throughout the night. He also kept to his promise and waited behind for his date to finish her shift after his companions left.

'I have a feeling that tonight will be unforgettable for both of us,' he told her, as she picked up her coat.

The only response that she could muster was a giggle. As they left the bar with their arms interlocked, one of his teammates fell into step alongside of them. She thought nothing of it as they would all be at the party together anyway. What she did not realise was that there was not going to be a party. These two drunken young men, to whom she had placed her trust, had something altogether different planned. Even they, however, could not have known that they were about to kick start a chain of events that would ultimately lead to murder.

Chapter 1

For the first time since leaving home he was genuinely lost. He had been away for a little under nine months and the time had passed quickly; too quickly. In order to keep the adventure going he had been left with just one option. Three months was the commitment he had made. Three months without beer, women and even fun; who knew?

Not Matt, that was for sure. He stood still whilst a throng of people moved around him. They were all in a hurry to get to wherever it was they were going. Everyone seemed to know exactly where they needed to be. Everyone, that is, except him.

'Harro, you go Ber'bandi?'

Matt turned to find himself facing a diminutive Japanese man. The speaker wore a chequered shirt and black skinny jeans held up with a metal studded belt. A soft guitar case was slung over his shoulder, leaving him to lazily drag his backpack along the floor behind him. The look was topped off with a red neckerchief and cowboy hat. If Kurosawa had made westerns, this would be his leading man.

'Yes,' replied Matt. 'I am going to Birribandi.'

He kept his speech slow and precise so that he would not

have to repeat himself. It was not the first conversation he had shared with a non-native speaker of English.

The stranger smiled before reaching into a pocket of his jeans from which he retrieved a small folded slip of paper. Matt already knew what information the note would hold before it was offered to him.

'Are you going for the harvest work?' he asked.

The Asian nodded with enthusiasm. He may not have possessed a great degree of skill with words, but his body language provided a more than adequate compensatory factor.

'I am Hiro,' he said.

Again, the image of the cowboy appeared to Matt; the valiant loner who rides into town to save the day.

'My name is Matt. I am from England.'

'Ah, Ingreesh. Very cold.'

Hiro wrapped his arms around himself, but the mime was not required. This was not the first time the reputation of Matt's homeland had preceded itself in this way and nor did he think it would be the last. He hoped others would soon arrive as he realised that he would have few insightful conversations with the Japanese man. Luckily for him, the two of them were soon joined by a pair of fellow travellers headed the same way.

One of the newcomers was short with unkempt dark hair and a plump, baby face. The other was taller and a few years older. He had a clean-shaven scalp and a countenance etched with experience. His skin was pale and he possessed impossibly green eyes bordered by crow's feet that were like bird prints in the snow. It was this second man who was to break the ice.

'Now there's a pair of stick pickers if ever I saw them. I take it you two boys are heading out for the harvest work.'

His accent was warm, relaxed and instantly recognisable to Matt.

'I'm guessing that makes four of us now. You're from Ireland, right?'

'Does the Pope wear a silly hat?'

For the first time that morning, Matt allowed himself to smile. The backpacker trail had introduced him to many people and he had become adept at gauging if he was likely to have anything in common with somebody from just the opening lines of a conversation. He felt an instant chemistry with this man. The journey ahead no longer seemed quite so intimidating.

He chose to initiate the introductions as he knew his original companion would be out of his depth in a group conversation.

'This is Hiro and I'm Matt.' he said.

'I'm Colin and your man here is Jonas; he's from Germany.'

There was something about the way the man spoke that simply invited mischief. Matt was keen to establish a repartee in order to calm his nerves regarding the journey ahead.

'Are you two a couple?' he cheekily asked.

'It's purely platonic so feel free to ask him out if you're looking for a boyfriend,' the other man replied, with comfortable ease.

'He's not my type so I'll have to pass on that.'

'I suspected as much. Once you've had Asian, you'll never want Caucasian.'

Colin suggestively nodded in the direction of Hiro. It was clear that if required he could continue the verbal rally for as long as it took for him to achieve the last word. Matt knew he could never win, but he had already taken what he wanted from the conversation. He had established a potential friend.

'Okay, I give up,' he conceded. 'So do you know much about this place where we're all headed?'

'I know its name and that it's full of sticks that need picking, but beyond that nothing. I have always preferred it that way. Life would be no fun without the surprises.'

'Maybe,' said Matt, a tad uneasily.

Colin chuckled.

'You're terrified, aren't you?'

Matt thought about telling a lie, but sometimes the truth, no matter how embarrassing, can be more productive.

'Completely,' he said. 'I mean, do any of us even know what this place is going to be like? I've heard stories that make some of these places sound no better than prison camps.'

'So why are you here?'

This was a question Matt had asked himself many times. He had joined the backpacker trail to have fun. It did not disappoint him. Casual sex, alcohol and cheap drugs were all easy to come by. The problem was that he was running out of time. His choice was simple. He could return to England and join the dole queue or spend three months doing harvest work in the outback to get another year added to his Australian visa. It was hardly a choice at all when he thought about it.

'Let's just say that I'm not ready to go home just yet,' he said. 'I've got no qualifications and from what my friends tell me, I'd struggle finding a job even if I had. There's nothing but an empty bank account and daytime television waiting for me back in England. That doesn't mean I'm happy about what we've all signed up to though. Do any of us even know what fruit we'll be picking?'

'I was told we'd be "stick picking",' replied Colin.

'What kind of fruit are sticks?'

'Who knows; sugar canes? The point is that we all get another year of partying in the sun at the end of it.'

Matt nodded, although nothing had really changed. He was still apprehensive about what lay ahead. Colin had merely

11

reinforced his conviction that another year in paradise was worth the sacrifice.

As the quartet continued to get to know one another a coach pulled into the berth opposite them. Its sides looked to be rusted through, but on closer inspection it could be seen that this was merely the iron rich dust of the outback clinging to its bodywork like a cheap spray tan.

An inspector dismounted and walked around to the side of the coach where he opened a large luggage compartment. He had no sooner raised the door, when a swarm of people began to haphazardly deposit their belongings into the newly revealed cargo hold. Being the least prepared, the backpackers were pushed to one side and found themselves at the back of the line. Until then, Matt did not even notice that so many passengers were waiting for the same service.

'Tickets for Birribandi,' the inspector called.

The crowd arranged themselves into an orderly queue, allowing Matt a better chance to look at them. He presumed from their ages and style of dress that they were all local to the destination. Half of them were Aboriginal and several had kids in tow. Their faces contained none of the fear or apprehension that those of the travellers did. They were merely going home.

Matt was the first of the foreigners to take his place on board the coach. He chose a window seat near the front as those at the rear had already been filled by families with noisy children. This was his first long distance coach trip and the last thing he wanted was to have a baby screaming in his ear for seven hours.

'Do you mind if I join you?' asked Colin, who was the next to board.

'Be my guest,' Matt told him.

He had never experienced such a long journey outside of an aeroplane, and without the benefit of in-flight entertainment he was glad to have some company to while away the hours.

'I cannot stand these inland journeys,' Colin said, as he took his seat. 'Every time you look out the window the view is identical; blue at the top and red at the bottom. You can travel five hundred miles, but feel like you're standing still.'

'Have you done this before then?' asked Matt.

'What, travel on a bus? Haven't we all?'

Rather than being rude, the Irishman's sarcasm was quite endearing. His enunciation was so laid back as to make the natives appear uptight. In Australia, this was no easy feat.

'I mean the outback,' added Matt. 'What's it like?'

'The scale of it is mind boggling, but you soon get used to it. It's the place where the centre of the universe overlaps with the outer edges of civilisation. Provided you can live without a few home comforts, you may even start to like it.'

Matt was pleased to discover that his neighbour had experience in this type of environment. There were a number of concerns he wished to resolve and he believed Colin would be the one to reassure him.

'Have you ever had any trouble when you've been in the bush? I mean, it's hardly the safest environment known to man, is it?'

A knowing smile appeared on the other man's face.

'Let me guess; you're worried about spiders and snakes, right?'

Matt shrugged. If the question was that obvious then surely the concern was justified. Everybody knew that the Australian Outback contained some of the deadliest creatures on the planet and he wanted to know which, if any, of these he was likely to face.

'Did a spider ever bite you back home?' asked Colin.

'Well, no, of course not.'

'So why do you think one would want to bite you over here?'

He had a point, but Matt knew it was not that simple.

'What about the snakes?'

Colin could do nothing to conceal a wry smile.

'I've done my fair share of tours throughout this country. I've been to the Top End, Western Australia and Uluru in the centre. At every one of these places the local tourist board goes to great lengths to reassure everyone that any threats that concern them are completely unjustified.'

'So it's all a myth then?'

'Not exactly; Australia is home to all ten of the world's most venomous snakes, but that doesn't necessarily mean they're the most dangerous.'

This was hardly the most convincing argument Matt had ever heard. He hoped there was more to it than that.

'That's like saying that the ocean is made up of water, but that doesn't necessarily mean that it's wet.'

This time Colin's smile opened into a small chuckle.

'Are you a mathematician or something?' he asked.

'No; why do you ask?' replied Matt, somewhat perplexed.

'You seem a little too focused on statistics that's all. Let me explain it the way your man told it to us on the tour. An Asian cobra will kill a man just as soon as look at him. It is responsible for more deaths per year than every snake breed in Australia put together, yet the strength of its venom doesn't even rank it in the top twenty of the world's most deadly. Snakes here may have the venom, but they're not aggressive. Besides, most of them have fangs too short to even penetrate your clothes. You'd be a fool to worry about them.'

This was exactly what Matt wanted to hear. He thought that if he kept Colin talking he would only receive more and more assurances that there was nothing for him to fear.

'So the snakes here are chilled out is what you're basically saying?'

'Pretty much, yeah. The only exceptions are the taipan and the death adder. Ever come across either of those and you're a dead man for sure.'

'But there isn't much chance of that, right?'

'No; not much. They're pretty rare everywhere apart from central Queensland.'

'We're headed to central Queensland.'

'Like I said; it's pointless worrying.'

Matt was beginning to wish he had quit whilst he was ahead.

'What do you mean "pointless worrying"? Is it pointless because I won't see any or pointless because there'll be nothing I can do about it if I do?'

Colin ignored the question. Instead, he put a set of earphones into place and reclined back into his seat with a triumphant grin on his face. Once again, his mischief making had proven successful. The journey was going to take seven hours, and for Matt, each and every one would be filled with the terror of wondering what horrors awaited him at the end of the road. He was headed into the outback and there was no turning back.

Chapter 2

The coach arrived at its destination just after sunset. Main Street was deserted, but Matt could not imagine it ever being otherwise. He could make out just two recognisable businesses; a hardware store and grocers. The other buildings all appeared nondescript except for the town hall and what was possibly a contender for the title of the world's smallest police station.

Despite being one of the first to dismount, Matt had to wait a short while to retrieve his backpack. The conductor opened the luggage compartment from the other side of the coach so even though Matt's bag had been one of the last ones on it was still at the rear of the pile. This meant that he had to stand aside and wait for the mob to clear away before he could get to it.

Once they had collected their belongings the locals soon shuffled off to their homes or wherever it was they were headed. This left behind four very confused backpackers, although they were now technically migrant workers, which did not sound quite so appealing.

After the coach left, the group endured several tense

minutes of waiting on the deserted sidewalk until a medium sized bus pulled up alongside of them. Its bodywork was completely white and a thick bull-bar over the front grille lent it a military like bearing. Peering through the windows revealed that the interior furnishings had been stripped to the bare basics, in some cases even exposing the metal framework underneath the seats making it harsh and uninviting.

The driver of the bus was a heavily set man who looked to be in his early to mid-sixties. He bore no uniform or nametags so it was impossible for the group to discern who he was or where he had come from. Leaving the engine running, the driver applied the handbrake and stepped off to greet the new arrivals.

'Welcome to Birribandi,' he said. 'My name is Joe. I run the local caravan park and I will also be your employer for the next three months.'

His accent was English, but his copper coloured, leathery skin suggested he had spent a long time living in Queensland's punishing climate. He directed the four travellers onto the bus, where they were careful to choose the least worn seats for fear of sustaining an injury. They were each too apprehensive to start a conversation.

The vehicle slowly pulled away and headed out of town. After about five minutes it took a detour from the main road and soon brought them to the caravan park.

'This is the oasis in the desert that you'll be calling home for the foreseeable future,' Joe said, as he brought the bus to rest.

Matt counted more than a dozen small caravans. They had all fallen into varying states of disrepair and it was impossible to ascertain which were in use and which were available as none emitted any interior lights or signs of movement. If they had Butlins in Beirut this is how Matt would imagine it to be.

'Do we get to choose which we want?' he asked.

Joe stood and turned to address the group from the front of the bus.

'Numbers one to three are already taken. You lot will take vans four and five, as it is more economical to share. All of the vacant vans have had the mains disconnected so don't get any ideas about switching once I've gone.'

He spoke with weariness in his voice, which suggested that he had conducted this orientation many, many times before.

'I take it that they aren't en-suite,' said Colin.

'There are toilets and a shower block on site,' replied Joe. 'The hot water doesn't last long though, so if you're selfish everyone will suffer. There is also a dining room where you will be provided with an evening meal and can buy alcohol at weekends. Do you have any questions?'

'How much do we have to pay for all of this?' Matt asked.

Joe had eight eyes fixed firmly upon him as he addressed the question of cost. Matt guessed he was not the only one who had entered into this endeavour with only a vague understanding of the figures involved. Like him, the others would have found the prospect of an extra year on their visas to be a far greater lure than any financial incentive.

'The accommodation and meals will be automatically taken from your wages, which will leave you with $90 a day to take home. The beer comes out of your own pocket and I suggest that you all drink responsibly. It's expected you'll want a relaxing drink or two after work, but save the heavier sessions for the weekend, okay.'

Joe made sure to establish eye contact with each person in turn when stating the point about the alcohol.

'So we do get the weekends off?' asked Matt.

'Depending on how productive you are during the week, you may have to work some Saturdays. Sunday will always be free though.' He paused for a moment whilst considering how to best phrase what he had to say next. 'I won't lie to you and tell you that the work is not going to be tough – it is, but everyone will get sufficient time to rest between shifts. I can promise you all that.'

'I think that's us sorted then,' said Colin. 'If you've not got anything else to tell us I'm happy to start settling in.'

Jonas was first off the bus and he immediately went to look over the caravans. He found that they all lacked one feature, which was an immediate cause for concern.

'There are no locks on these vans. Where do we store our valuable stuff?'

Joe was in the process of removing everyone's bags from the bus and he did not stop whilst answering the question.

'I recommend that you keep your wallets and passports on you at all times, but everything else will be fine. There are no thieves in this town. If you need anything else just give me a call. My contact number is written on the evacuation plans in each of the vans. For now though, I will wish you all good luck and expect to see you again sharp and early on Monday morning.'

He got back onto the bus and drove away. Colin picked up his bag and walked past Jonas to enter the next available van. Since Matt was yet to establish any kind of relationship with the German he followed Colin.

There were two beds and Colin had already claimed his by placing his backpack upon it. As the Irishman began to unpack, Matt noticed that his bag contained a large amount of what looked suspiciously like weed. It was easy for him to guess at how his new roommate planned to get through the next three months.

After taking a seat on the other bed, Matt removed his mobile phone from his pocket and checked for a signal. Not a single reception bar was showing.

'Is yours dead too?' asked Colin, picking up on his disappointment.

Matt nodded. He supposed it was too much to hope that his phone would have coverage in such a remote location.

'I guess technology is pretty useless here,' he said.

'You just have to look at the positives,' replied Colin. 'I don't have a watch so I'll still use mine as a clock and the camera always comes in handy. Nothing is ever useless unless you allow it to be.'

'That's all very well; I only wish I hadn't topped it up with $100 worth of credit yesterday.'

He had only been in town for five minutes and already he had made a rookie mistake.

'I'm guessing you only have a certain time limit to use your credit before you lose it,' said Colin.

'Three months,' replied Matt.

His new roommate laughed. Not to be patronising or condescending, but simply because he found it funny. Matt wondered if it was a bad omen. He looked around for an excuse that he could later use as a get-out clause should he wish to take an early retirement from the harvest industry. The caravan held many options.

'If it rains, I'm out of here,' he said, pulling away a sheet of cardboard by his bed to reveal a gaping hole. 'This place isn't even watertight.'

'You'll soon change your tune. After a week in the field you'll be praying for rain to come and give you a day off work.'

'Are you kidding me? Judging by what we saw on the way in I doubt there would be much to do around here at the height of summer never mind on a rainy day.'

Colin sighed.

'If that's your opinion why did you come here in the first place?'

That was a question Matt was beginning to ask himself with increasing regularity.

'I already told you; three months of hell is a fair trade off to get another year on my visa.'

'Well, just remember that those two out there haven't got advanced language skills and therefore don't have the luxury of being able to take a high paying office job in Sydney or Melbourne. They're here out of necessity, not luxury, so it's probably best not to complain too much around here.'

Like many backpackers, Matt liked to revel in the preconceptions others held about his national identity. If anything, it always made for an easy way to break the ice.

'You're asking a Pom not to whinge. You've got more chance of finding a pot of gold at the end of a rainbow.'

'Well, let's hope there are no more of your kin around here then,' said Colin. 'Are you coming out to meet the others?'

'Others?'

As far as he was aware, Matt assumed it was just the four of them.

'You didn't think it would be just us, did you? Your man said that some of the other vans were occupied and I don't think Birribandi attracts many holiday makers.'

B usiness was not running smoothly for Joe. He had been just three weeks into a major contract when half of his workforce deserted him. If he fell any further behind schedule he run the risk of being taken off the job, which would be nothing short of a disaster. Normally he could offset his sparse returns taken during the dry season with the summer harvest, but thanks to one of the worst cyclones in the past twenty years the previous crop had offered scant profits and he was now more reliant than ever on his off-season income.

Thirty years he had spent building up his company and he was not prepared to let it fall apart so easily. He was left with no choice other than to go to the city to take up some extra work. This required him to appoint a caretaker to take charge of the business during his absence. The man he had chosen for the position sat opposite him at the table. Their meeting was being held at the local pub as this was the outback, where office space was deemed about as necessary as a shearing shed was in the city.

'So what do you think?' Joe asked.

His companion took a long draw on a cigarette, which was clasped tightly between his index finger and thumb. So miniscule was the hand rolled tobacco tube that to any casual bystander it would appear the man was simply giving his partner an OK sign.

'So long as the four newbies can handle the strain, we should be able to clear the fields in twelve weeks.'

Joe had made the same estimation. He hoped that by advertising for a three month contract, which would guarantee anyone who took the job a visa extension, would be enough of an incentive for them to stay.

'I've stipulated a minimum term in the contract so they should all be in it for the long run.'

'The job's done then. All that leaves for me to do is to keep them...focused.'

His counterpart finished his sentence with a sneer that Joe was not wholly comfortable with. Entrusting the business to this man was certainly a risk, but a necessary one. Due to the short notice with which he had to fill the role there was nobody else in the town with the experience or the know how to do the job. He just hoped the decision would not be one he would later come to regret.

'I'll pick them up on Monday and get them to work, but after that, they're all yours.'

Joe extended his hand across the table. The other man casually flicked his cigarette onto the floor and then stubbed it out with his foot. The only effect a state wide smoking ban had on him was the absence of a proper ashtray.

'It's a deal,' the man said, firmly meeting the grip of his new employer.

'So what attracted you to the glamorous world of stick picking?' asked Niall

'If I knew what stick picking was, I'd be better placed to answer,' replied Matt. 'Would I be right in guessing it involves sugar canes?'

Niall managed to keep a straight face, but his three friends could not.

'It's not sugar canes,' he said.

Along with Stephen, Rose and Jenny, Niall had been in Birribandi for three weeks. In the eyes of the newcomers this made him a veteran.

'If you will be so kind as to place another log on our campfire I will tell you what stick picking is,' offered Rose.

She spoke with an eloquence that was matched only by her delicate good looks. The archetypal English beauty, she was as out of place in the desert as a farm hand would be at the Royal Ballet. There was a small stack of wood propped against the nearest caravan. Matt took a block from the top and dropped it onto the flames. This elicited a rapturous cheer from his new friends.

'Congratulations, Matt,' said Rose. 'You have passed the training. You are now a fully qualified stick picker.'

This again brought giggles from the group. He assumed it was just the alcohol, but sought further clarification anyway.

'You still haven't answered my question,' he said. 'What is stick picking?'

'Stick picking is...picking sticks,' Niall answered, rather lamely. 'Basically, we are driven to a field littered with dead wood and we have to clear it.'

'And what do you do with the sticks when you have collected them?'

'We burn them.'

'If you would prefer a more positive job description you could try calling yourself a bonfire technician,' suggested Stephen.

This was the first time he had spoken and his humour was drier than the desert around them. Both he and Niall were compatriots of Colin and it was clear the three were going to get along.

'It sounds easy enough,' said Matt. 'There are certainly worse jobs out there. At least it doesn't involve children or animals.'

'Matt's very nervous about the local wildlife, so he is,' said Colin.

'I am not. It's just good to know what I need to avoid.'

'If it slithers or crawls give it a wide berth. That's the basic rule in these parts,' said Niall. 'Have you checked your van for any unexpected roommates?'

The question made Matt uneasy. They were all sat on logs around the open campfire and he had taken his seat without giving a second thought to what could be lurking between the cracks in the wood. Colin picked up on his nervousness instantly.

'You should double check that patch up job when you get back to the van,' he said.

'Find a few holes, did you?' asked Niall.

'Just the one, but it was huge. Right beside Matt's bed.'

'I'd make sure that's securely covered if I were you,' advised Niall. 'You don't want any red backs sneaking in whilst you sleep.'

'Red backs?' Matt asked.

'Spiders; they're the only deadly ones they get in these parts, but there's a hell of a lot of them about.'

'I hung my washing up to dry and one crawled into my knickers,' said Jenny, who was the younger sister of Rose. She was also a little tipsier than the others.

'It was attracted by all of the cobwebs in there,' said Stephen. 'Jen hasn't had a boyfriend in over four months, you know, lads. Perhaps either of you may be the one to change that.'

The Irishman gave a wink to the embarrassed girl to show that he was only playing with her. Both Matt and Colin laughed off the suggestion. The camp pecking order was quickly becoming apparent and they each knew that how they acted on this night would decide their own places within it.

'Do any of you guys smoke?' Colin asked.

'There isn't much else to do in these parts,' replied Niall. 'Tobacco is like gold dust around here though. We tend to share what we have to keep it social.'

'That's all very well, but do you *smoke*?' Colin again asked, with a more suggestive inflection this time.

The pair were quick to catch on and the three soon repaired to Colin's van, where his stash was waiting for them. This left just Matt and the girls, which placed him at a disadvantage.

'I take it there's not much of a social scene in this town,' he said.

'This is it,' said Rose. 'Unless you want to venture down to the local pub, but that's probably something you would only want to experience once.'

'Is it that good?' he asked, reaching down for another beer.

'The highlight of the week is on a Friday when they have skimpies night. When you are this far from civilisation a few scantily clad barmaids is as good as it gets, apparently.'

'And you don't approve? Back in Cairns the barmaids wore bikinis all the time. I thought it was the norm in this climate.'

'This is a desert not a beach and these girls do not wear bikinis. Come to think of it, even the term girls may be stretching it a little. Stephen described them as belonging more to *Ripley's Believe It or Not* than *Victoria's Secret*.'

'So the guys have been along then?'

'They only go when they want to score some weed. Ben, who left a few days ago, had a contact there.'

'There probably won't be much reason to go there in the foreseeable future then. I caught a glimpse in Colin's luggage when he was unpacking and he came prepared, if you know what I mean.'

'You boys are terrible,' said Jenny, whose tone had settled considerably since she had last spoken.

Unlike her elder sister, who had luxuriant blonde locks and delicately pale skin, Jenny had dark hair and a warm, tanned complexion. Although clearly in the shadow of her sibling there was something about the girl that Matt found most appealing.

'At least Matt here likes to keep a clear head,' said Rose.

'I wouldn't say that,' he replied, raising his bottle for another gulp.

'And what about your other friends; weren't there four of you arrived today?' she asked.

'Yes, there was. Do you want to go and meet them?'

Her face lit up.

'I thought you would never ask.'

The bar was now full. That is to say the majority of seats inside were taken. Standing room only was a term that would rarely apply outside of the men's dunny in the Birribandi Tavern. Even on a Saturday night. Being the only watering hole within a hundred kilometre radius, the tavern had not been appropriated by a single group and instead represented a full multigenerational cross section of the entire town. Under the watchful eye of parents, uncles and grandfathers, the town's youngsters rarely stepped out of line. Amidst the revelry and conversation, a lonely figure sat at one corner of the bar.

Joe had gone home leaving his new business partner to drink alone. Rhett was onto his fifth schooner, but had barely even begun to warm up. He always stuck to beer in public, never spirits, as drink was just one of the many demons he had battled over the years. Once despised by the entire town, he was now looked upon the same way one looks upon a wild animal neutered with age. Character traits that would have been considered deplorable thirty years ago were now regarded as merely colourful.

He emptied his glass and deposited it back onto the bar in one fluid movement.

'Same again?' offered the barman, pouring the drink without waiting for a reply.

'Too right, but it'll be my last,' replied Rhett. 'Don't want to overdo it now, do I?'

The barman smirked to himself, but not so that the old man could see him. The pub doubled as a bottle shop and it was the only place in town where alcohol could be purchased. Rhett was one of the most frequent customers. Just that very afternoon he had been in and bought a bottle of rum. The only reason he hung around after Joe left was to see if he could drum up a bit of business.

He had a brief stroll around the tavern to look for potential customers, but none of his regulars were in. Those that were present seemed to either tense up or lean away as he passed them. It was a reaction that he evoked with great frequency.

Thirty minutes later, the atmosphere in the tavern had improved considerably. This meant nothing to Rhett as he was already back home, tucking into his rum. He lived close enough to the pub that the walk back barely interrupted his drinking time. The only concern he had was that maybe one bottle would not be enough.

It never was.

Colin took a protracted drag on the joint before passing it on to Stephen.

'Man, that was a long journey,' he said. 'If I'd had to wait much longer for this I'd be going cold turkey by now for sure.'

'I reckon you could've had a crafty smoke on the bus provided you were discreet enough like,' said Niall.

'Are you kidding me? I tried that on a tour once. We were on a four hour drive from Alice Springs to King's Canyon. Since I was on the back seat and everyone else seemed half asleep I thought I'd get away with it. Little did I realise that the bastard air-con unit was circulating my smoke throughout the entire bus. We pulled in for a rest stop at this dried up salt lake and everyone was stoned; even your man driving the bus.'

'It sounds like you livened their day up a bit,' said Niall.

'It was brutal. People started stripping off and marching into the salt lake thinking they could go for a swim. We were in the middle of a fucking desert for Christ's sake. The only water within a hundred miles was what we had on the bus. Some Korean guy even started digging a hole through the salt. I asked what he was doing and he just kept repeating "too shallow" over and over again. You can get away with that shit on a bus full of backpackers, but no way would I take any chances on a public bus. If they kick you off, you're dingo food.'

'Well, you're gonna love it here,' said Stephen.

'Birribandi is a stoner's paradise,' added Niall.

The joint had now returned to Colin, who took time to contemplate it in his fingertips.

'Has either of you boys heard of a town named Nimbin?' he asked.

'I have,' replied Stephen. 'Isn't that the place where they legalized cannabis?'

'It's not legal, but the law chooses to turn a blind eye in order to provide a gimmick to get the tourists in. The entire town is one big shrine to all things hemp. I actually bought this, just fifty yards from the local police station.'

He pulled back the door of the caravan and showed them his open backpack inside. The contents of which were clearly visible for the other two men to see.

'Christ, I've never seen so much weed before,' said Stephen.

Colin passed over the joint once more.

'I figured that I'm here for the next three months and what else would there be to do? Besides, I wasn't sure if I'd find a supplier in the outback, so best come prepared is what I say.'

'Prepared for what; Woodstock? We're gonna have to put in some heavy sessions to help you get through that lot,' said Stephen.

'Well, I'm always happy to share. I take it things were a little dry before I arrived?'

'A couple of the guys who left had a contact they bought from in town' said Niall. 'I never met him myself, but he sounded like a real creep. Apparently, he was reluctant to accept the payment and it was as if he preferred to have them in his debt. That's certainly not someone I'd want to do business with.'

'What about the girls?' asked Colin.

'I was beginning to wonder when you would ask,' replied Stephen. 'Which one have you got your eye on?'

Colin shrugged, careful not to tread on anyone's toes.

'They're both fair game if you're interested,' said Stephen. 'Rose had a thing going with one of the guys that left so you may catch her on the rebound. The younger one's very idealistic though, which would rule you out for a start.'

'My reputation precedes me. Even amongst strangers on the far reaches of civilisation the legend of Colin O'Meara lives on.'

Stephen laughed, before reappraising the situation to offer his countryman a slight glimmer of hope.

'Then again, she's also quite naive so you may stand a slim chance.'

'Glad to hear it. How about you two?' asked Colin. 'At least one of you must have had a crack at it.'

'After three weeks together they feel more like sisters,' replied Stephen. 'Besides, there are always other avenues to explore.'

'You haven't met Celeste yet,' added Niall.

Colin raised an eyebrow.

'Celeste?'

'She's Canadian, but from the French side. Which, may I add, she reminds us of almost constantly. She's seeing Pierro, who is the chef, so if anyone gets caught fooling around with her we will all starve.'

'Well, isn't this turning out to be quite the soap opera you have going on here,' said Colin. 'So where is Celeste tonight?'

'She doesn't always mix with the rest of the group. From what we gather, she suffers from epilepsy and Pierro doesn't like her drinking when he's not around. He's terrified that she'll get into trouble when he isn't there to look after her.'

'There are eight other people here. Is it really concern or is he worried about the competition?'

'I think you'll figure out the answer to that yourself soon enough. Tonight though, is about celebrating new arrivals and the possibilities that they bring.'

Niall took a long draw on the joint before passing it on.

'I'll toast to that,' said Colin.

He looked around for his beer, but he had left it back at the campfire. Instead he raised the joint.

'To new beginnings.'

'New beginnings,' the other two echoed.

Colin knew exactly how he would be spending his free time over the coming months and he could not have been more pleased with his prospects.

Jonas was sitting on one of the steps leading into his caravan smoking a cigarette when Matt approached with the girls.

'Hey man, you don't waste any time,' the German said. 'Who are the beautiful ladies?'

Rose smiled, but Jenny rolled her eyes skywards. Being less experienced than her sister she did not feel as comfortable with such comments.

'This is Rose and Jenny,' said Matt. 'They're our new neighbours and soon to be co-workers.'

He extended the introduction to Hiro who was sitting on his bed playing the guitar. The Asian had earlier impressed

Jonas with his infusion of Japanese gothic poetry and death metal. It was a performance he repeated for the benefit of the English trio, who were not so easily won over. This was largely due to the fact that his music resembled the sound of a geisha giving birth on a runaway bullet train. The Japanese man had very little confidence in his ability to speak English and preferred to listen, so he kept on playing as a way to distance himself from taking an active role in the conversation.

Matt, meanwhile, took the opportunity to cast a glance around the interior of the van to see how it compared to his own. If anything, he found it to be in even worse shape.

'Are the ladies quarters as classy as this?' he asked the girls.

'You have to be kidding,' replied Rose, her eyes taking on a faraway dreamy expression. 'My sister and I insist upon only the most opulent 5-star luxury. We each have four poster beds covered with the finest silk and Egyptian cotton. There is also a diamond chandelier for optimum illumination and a mini bar stocked with only the most expensive Kristal champagne. Our butler makes sure that it is all kept in tip top shape too, may I add.'

Jenny shot her a frosty look.

'Our van is exactly the same as this,' she insisted. 'Everyone is equal here.'

Matt noticed that the younger sibling had stopped drinking following Stephen's earlier teasing. He now wondered if maybe Jenny was the more reserved of the two. Luckily, any resulting tension was avoided as they were soon interrupted by Colin, who was returning along with Niall and Stephen.

'I hope you aren't having a party without us,' he said, 'What have I missed?'

'Jenny was just explaining how we all are equal here in Birribandi,' said Matt.

'That is something I simply cannot agree with,' said Colin,

placing an arm around each of the girls. 'You two are far more beautiful than the rest of us put together.'

Jenny shrugged away his arm, but Rose welcomed the attention.

'It's a real shame to waste a good fire. Shall we take this social gathering to somewhere a little warmer?' suggested Colin, who had read both girls' body language and was now clearly directing his conversation toward the elder sister.

They all returned to the campfire, where Matt noticed that Colin was quick to disengage Rose from the rest of the group. His friend certainly wasted no time, but Matt did not fancy his own chances with the sister just yet. Her earlier tipsiness had been misleading, as he could now tell that she was unlikely to be a pushover. It did not deter him from trying though.

'I never pictured travelling to be quite like this,' he said, 'but I think that I may grow to like it here.'

He hoped the statement would be sufficient to invite a response from Jenny. She briefly glanced directly into his eyes, as if searching for something. If she was trying to gauge his intentions, they did not betray him.

'I suppose it's not so bad,' she said. 'You would probably be wise to hold your judgement until after work on Monday though. The guys you are replacing couldn't stick it out.'

'You seem to be coping okay. Or are you just dead set on extending your visa?'

She laughed, but to a private joke that he was not privy to.

'You men are all the same. Only thinking about what you can gain from something. I may return someday, but I'm not planning on extending my stay during this trip.'

'So why are you here; surely not just for the love of stick picking?'

'Would that be so bad? With the skills that I acquire here I am hoping to set up my own timber disposal business back in the UK.'

The lack of familiarity made it impossible for him to discern with any certainty whether she was just messing with him. She could seem at one moment playful and then confrontational the next. There was, however, always a detectable trace of defensiveness in everything that she said. This made her come across as more of a reluctant optimist than a cynic, which he found appealing.

'If you are always this gullible I shall have to keep my sister away from you or she will torment you night and day,' she added.

'Luckily I'm not always this drunk. So why did you come here if not to work?'

'I came to work. Rose has no conscience about spending our parents' money, but I am determined to pay my own way during this trip.'

'So why did you choose Birribandi? I'm sure a smart girl like you could earn a lot more money in the city.'

Jenny's features lit up instantly. The question seemed to be the one she was waiting for.

'I came for the stars.'

Matt found the opening too hard to resist.

'Do you get many celebrities here?'

She shook her head, pityingly.

'I shall definitely have to keep Rose away from you. The stars I am talking about have much more longevity than the ones that dwell in Hollywood.'

She looked up to the heavens and Matt craned his neck to follow, but his eyes had yet to adjust from the light of the campfire. The sky appeared no different to any other that he had seen before.

'Your eyes may need a little time to acclimatise to the darkness,' she said.

He was a little impatient and worried that this was another of her games.

'Maybe tonight is not the best night,' he replied and instantly regretted it.

She glanced away and crossed her arms over her chest as if suddenly aware of the cold.

'You're right,' she said. 'It's getting late. I should go to bed soon.'

He inwardly cursed his own stupidity and lack of tact. It was now obvious that she had been opening up to him, but she may have now misread his nervousness as apathy.

'It's not that I don't want to see them. I'm sure they're spectacular, it's just that my eyes aren't really focusing as best they can right now.'

He held up his beer bottle as evidence of his visual impairment. The moment was clearly lost, but he was determined to reassure the girl that it was not down to anything she had said or done.

'That's okay,' she replied. 'We have many nights ahead of us and the sky is not going anywhere.'

He offered her a feeble smile as she turned and left. When he reclaimed his seat around the campfire he was frustrated to see that Colin had fared much better with the other sister. The pair of them were smiling and giggling amongst themselves like teenage lovers.

'You, my friend, look like you need another beer,' said Niall.

Matt took a fresh bottle from the crate.

'It's ironic, but when I signed up for this job I was actually worried that I wouldn't know when I would get my next taste of alcohol.'

Niall laughed at the suggestion.

'That certainly won't be a problem for you here. After

three months, you'll view the return to civilisation as an opportunity to detox. There are three things you will never be short of in this town.'

'And they are?'

'Sand, beer and...' He glanced towards the budding couple seated opposite, '...disappointment,' he finished.

'Some of us are just lucky, I guess,' said Matt.

'In that case, let me propose a toast to those who aren't,' replied Niall.

They clanked their bottles together before consoling themselves on the contents. Matt thought that just maybe, the next three months were not going to be so bad after all.

Chapter 3

Sundays in Birribandi were no different to any other day in Birribandi. The harsh conditions of the outback did not allow time to devote an entire day to rest. For the residents of the caravan park it was laundry day, and with just one washing machine on site it paid to be an early riser.

Morning had usurped the night long before it was welcome, and as a consequence it was midday by the time that anybody set about their daily chores. Since the four new arrivals were still fresh from the coast they could afford a more relaxed day ahead of them. Matt was the last to wake and it was with great reluctance that he left his bed. Without the luxury of air conditioning his sleep was not settled, leaving him feeling hollow and tired.

'Remind me why I do this to myself,' he said to Colin, before taking a substantial drink from a water bottle, which he kept by his bed.

His throat was coarse and the fluid dislodged some dried phlegm, forcing him to suppress a gag reaction.

'It's the English weakness,' replied his friend. 'Your bodies aren't as well adapted to cope with the effects of alcohol as those of your better cousins across the sea.'

Infuriatingly Colin did not display even the slightest indication of as much as a mild headache.

'Well, this is the last time. Back in Cairns I had a part time job at the hostel. Bar work was one thing, but I don't fancy spending a day lifting wood with a head like this.'

'That's the spirit. Now what are your plans for the rest of the day?'

'I thought I'd check out the town. That should take all of five minutes and then back to bed.'

He was now sat on the edge of the mattress with his eyes shut and his head in his hands. His roommate sat opposite and did not appear at all sympathetic to his condition.

'I'm going into town soon if you want to tag along,' offered Colin. 'Joe came around while you slept and dropped off our weekly provisions. We now have two loaves of bread, some processed cheese and a packet of Tim-tams.'

The mention of the chocolate biscuits perked Matt up a little.

'Well, isn't he pushing the boat out. What more could we possibly need?'

'Sunscreen for a start. The rays out there are relentless. Whatever factor you used on the coast, I would consider doubling it here.'

Matt glanced down at his bare arms. He put a lot of effort into getting his tan just right, but was now beginning to realise that vanity had no place in the outback.

'Anything else?' he asked.

'I didn't want to be the one to tell you this, but you may want to think about investing in some deodorant,' Colin paused for a moment before adding; 'especially if you want to impress that Jenny bird.'

Matt looked up at his roommate inquisitively.

'Something tells me that this is more than just neighbourly advice. You wouldn't happen to have a vested interest in my love life at the moment, would you?'

'Don't worry about me. Just you keep little sister occupied and everyone's happy.' He stood up. 'Now hurry up and put some clothes on, will you.'

Matt quickly threw on a pair of board shorts and a plain t-shirt. Beach wear, desert wear; it was all the same. He was a thousand miles from the coast, but he still had the sun on his back and sand between his toes.

'Is anyone else coming?' he asked.

'I told Jonas and Hiro that we would call on them once we were ready. The others are all pre-occupied with their laundry. If you have any clothing that you don't want to turn orange, you may want to refrain from wearing it in these parts.'

The town, if that is what you could call the ramshackle collection of houses that made up Birribandi, was located about one kilometre from the caravan park. It had a population of just three hundred and fifty two. Forty percent of the inhabitants were indigenous and it was not uncommon for family groups to extend into double figures. The average household had just one bread winner and in total the workforce accounted for only fifteen percent of the population. Many of these worked out of town, sometimes travelling up to 300 kilometres for their daily commute.

Main Street was yet to be appropriated by the large retail chains and was composed of a small collection of locally owned businesses. Despite the seemingly endless expanse of space the town was set within, commercial real estate was at a premium, meaning that every business had to fulfil more than one purpose. This led to some unusual bespoke combinations.

The supermarket was also a bank. The post office doubled as a pharmacy. The barber's shop was a laundrette. Only the police station stood alone, but given the low crime rate in such a close-knit community it would often be called upon to cater to more than just the upholding of the law to justify its existence.

There was a group of Aboriginal teenagers loitering on a street corner. They laughed and whispered amongst themselves as the four strangers approached.

'This is one crazy town,' said Jonas, as he took in the antiquated store fronts. 'In Germany, this is like theme park.'

'Well, then, that explains why Disney chose to build in France now, doesn't it,' said Colin, whose humour was less direct, but no less caustic with the foreigners. 'I'd choose a rollercoaster over this place any day.'

'You've been to Euro Disney?' asked Jonas, not quite grasping the crux of the Irishman's wit.

'Never mind him,' said Matt, choosing to lend the German a helping hand. 'He's just on the defensive because he's strayed a bit too far from his comfort zone.'

Colin turned to face Matt, throwing his arms up into the air in feigned astonishment.

'You wouldn't be suggesting that I'm out of my depth now, would you?' he protested, clearly relishing the challenge. 'I'll have you know that I'm more than capable of handling myself in a dustbowl like this.'

'Are you kidding me,' said Matt. 'You stick out like a bald Irishman at a Rastafarian convention. Even Hiro blends into this town better than you do. He's got the cowboy look down to a tee. Isn't that right, Hiro?'

The Asian responded by forming a gun with the fingers of his right hand and then firing a mimed shot at one of the youths as they passed, whilst repeating the word "cowboy". The gesture seemed rather creepy.

'If we get attacked by marauding Indians I'll be happy to let the Kyoto Kid here take charge,' said Colin, 'but right now you'd all be wise to follow my lead. I've spotted a supermarket just ahead and I can suggest a purchase or two that you'll definitely thank me for later.'

They entered the shop to which they brought the only custom. Its shelves were stocked with all the usual luxuries that would be found in the coastal cities, but the price tags differed greatly. The inflated economics of rural life were immediately picked upon by the outsiders.

'$5 for fucking milk,' said Matt. 'Maybe Joe wasn't being such a tight arse after all.'

'Wait until you see the price of Tim-tams,' replied Colin.

The Irishman was the only one to be taking anything from the shelves. He had several packets of tobacco papers, a pair of gardening gloves, a 2lt bottle of water and some insect repellent.

'Why are you buying gloves?' asked Matt. 'Surely we'll get them provided tomorrow.'

Colin took a second pair from the rack and handed them to Matt.

'You will, but from what the guys told me last night they'll have dissolved by first break. It would definitely be a smart idea to get a heavy duty pair like these. Of course, even they will probably need replacing by the end of the week.'

'I'll take your word for it. What about sunscreen? I didn't see any with the pharmaceuticals or the cosmetics.'

'It was the first thing that I noticed when we came in.' He beckoned Matt to take a look over toward the checkout. 'I guess that's what you could call the cancer section – cause of and prevention.'

Behind the service desk was the usual display of cigarette brands with several bottles of sunscreen nestled on the shelf above.

'Are they expecting them to be stolen or have you got to be of a certain age to protect yourself from the sun in this town?' asked Matt.

'The way that your man has been keeping his beady eyes trained on us the whole time we've been here, I'm going to go with your first guess,' replied Colin.

A bell rang to indicate that another customer had entered the shop. It was one of the youths they had passed earlier. He walked with a cocky swagger and Matt noticed that he was taking things from the shelves and stuffing them under his top. He tapped Colin on the elbow.

'Check out the five fingered discounts over there.'

Colin shrugged.

'That's not our problem. Let's just pay for this stuff and get out of here.'

Matt glanced again at the thief. It was so blatant that he actually felt guilty having witnessed it. It was not his place to say anything more, so he just decided to ignore it. They took their baskets to the counter. Matt was the first in line and he was horrified to see that the sunscreen was priced at $30 for a standard bottle. This was a mark-up of almost one hundred percent on the amount he was accustomed to paying. It was a price that he would rather avoid.

'Do you wanna go halves; fifteen bucks each?' he asked, turning to Colin.

'No chance,' replied his friend. 'I got mine before coming here. Besides, if you don't pay for your mistakes how can you expect to learn from them?'

Matt begrudgingly handed over the cash and waited for his change. Then as he was about to leave the shop, a security guard stepped in front of him, blocking the way. Before then he had not even been aware of any other store employees.

'Can I see inside your bag, please?' the security guard asked.

'Er, sure,' Matt replied.

The guard rummaged for a moment before handing it back, satisfied nothing had been taken. The interaction annoyed Matt and he left the shop feeling frustrated.

'I hate that,' he said, when the others joined him outside. 'For such a supposedly laid back nation they're certainly paranoid about people nicking stuff. Even in Sydney I could never go into a shop without having my bag searched.'

'Tell me about it,' said Colin. 'Do you remember all that weed I showed you back at the caravan. I went into a shop in Brisbane with that in my bag just before getting the bus here.'

'How did you avoid getting searched?' Matt asked.

'I didn't,' replied Colin. 'If I refused, they'd obviously think I'd stolen something so I just showed them what I had in my bag; a half empty water bottle, a couple of battered old paperbacks and a shit load of weed. None of which they sold in that store, I pointed out.'

'Well, you've certainly got balls, I'll give you that. I just hope I'm not around when they finally land you into trouble that you can't talk your way out of.'

As he finished speaking he noticed the Aboriginal boy was leaving the shop. The security guard was nowhere in sight. This annoyed Matt further as he watched the boy walk back to meet up with his friends, where he distributed the illicit goods that had been hidden under his shirt. He could not be certain, but he thought that the boy looked back at him at one point and appeared to be gloating.

They took their shopping back to the park, where after leaving Jonas and Hiro they bumped into Rose and Jenny returning from the laundry room. It was the first time either of them had seen the girls since the previous evening.

As soon as Colin's eyes met with those of the elder sister a shared secret passed between them, which at once made the atmosphere seem a little uncomfortable for the other two.

'Are you boys ready for work tomorrow?' Rose asked.

Her eyes remained locked on Colin's, searching for the answer to a different question entirely.

'We're as prepared as we can be,' he answered, matching the intensity of her stare, and in doing so telling her everything she needed to know.

Matt was eager to cut the tension and felt relieved when Jenny did it for him.

'So what did you think of Birribandi?' she asked.

It was fair to say that the town had not made the best first impression on him. However, since he could tell that the girl was quite sensitive, the answer he gave was very different to the one he would have given to the males in the park.

'I liked it.'

'Really?' she asked.

'Yeah, really,' he glanced downward to avoid looking her in the eye. 'It's good to experience a different pace of life.'

He knew that the lie was obvious, but she seemed to accept his attempt to be positive. If he was going to get anywhere with her it was important that he made a good early impression. So far he felt that he was succeeding.

'Most of the guys that come through here cannot see past the desert,' she said. 'They think it is boring and lifeless, but they are missing out on so much.'

Matt nodded in what he hoped was a thoughtful way.

'As soon as we get a clear night, you'll see the true beauty of this place,' she added. 'You are in for a real treat, I promise you.'

'I certainly hope so,' he replied.

Colin glanced over at Matt to check on his progress. Matt saw this as a good time to break off the conversation. He thought it better to play it cool and quit whilst he was ahead rather than risk jeopardizing all the groundwork he had put in.

'I guess I'll see you at dinner,' he told Jenny. 'Right now we better get this stuff back to the van.' Then turning to Colin, he added; 'are you ready?'

The Irishman offered Rose a shrug and waited for the girls to be out of earshot before responding.

'I'm readier than you are, you bastard.'

Though his friend's tone was playful, Matt could sense an undercurrent of frustration in it.

'What's that supposed to mean?'

'This nice guy routine of yours is never going to work. You need to lay your cards on the table from the start. If she doesn't see through your bluff you still run the risk of becoming the gay best friend.'

'Don't go judging me by your own standards,' Matt protested. 'Not everyone is as shallow as you. Besides which, she is starting to warm towards me.'

'Is that so,' said Colin. 'In case you haven't done the math, you aren't the only guy around here without regular female companionship.'

Matt had not really considered that he may have competition. He assumed Stephen and Niall were not interested, because if they were they would surely have made a move already and Hiro could barely even speak English. This left only Jonas as a possible rival.

'You're referring to our young German friend, aren't you?'

'I will admit that he's got less of a chance than you, but if he makes a play for her it could make things awkward.'

Matt fully understood the point being made. Once a friend stakes his claim on a girl, it is extremely bad form to try and take her away from him.

'Do you think I should let him know that I'm interested in

her?' he asked.

'Only if you want to speed up his own advances. Until one of you makes an actual move, it's a level playing field; trust me,' advised Colin.

This certainly gave Matt something to think about. When they visited the dining block for dinner he wanted to make sure that he chose a more advantageous seat at the table than Jonas. It was obvious to everyone that Colin and Rose had coupled up, so to establish all of them as a foursome would hopefully convince the others that Jenny and he would soon be an item too.

Other than the shower block, the dining hall was the only permanently fixed part of the caravan park. It was comprised of four large ten seated tables, although only one was covered with a table cloth and cutlery when Matt entered. The others, though not in use, did hint towards a time when the town may actually have been frequented by tourists. Jenny was seated at the end of the table with her sister beside her. Stephen and Niall were opposite and Colin took the seat next to Rose, leaving Matt to take the seat facing him. It was not quite what he had hoped for, but it at least kept Jonas out of the picture.

Last to enter the room was Celeste. This was the first time that the newcomers had seen her. She wore a simple vest top and jeans, but had the type of body that required no dressing up to receive compliments. Stephen was the only one not to stop and stare when she entered. As she took her seat she brushed a lock of delicately curled strawberry blonde hair from her face. The slowness of the action suggested it was not merely for her own benefit that she did this.

Rose reluctantly made the introductions. It was unlikely she saw the girl as a threat, but it was obvious to everyone that she did not like her. In fact, Celeste did not inspire solidarity in either of her female acquaintances. Jonas, however, took an instant shine to her, which could not have turned out better for Matt. If this new distraction kept his rival preoccupied it would pave the way clear for him with Jenny.

Once everyone was seated the food was brought out. The meal was composed of just one course and it was simple, yet substantial. Since the daily lunch rations would consist of nothing more than processed cheese sandwiches and a chocolate biscuit, the evening meal was a treat to be savoured.

As they ate, the young backpackers talked about their homes and families. They shared traveller's tales of adventures past and those yet to come. Not once did they broach the subject of what had brought them all together in the first place; work. For the next hour, it was as if they could have been sat at any table, in any hostel, anywhere in the world.

Chapter 4

The window of the caravan was permeated by a blinding light. This was followed by a blaring horn, which had the effect of applying a defibrillator to the dead of night; a sudden shot of electricity bringing life to the predawn darkness. The work bus had arrived.

'Jesus Christ!' said Colin, but before he could elaborate further he was interrupted by a knock at the door.

'It's Joe,' said Matt, peering behind the flimsy curtain that covered the window.

He opened the door slightly, where he was simply told 'fifteen minutes' by his boss.

The two men fumbled to get dressed in the cramped van. They then hurried along to the shower block to brush their teeth before joining their workmates outside. It was bitingly cold and everybody shivered beneath their hastily applied layers of clothing.

'Nobody warned that we were on the nightshift,' said Matt. 'Please tell me we aren't expected to get up this early every day.'

'It's a quarter to six,' said Niall. 'It'll be light soon and that will wake you up. We have to start this early to avoid the worst of the afternoon sun. You'll quickly get used to it.'

They all shuffled onto the bus for the hour long drive to the field where they would be working. There was no conversation during the journey. Some of them drifted off back to sleep, whilst others merely stared blindly out the windows. Matt was in the latter group. Looking out onto the flattest horizon he had ever seen he could begin to see signs of why Jenny liked it so much out there. The rising sun painted thick, even bands of colour along the bottom of the skyline, which contrasted heavily with the darkness below. As the light increased, kangaroos could be seen bounding away from the roadside with an almost balletic elegance. It was the Australia he had previously only dreamed of.

Everyone was woken with a jolt when Joe pulled the bus off the smooth tarmac of the highway and onto a rough unsealed road leading to the field. When they arrived, there were two other vehicles waiting for them. Both automobiles were white, as had been the clear majority of those parked around the town the previous afternoon. Colour was an extravagance that it seemed could be done without in rural Australia. The first car was a dust battered saloon from out of which stepped two Aboriginal men.

Joe introduced the Aboriginal men as Sam and Paul. They were father and son. Sam, who was the elder, drove the tractor and his son Paul would be labouring with the backpackers. The younger man was greeted warmly by the original workers, showing that he was one of the gang. The driver of the ute was not as personable. He had a permanent scowl fixed in place as he looked over the new recruits.

'This is Rhett,' said Joe. 'He will be managing things here for the next few months as I have to attend to business out of town.'

The man did not look like management material. He possessed harsh, almost feral features and was dressed in scruffy blue overalls, which were a remnant from some previous factory job. The garment had a nametag sewn onto it bearing the name of *Rhett Butler*. Colin gave Matt a nudge in the side and sniggered when he saw it.

Once the introductions were dispensed with, the backpackers were placed into formation around the tractor and trailer. Whatever crop once grew in the field had been bulldozed, leaving behind a load of wooden debris. Before a new plantation could begin, this all had to be cleared, which is where the stick pickers came into the equation.

Colin and Hiro were placed in an advanced wide position covering the flanks. They were to throw wood in towards the centre, where Matt and Jonas would then deposit it onto a trailer, which was attached to the tractor. The three girls occupied the central channel directly behind the vehicle, which carried the least heavy lifting as they would deposit their wood directly onto the open back of the trailer. Stephen and Niall had a slightly different job. They were responsible for lighting the bonfires and taking care of any larger immobile logs that could not be lifted onto the trailer easily by hand. That left just Paul, who acted as a floating hand, helping out when and where he was needed.

With everyone in place, it was time to begin. Rhett and Joe remained by the vehicles to talk over their plans, whilst the tractor pulled away at a comfortable pace for the pickers to keep up. Even though the days were hot, they did take time to get going. The early morning was cool and everyone took to the work with enthusiasm, if only to keep the blood flowing and generate some heat.

Conversation was light to begin with. Rose and Jenny were clearly not at ease with the Celeste around them and the boys were too busy concentrating on learning their job. Although Matt was placed closer to the girls, he soon became envious of Colin and Hiro. They both threw with reckless abandon as they simply had to move the wood with the security of knowing that whatever they missed could be later picked up by somebody else. Those around the trailer were not afforded such luxury.

'They got the easy job,' said Jonas, who had noticed the same thing. 'Do you think they will swap with us after our break?'

'Would you?' asked Matt, who was behind Hiro and struggling to keep pace as the Japanese man kept on adding to the already substantial debris in his catchment zone.

'I see your point,' Jonas conceded. 'Maybe if we ask one of the bosses they will make them swap.'

Matt glanced back to where Joe and Rhett remained locked in conversation over some plans that they had lain out on the bonnet of the ute. Neither man seemed particularly interested in the heavily guarded motorcade as it advanced across the field.

'I wouldn't bet on it,' he replied. 'They have a strange mentality in these parts. Complaining would almost certainly guarantee that we end up doing this job until the day we leave here.'

'So let's have fun then,' said Jonas. 'Maybe they move us to the easy job as punishment.'

Their conversation was interrupted by a voice from behind. The girls had previously been so quiet that Matt had almost forgotten they were there.

'I hope you boys aren't struggling,' teased Rose. 'We girls will be counting on you if we need help, won't we Jen?'

Her sister ignored the insinuation. Although she did not struggle physically, she was focused mentally on the job in front of her. This was an attitude that could not have contrasted more heavily with the third girl in the group. Celeste could not have been any more disengaged from the task at hand. She ambled lazily behind the sisters, stopping only to shift the most obvious objects that could not justifiably be left alone. If the girls complained about her not pulling her weight, she ignored them. If one of the guys complained, she would simply flirt with them until the indiscretion was long forgotten.

'I would gladly help out,' said Matt. 'The only trouble is that I cannot leave my post while Hiro continues to provide so much work for me.'

'Maybe you should switch sides with Jonas,' Rose suggested. 'I don't think that Colin has such a strong work ethic.'

She gestured to where Colin was lazily throwing wood in toward the centre, whilst a bewildered Paul tried to demonstrate how he should be doing it. Jonas was quick to prove that he, however, was pulling his weight. He deposited two logs together onto the top of the trailer, which took it to capacity. The young Aboriginal man immediately noticed this and jogged over whilst signalling for his father to kill the engine.

'Who wants to unhook the trailer?' he asked.

Although Jonas was the closest, he made no effort to volunteer himself, so Matt stepped forward. If first impressions counted, he decided that he may at least try to look keen on his first day at work.

Paul explained the procedure to him. The trailer was released by pulling a simple leaver, but the real skill was in the timing. Once the connection was broken it was imperative to get out of the way as quickly as possible. The tractor would reverse, which tipped the trailer into an upright position, depositing its contents onto the dry soil. When all the wood was offloaded, Sam would accelerate forward to right the trailer, which was then reattached by pulling the lever in the opposite direction. With practice the sequence could be completed in mere seconds. Matt took a little longer, but he performed the task well.

'Too easy,' he declared, proudly displaying his grasp of the Aussie vernacular as well as the instructions given to him.

'Don't get cocky,' warned Paul. 'If you do not move out of the way before the tractor reverses, things could get very messy. Last year a fella broke his back in a tractor accident not too far from here.'

The Aboriginal's statement grabbed Matt's attention. He knew that the job would be boring, but he never expected it to be dangerous as well.

'Are such accidents common?' he asked.

'Not the serious kind, but you could easily lose a finger or a thumb if you aren't quick enough.'

'Are you kidding me? Is nobody here the least bit concerned about health and safety?'

'Of course,' said Paul. 'If you die it can take up to a week for the boss man to get a replacement. A lot of work can be lost in a week.'

Matt had no response. He was completely dumbfounded by Paul's remarks, much to the amusement of the young Aboriginal.

'You white fella's are priceless,' Paul said, before giving Matt a reassuring pat on the back. 'With dad driving the tractor you have nothing to worry about. He's done this most of his life and he never hit nobody yet.'

'Glad to hear it,' replied a much relieved Matt. 'We should probably make up a rota though. It's only fair that everyone gets their turn.'

By the time the second load was filled the group had been working for close to two hours so they took the opportunity to have their first break. Talk immediately turned toward the stranger who would be taking charge the next time they started work.

'Have any of you seen that guy before?' asked Colin, who then lit a cigarette before taking a prolonged drag.

'He's never been here while we were working,' replied Stephen, who took the lighter from Colin. 'There is something familiar about him though, something I cannot quite place.'

'I don't trust him,' said Colin. 'I think he's an ex-con.'

All eyes turned toward the Australian. Rhett was in his early fifties, but could have passed for twenty years above that. It was fair to say that the years had not been kind to him. His skin was worn and creased, with thick grey stubble spread over it like moss on the bark of a tree. From this unkempt mess around his mouth, a small white stick was visible.

'He looks more like a cop,' said Matt. 'Didn't Kojak used to suck on a lollipop like that?'

'That's not a lollipop stick,' said Colin. 'It's a cigarette.'

'That's ridiculous. It's much too small to be a cigarette. How could anybody even roll one that small?'

'Like I said; I think he's an ex con.'

Matt failed to make the connection that his friend had.

'So he's running low on tobacco. That's not illegal, is it?'

'It's a prison rollie. Convicts always roll them that tightly. Obviously, it's a habit that sticks.'

Matt still failed to make a connection.

'I think you're just being paranoid. You can't go accusing people of things because of the way they roll their cigarettes. We should at least give the guy a chance.'

'I wasn't accusing anyone of anything,' said Colin. 'I was only making an observation, that's all.'

'Maybe your man Paul knows something about this guy,' suggested Niall. 'We could ask him.'

The young Aboriginal was still stoking the most recent bonfire when he was called over to shed some light on the mystery man.

'Do you know anything about the new gaffer over there?' asked Niall.

Paul did not give an immediate response. He instead looked to his father for guidance. The struts of the tractor cab obscured the older man's face, so the group could not see what gesture he made to his son. Paul nodded his understanding before speaking to the backpackers.

'He's the new boss man. That's all you need to know.'

Nobody was convinced.

'Come on, Paul,' urged Rose. 'You obviously know something. We're all friends here, so there's no harm in sharing whatever it is that you know with us.'

'There's nothing to tell,' he insisted.

Before anybody could badger him further, Joe signalled that the break was over and for everyone to return to their positions around the tractor.

The next few hours passed quickly and they had all worked up large appetites by lunchtime. However, the final section after lunch would prove to be the toughest part of the day. With the sun at its highest point in the sky there was to be no escape from its energy sapping rays.

The ground had become baked solid by the heat, but it still had to yield to the overpowering weight of the tractor as it carved deep trenches into the soil with its relentless progress along the field. This made walking a tricky affair, somewhat like spending hours on a stepper in the gym. Matt had on more than one occasion come perilously close to losing his footing, and as such became more and more distracted by where he placed his feet. It was whilst his attention was thusly diverted that he failed to see the foot long, three inch thick log that was headed directly for the back of his head.

He did feel it though. Boy, did he feel it.

Chapter 5

An intense pain gnawed at the inside of his head like a rat trying to tunnel its way out of a hollowed-out pumpkin. If he closed his eyes and discarded all thoughts from his mind, it helped. It did not help much, but it was the difference between tolerance and giving in to the desire to beat the pain out of his head on the dashboard.

The sound of an engine pulling up alongside of his ute brought him back to reality. Joe had finally arrived with the backpackers. He already knew that half of them were fresh from the cities or whatever tourist Hell-holes these foreign kids were despoiling these days. This meant that they were untested and would possibly not be able to take the strain of doing the job. He hoped for their sake that if they were too weak that they would have the sense to quit after this first day. The pom would probably even offer to drive them back to the city. They will get no such molly codling on his watch.

'This is Rhett,' said Joe. 'He will be managing things here for the next few months, as I have to attend to business out of town.'

'Managing,' now that was a word he liked to hear; it was

about time that people had cause to show him some respect in this town.

He watched as they gathered around the tractor. Straight away he could tell which were going to present the most problems. The three who weren't native English speakers were an obvious cause for concern. If they could not understand the orders that were given how could they be expected to follow them? At least the girls provided some much needed eye candy. It was a real treat watching their pert little behinds as they made their way out to the field.

Once the tractor was underway, it was time for him to go over the plans for the coming weeks with Joe. There were four fields that needed clearing and timing was imperative if all were to be completed on time. If they weren't, he would miss out on a healthy bonus payment at the end of the contract.

Joe pulled out a large map, which he unfolded and placed onto the bonnet of Rhett's ute. It had the four fields clearly marked, but this being the outback the scale was vast. Three of them were within one hour's drive from the town. The other was twice that distance away.

'This last one is going to be a tough one to complete,' said Joe. 'We lose an extra two hours each day to travelling, so you're going to have to allow for maybe just four and a half to five lengths in a day.'

'Why?' Rhett asked. 'We'll just get home a little later than usual. An extra couple of hours at the end of the day is no real hardship. Probably do those layabouts some good too, as it would eat into their drinking time.'

It was obvious that Joe had already made up his mind and would not be budged, but that never stopped Rhett. Arguments were not about winning or losing. To him the outcome was always secondary to the fun of the fight involved in getting there.

'Their day begins at half past five,' said Joe. 'If we keep them out until seven, then by the time they have showered and had dinner they'll have to go straight to bed. You have to give them time to recharge or they'll all be burnt out long before the job's finished. They are only kids after all.'

'You're the boss,' conceded Rhett.

In twenty four hours, Joe would be gone so his opinion did not matter so much anyway. Rhett looked out to the field where Sam was shamefully overcompensating for the slowness of the rookies. They really were clueless. #

The pommie one was the worst of the bunch. He kept looking over his shoulder to see what those two posh slags were doing instead of keeping his eye on what was happening ahead of him. It could only be a matter of time before the Jap hit him with a mistimed throw. It would certainly make Rhett's day to see that happen and he mentally tracked the trajectory of each wayward throw, hoping that it would be the one to cause the damage.

He found it a welcome relief when morning smoko finally arrived, as he badly needed a break from Joe's fussing over every minor detail. All that was required of him was to babysit a bunch of kids picking up sticks and give them a kick up the arse if they got complacent. How difficult could that be?

He rolled a cigarette and placed it into his mouth.

Where had he put his lighter?

He patted down the pockets of his overalls before eventually finding it. He was always losing them, which was a continual pain. The baccy that he rolled never stayed lit for long and he was always having to fidget about to get it relit. He would, of course, have preferred something a bit stronger in there, but never in front of the boss.

After the break, Joe moved on to giving endless instructions regarding the caravan park. He talked and talked about how it was important to give the kids their space. Space for what exactly? Drinking and screwing was all they were likely to get up to. Rhett planned on paying as few visits to that place as was absolutely necessary.

After yet more needless instructions from the man in charge, the day finally picked up following lunch. The soppy English kid, who had spent the entire morning trying to impress one of the skinny girls, took a hefty whack to the back of his head from one of the Jap's wayward throws. The ferocity of the impact had Rhett hoping it had been a deliberate act, but that was unlikely with a bunch as soft as this lot.

As soon as everyone became aware of what had happened the tractor came to a halt and they all used it as an excuse to shy off from doing work. Joe looked to be concerned as he jogged out to the field to investigate. He had good cause to be worried given the lack of work being done, but no doubt the fool just wanted to check up on the kid to see if he was okay.

Rhett walked out to the scene of the commotion with a lot less urgency than everyone else. This gave him time for another smoke and also a chance to survey what work, if any, had been achieved. He could not believe the amount of wood that was being left on the ground as he followed the freshly laid tractor tracks. Why Joe insisted on hiring these outsiders was a mystery given the wealth of cheap labour in the town.

The two Irish boys, who Joe had earlier told him were part of the original crew, caught up to him as he walked. They had been stoking a bonfire and therefore missed what happened.

'What's going on?' asked the taller of the two.

'Nothing that needs to concern you; one of the new starters got a bit clumsy, that's all,' replied Rhett.

'Is it Matt? What happened - is he alright like?'

Here was yet more slacking off. Rhett was tempted to take

them by scruff of their necks and force them into getting back to work, but it would pay to keep these two onside; for the time being at least.

'He's still on his feet so it can't have been serious,' he told them.

'Maybe one of us should switch with him for the rest of the day. It's not as hectic what we're doing.'

Rhett was surprised to hear such a common sense idea from a backpacker. This one clearly had leadership potential. Well, to lead this ramshackle group at least. Once Joe was out of the way he would approach this one with his proposition. For now though, he just needed to keep him on side.

'That's a good idea. Why don't you run up and swap with him,' he said. Then turning to the other; 'you can get back to work now. The imbecile will come and help you when he's ready.'

The two exchanged a look of uncertainty before splitting up and jogging off their separate ways. It really was pathetic how they could not so much as wipe their own backsides without seeking one another's approval.

Rhett met Joe and the injured boy halfway between the tractor and the edge of the field. The latter had a slight cut to the back of his head, but the bleeding had already stopped so it could hardly have been serious.

'I'll take him down to the bus to put a plaster and some antiseptic on it,' said Joe. 'You keep an eye on the others to make sure there are no more mishaps.'

Rhett offered a shrug of acceptance then headed towards the tractor. Once he caught up to it, he climbed onto the back where he had a good vantage point to see everything around him. Most were getting on with their work, but two of the girls were gabbing about what just happened. He found that a long, cold stare soon shut them up.

With his authority established, he placed a roll-up in his mouth and continued to survey his new kingdom. Life was definitely looking up. He not only had a job, but it came with underlings too. It was like he had inherited a readymade supply chain. If all went to plan this was going to be his most profitable venture yet.

Chapter 6

Matt's body felt like crumpled steel by the time he got back to the caravan after work. Eight hours of constant bending had left him wanting nothing more than to just collapse onto his bed and remain there until it was time to repeat the whole process again in the morning. Of course, for him to hope for a moment to himself in such a close-knit environment was pure whimsy.

'I wouldn't get too comfortable if I were you,' warned Colin, as he took off his mud caked boots. 'The guys are meeting for a few after work drinks and I'll be damned if you think you're getting out of having a few beers with us.'

'What do you need me for?' asked Matt. 'Between Rose and your little smoking circle I'm sure you have more than enough to keep you entertained.'

'Jenny's going to be there and so is Jonas,' said Colin, knowing exactly which buttons to press.

'I'm sure they'll make a wonderful couple,' Matt replied, whilst raising himself up on the bed.

'Come on,' urged Colin. 'That was a nasty whack you took to the head today. If you're suffering from concussion the worst thing you can do is sleep.'

'Whereas drinking will do me the world of good, I suppose.'

He rotated his body and placed his feet on the floor, ready to get up.

'Best cure there is,' said Colin.

Despite the protestations of his body, Matt followed his friend outside to where a gathering had once more formed around the freshly lit campfire, with only Hiro and Celeste missing from the group. Alcohol was not the focal point this time, as the drinks were merely an aid to relaxation rather than a means of intoxication. Matt promised himself that the minute anybody brought up the subject of sticks he would leave.

'How's the head?' asked Niall.

Matt rubbed a hand over the plastered cut. The swelling had died down considerably, leaving only a minor bump and a hint of residual pain.

'I'll live,' he told them. 'Where's Hiro; he isn't missing because of me, is he? I wanted to talk to him about it on the bus, but I could hardly keep my eyes open.'

Colin started to laugh.

'He's in his van right now committing Hare-Kari. He told us that he couldn't live with the dishonour he'd brought upon himself.'

'Very funny,' replied Matt. 'Seriously though, where is he?'

'Don't worry,' said Rose. 'He's just having a shower. There's always a big queue for them at this time as hot water is a luxury that runs out quickly in this place.'

'Just as long as he knows there are no hard feelings,' said Matt.

'I'm sure he'll buy you a beer later,' she reassured him.

The door to the female shower opened and Celeste

stepped out. She was barely covered by the flimsy towel that she had wrapped around her and all the guys secretly hoped it would slip as she walked past. They had no such luck, but the thought alone was a small reward in itself. The Canadian girl had a body that could look good in anything, but would always look better in nothing.

'I think I'm gonna go and have a quick nap before dinner,' said Stephen, rising from his log seat ready to leave.

A cheeky smile was exchanged between Rose and Niall.

'You must be feeling really stiff after working so hard,' said Niall.

'I bet you cannot wait to get into bed,' added Rose, before they both saw him off with an 'Au revoir.'

He held his middle finger aloft as he walked away, showing them exactly what he thought of their teasing.

'Am I missing something here?' asked Matt, who was finding the pair's behaviour a little strange to say the least.

'Let's just say that our Irish friend is somewhat of a dark horse,' Rose answered, rather coyly.

'I must have hit my head harder than I thought,' said Matt. 'Nobody seems to make any sense anymore.'

'We live in a desert and we spend our days picking up sticks. It would take a brave man to try and make any sense of that,' said Rose. 'I fear that the answer would lead only to insanity.'

Matt let out a deep sigh, before throwing his arms into the air.

'See what you've done now,' he said. 'You've only gone and mentioned the "s" word. I promised myself that the moment anybody brought that up, I would leave.'

'Insanity?' she queried.

'That doesn't begin with an "s". I'm talking about sticks. If I have to spend all day bending down and picking them up, they're the last thing I want to talk about when I get back here.'

'What else is there to talk about? Sticks are what we live for.'

Matt placed his hands over his ears.

'I'm not listening to you.'

'Sticks, sticks, sticks and sticks,' she replied, leaning in to face him nose to nose.

'Do you want me to leave, because if you do, you should just say so?'

'Don't be silly; of course I don't want you to leave. I'd much prefer it if you were to stick around.'

'That's it, one more time and I'm going.'

'Sticks; now fuck off,' interjected Colin, waving his arm dismissively.

'Well, if that's your attitude, I'll stay just to piss you off,' said Matt.

The boys could have kept this childish behaviour up all night, but the girls were already beginning to tire of it. As if to prove this point, Jenny got up to leave.

'I'm going for a shower,' she said. 'I'll catch up with you all after dinner. Hopefully, the pair of you will have grown up a bit by then.'

'I'll join you,' said Jonas.

'I beg your pardon,' said Jenny.

The girl's shock was matched only by Matt, but Colin and Rose found the German's apparent proposition hilarious.

'I will shower too,' he said. 'By the time I get ready, Hiro will be finished.'

'Oh right,' said Jenny.

She turned to Matt and let out an exaggerated sigh of relief. He took this as a positive sign. Once Jenny was out of earshot the remaining three rounded on him. He had been starting to sense a spark of chemistry between himself and Jenny and did not expect it to have gone unnoticed by the others.

'So when are you going to ask my little sister out?' asked Rose.

The question seemed an immature one. This was the way relationships were made on the school playground, with friends scheming behind one another's backs. Surely they were above that kind of thing.

'Ask her out; like on a date?'

'What else do you think I could mean?'

'Well, this isn't exactly Paris. The local bar is like a cowboy saloon from what I've heard, the nearest cinema is five hundred miles away and the only restaurant is the one that we eat in every night. This place isn't exactly conducive to building a romance.'

Matt may have been talking to Rose, but he soon realised that he should have chosen his words more carefully given the other ears privy to their conversation.

'Romance? Listen to Casanova here,' said Colin. 'You're not taking Cinderella to the ball, you know. All you have to do is show a girl a bit of fun and I'm pretty sure you're equipped for what that requires.'

Rose turned and presented him with an open jawed look of disgust.

'That is my little sister you are talking about.'

'That's my point. If she takes after you he would do well to use a more direct approach.'

Colin's proclamation was met by Rose with a delicate slap across his arm.

'How dare you!'

Colin placed his hand on her thigh.

'Oh, I dare alright,' he said.

She motioned to give him a second slap, but he caught her

hand in mid swing. They then started to play wrestle, which made the other two feel uncomfortable.

'Shall we leave these two lovebirds to it?' suggested Niall.

He stood with Matt, ready to leave.

'Wait just a minute,' said Rose, struggling to push Colin away so that she could address Matt directly. 'I haven't finished grooming Matt yet.'

'I'm not sure that I need grooming,' he said. 'I do have experience with women, you know; just not in such unpromising surroundings.'

'That is where you are wrong,' said Rose. 'To Jenny this place is the most romantic on Earth. All you have to do is take her for a walk under the stars. She loves it here.'

'I did already get that impression.'

Despite the encouragement, Matt was not wholly comfortable with his love life being turned into public property in this way. It only served to place undue pressure on him, which he could most definitely do without. The problem was that in such a secluded locale, he could not be sure if it was even feasible to experience anything without it soon becoming public knowledge.

He went back to his caravan where he had the solitude to think things over. It had been a long day for him and the thought of keeping that pace for the next three months was not a prospect that he relished. Of course, if Rose was correct and her sister did reciprocate the growing desire he felt for her, those three months would not appear quite so daunting at all.

Chapter 7

The second pre-dawn start came more easily than the first. This time Matt was anticipating the bus's arrival and leapt straight from his bed the moment he heard it pull into the park. He did not do this out of enthusiasm. He simply knew that the longer he remained in bed, the more difficult he would find it to get up.

'Jesus, you're keen,' said Colin, who was not quite as prepared for the day to begin as his roommate.

'We have another wonderful day ahead of us in the field. Who wouldn't be keen?' joked Matt.

He put on fresh underwear, but the rest of the clothes he dressed in were the ones he had discarded after the previous day's graft. They were caked in mud, but dirt was the least of his concerns. There was no escaping the grime of the field, so why try? After all, there was little point in spoiling another set of clothes simply for the sake of feeling a little bit fresher for a few hours.

Rhett did not prove to be as patient a chaperone as Joe and he repeatedly honked the horn until everyone was out of bed, dressed and on the bus. Even though he was now the boss and had arrived to take them to work, he sulked as if merely being there was an inconvenience. It was like he was an annoyed parent dragged out of bed in the middle of the night to go and collect a group of recalcitrant teenagers who had long outstayed their curfew.

Once all the kids were accounted for it was time to leave. The road they traversed was the same as the previous day, but Matt was surprised by how little of it he recognised. That is to say that there were no specific landmarks or unique features that he recalled from the earlier trip. The road itself was all too familiar. It started out in complete darkness until the rising sun split the world in half; blue at the top and red at the bottom.

Sam and Paul were again the first to have arrived at the field and this time they set a small bonfire to welcome their fellow workers. Once off the bus, everyone huddled around the flames to warm themselves in its protective heat. Rhett allowed them all ample time to bring their body temperatures up to a comfortable level before beginning work. This was, of course, to ensure that he would get the most out of them in the field, rather than an act of genuine kindness.

Once sufficiently warmed, the gang took their respective places around the tractor. As usual, Stephen and Niall were separated from the group as they took on the duty of clearing the large, deeper buried and harder to shift wood. Rhett went with them, which came as a welcome relief to all but the two Irishmen.

Matt was fortunate this time to be given wide duty so he took the side where he would be throwing to Colin. His friend had insisted on this as he said that the temptation for Matt to take revenge on Hiro was much too great for them to chance working together so soon after the accident. Matt took this in good spirits, but it left him wondering if the Japanese man was harbouring more guilt than he let on.

The shift in duties also afforded Matt with a more relaxing morning. He missed the camaraderie of working as part of the pack, but solitude had advantages of its own. He was pretty much free to set his own pace for the day. Naturally, he decided to take it easy. So long as there was nobody standing over him cracking a whip he reasoned that there were certainly worse jobs than stick picking.

Morning smoko provided him with his first opportunity for a bit of social interaction. Having spent the morning further out in the field he was the last to make it back to the tractor. By the time he got there, several different groups had already formed. He knew instantly which of these he wanted to join.

The three Irishmen were standing behind the trailer smoking and Matt guessed they were talking about Rhett as they regularly glanced in his direction. The Australian remained deeper in the field to tender one of the fires, which he had earlier made with Niall and Stephen. This was most likely just an excuse for him to avoid having to attempt any sort of socialising with the backpackers as there was nothing he could possibly have in common with any of them.

Jonas and Hiro, meanwhile, were sitting on the back of the tractor. The German was talking animatedly, which was quite common for him to do. Hiro did not seem to be listening too intently. Although he probably would not have understood much if he did. He was preoccupied with staring at Celeste who was pacing up and down with a cigarette about twenty feet or so from the tractor. She, too, liked to keep her distance.

Even in her scruffy work clothes Celeste oozed sensuality. Matt had known many girls like her in the past. If they were on the coast she may even have been the kind of girl that he would have gone for, but not here. In such a close knit environment a girl like that could only spread discord. When living in such a tight community harmony took precedence over hormones.

The sisters were standing at the front of the tractor cab with Sam and Paul, laughing and joking with the two generations of indigenous men. This was the group that Matt wanted to be party to, but as he approached, he was called over from elsewhere.

'Hey, Matt,' Jonas hollered. 'How are you doing; this job is good - yes?'

Matt was left with no choice but to join the German and his Japanese companion. It would have been rude of him not to.

'It's certainly a lot easier,' he replied. 'A little on the quiet side though. Do you not miss having anyone to talk to?'

'Sometimes, but it is also good to have one time.'

The expression was not familiar to Matt; he assumed that it was a German saying.

'How about you?' he asked, turning to Hiro. 'Do you like working alongside the girls?'

The Japanese man was clearly still distracted by Celeste and averted his attention only long enough to give a brief answer.

'Is good,' he replied, whilst nodding his head enthusiastically. 'They talk fast, but if concentrate, I understand.'

'That'll be Rose,' said Matt. 'She could talk for England that one.'

Hiro again nodded before refocusing his attention on the Canadian girl. Being unable to keep up with most of the conversations that went on, Matt could understand why he chose to occupy his attention with a more visual stimulus and there were few sights more stimulating than Celeste.

'What do you think they will plant here when the field has been cleared?' Jonas asked.

It was not a question that Matt had given much thought to, but what they were doing had to have some purpose. Although what crops could possibly grow in such a dry wasteland he could not begin to guess.

'Perhaps they will just litter it with more wood,' he joked. 'That will keep the stick picking industry going strong.'

'That is what I think too,' replied Jonas, oblivious to the sarcasm as ever. 'People would not come to this town otherwise, so this is how they bring us in.'

'And then what?' Matt asked, interested to see if his companion was going anywhere worthwhile with his theory. 'Our contribution to the local economy is a lot less than what they are paying us for the job.'

'They breed with us,' Jonas answered, triumphantly.

'They breed with us?'

'Think about it. This town is tiny. There are only about two hundred people, which means they are all, how do you say - relative.'

'You mean everybody's related,' Matt corrected. 'There may be one or two potential inbreeds about (he was thinking about Rhett in particular), but I don't think it's become a pandemic just yet.'

'You wait and see,' Jonas promised. 'The local girls will be queuing up outside of my door before long; all wanting my strong Deutsch seed.'

Jonas's seed was the last thing Matt wanted to think about. On the other hand, it was reassuring for him to discover just how immature the young German was. With a sophisticated girl like Jenny he did not think that he had much to worry about in regards to any rivalry from Jonas' quarter. As conceited as it sounded, he knew that he was the one with more to offer the girl.

*

Colin was feeling troubled. During the morning break he had received some unsettling news from Stephen and Niall. They had both spent the morning working alongside the gaffer and in doing so picked up some interesting information relating to the man in charge of them. He hoped that the concern they had shown was not warranted. To try and take his mind off it he attempted to strike up a conversation with Hiro. Success was proving elusive.

'Jeez, you're a tough nut to crack, aren't you? I'd pay a hundred dollars to know what was going through that head of yours right now.'

The Japanese man merely smiled and bowed his head. It was a gesture that Colin was receiving with frustrating regularity. He knew Hiro possessed basic English skills, so there had to be some way to get through to him.

'You can hardly blame him for his lack of comprehension,' said Rose, who had been amused from afar by Colin's failed attempts at bridging the lingual divide.

'What's that supposed to mean?' Colin asked.

'Well, your accent can be a little strong. Even Jenny and I have trouble understanding you sometimes.'

'That's right,' added her sister. 'A lot of the time I can only guess at what you are saying.'

Colin may have walked all too easily into their ambush, but he was not about to let two private school girls tell him how he should or should not be speaking English. There was nothing incomprehensible about his accent. If anything, he thought that their airs and graces made them the ones that were difficult to understand.

'I'll have you know that the Gaelic accent is considered to be one of the most down to Earth and friendly accents spoken anywhere in the world,' he said. 'Everyone loves the Irish.'

'Well, you cannot really hold a grudge with someone if you

do not know what they are saying,' replied Rose, who was clearly in the mood for some flirtatious teasing.

'Is that why you find me so irresistible, because you cannot understand a word that I say to you?' he asked.

'I have no idea what you just said, but it makes me feel hot.'

She had a stick in her hands and she began to suggestively run it through her fingers.

'Oh please!' exclaimed Jenny, snatching the phallic branch away from her sister. 'Will you two get a room. You are not only embarrassing each other, but also Hiro and myself.'

'A minute ago he couldn't understand us and now he's getting embarrassed,' said Colin. 'Make your mind up.'

'I only said that he could not understand you. I imagine he has no difficulty whatsoever with what my sister has to say.'

'Well, let's ask him, shall we?' He turned to face Hiro. 'Who is the easier to understand; me or the girls?'

'Ah...' the Asian began, before turning towards Rose and Jenny for guidance.

'Hiro, do we speak clearly enough for you?' asked Rose.

'Yes. Is hard for me, but okay,' he replied.

She offered Colin a satisfied smile before turning back to Hiro.

'What about Colin; can you understand him?'

'No, no, no,' he replied, whilst shaking his head with a greater than required enthusiasm. 'Ingreesh difficult, but Irish - impossible.'

The girls laughed.

'They're both the same language,' protested Colin.

Hiro again looked to the girls.

'He says that English and Irish are the same,' said Rose.

Hiro laughed.

'Ree-ry?'

'Colin speaks English too,' confirmed Jenny.

The Japanese man looked genuinely surprised.

'My Ingreesh not good, but his terrible.'

'In that case, I will keep quiet from now,' said Colin. 'It's not like anyone understands me anyway.'

'Can you say that again when Niall is around?' asked Rose. 'Communication would be made much simpler by an interpreter.'

'I'm not saying anything to you ever again,' he sulked.

'I hope you are not planning on keeping this vow of silence on Saturday.'

'What happens on Saturday?'

'It is Paul's birthday so we are having a party for him.'

Colin looked at her with feigned disappointment.

'And when were you planning on inviting me to this little shindig?'

'I just did. Paul does not drink alcohol, but I thought that we could get him a cake.'

'Pierro will make cake,' said Celeste.

Her interruption was a statement rather than a suggestion. Her inclusion in the conversation quickly cooled the other girls' enthusiasm to speak freely.

'I'm yet to meet the famous Pierro,' said Colin. 'How come he isn't out here dirtying his fingers with the rest of us?'

'Pierro does not do manual labour,' she replied, condescendingly, 'he is the camp chef.'

'That explains it then; I didn't realise he was camp. Nancy boys are always into baking and things. I prefer to do a man's job myself.'

He noticed that Rose was smiling. His banter was lost on the Canadian girl, but it seemed to amuse Rose no end. She obviously liked it when he stood up to Celeste, which was all the encouragement he needed.

'Will Pierro be coming to the party?' he asked.

'Of course,' she replied. 'He will be there.'

'I'll have to see if I can tear him away from your side long enough to have a drink with the lads.'

'Pierro can drink any of you little boys under table.'

'If he wants a challenge, we'll certainly provide him with one. The three foreign boys here are not much cop, but we Irish can out drink anybody.' He paused briefly before adding; 'especially Stephen.'

Rose was now biting her bottom lip to keep herself from laughing. Celeste, however, ignored the insinuation.

'My Pierro is more of a man than all of you put together and he will prove it.'

Colin decided that he could now take his foot off the pedal as he had toyed with the girl long enough. He knew that he would have plenty more opportunities to make fun of her later; especially after the proposed drinking contest.

'We'll see,' he told her.

Following lunch, Rhett took up a perch atop the back of the tractor. With his burning gaze analysing their every move, the workers were spurred on to completing their required number of lengths ahead of schedule, but they did not get to finish any earlier. Their boss insisted that they kept working until exactly three o'clock. Although the work rate was more productive with him in charge, it was certainly a lot less fun. The girls in particular felt uncomfortable in the old man's presence.

'That guy really unsettles me,' said Rose, as she and the others made their way back to the bus.

'Tell me about it,' replied her sister. 'The only time that he stopped staring at us was when he was shouting at the guys for not working fast enough.'

Rose nodded.

'I cannot believe that Joe would hire such a creep.'

If there was any lingering doubt about the character of the man that had been placed in charge of the backpackers it was irrevocably removed during the drive back to the caravan park. What should have been a straightforward journey back to camp proved to be anything but. The complications began when the usual subdued hush of the tired workers was abruptly broken by a loud thump and then a screech as Rhett roughly applied the brakes.

'Fuck!' the old man shouted, with more venom than a taipan.

Everybody was shaken by the unscheduled and extremely jerky stop. They each looked to one another for clarification of what happened.

'We've hit something,' said Stephen.

'What do you mean?' asked Jenny. 'There is nothing for us to hit; we are in the middle of a desert.'

Colin and Stephen exchanged an awkward look. Neither of the men wanted to be the one to explain what had happened to the girl, who was quick to pick up on their apprehension.

'What are you not telling me?' she asked.

'Well, you must have noticed that there is an awful lot of road-kill around these parts and it has to come from somewhere,' replied Colin.

Jenny covered her mouth with revulsion. She tried hard not to think about what ghastly scene may be unfolding on the roadside. Whilst Stephen and Colin got out of their seats and made their way to the front of the bus, Rose put her arm around her younger sister to try and offer her comfort. Rhett, meanwhile, had already dismounted and the two Irishmen joined him outside.

'What did we hit?' asked Colin.

The old man looked back at the backpacker with a scowl as if inconvenienced by the question.

'Kangaroo,' he replied, bluntly.

The animal lay still by the side of the road. The force of the collision had knocked it a good distance from the vehicle. Rhett, however, was more concerned by what damage might have been inflicted on the bus than the kangaroo. He crouched down to examine the impact point and fortunately for him he could see that the bull-bar had fulfilled its role effectively. Apart from a small spatter of blood there were no visible signs of the accident.

'Come on,' he said, 'luckily there's no harm done so we can get going.'

'No harm done,' repeated Colin, incredulously. 'What about poor Skippy over there; shouldn't we check for any signs of life?'

For once Rhett smiled. The gesture did not make him any more endearing.

'Be my guest,' he beckoned.

Colin edged tentatively towards the stricken animal. As he neared he could see its chest rise and fall and hoped that it had not sustained too serious an injury. When he got to within just a couple of feet of the animal it violently bucked, launching itself up into the air with its powerful legs. Colin fell onto his backside and instinctively raised his arms to fend off any subsequent attack, but the kangaroo merely dropped back to the ground before rolling onto its side.

'Jesus!' exclaimed Colin. 'The little bastard scared the life out of me. I guess we didn't hit it as hard as we thought we did.'

Stephen was shaking his head as he helped his friend back to his feet.

'Look again,' he said.

This time when Colin looked at the animal the full extent of its injuries became all too apparent. Its head was bent to an impossibly obtuse angle and trickles of blood could be seen to have formed around its mouth. The creature was clearly suffering and it was obvious to him that it would not survive for long on its own.

'What should we do?' he asked.

The rest of the boys had gotten off the bus when they heard the commotion and they all eagerly waited on Rhett's answer. Each one of them was hoping that their first encounter with the local wildlife would not leave behind a bitter taste.

'We don't do anything,' the Australian replied. 'It's as good as dead, so why bother.'

This was not the response that anybody wanted to hear.

'Could we take it to a vet?' asked Niall.

Rhett laughed.

'If you are so concerned about helping the thing the best you can do is to put it out of its misery.'

'You mean kill it?'

'Like I already said; it is as good as dead anyway. If you want to speed things up I won't stop you.'

Niall did not anticipate being placed on the spot in this way and had no answer. His silence was enough to convey to Rhett what it was that the backpackers expected from him.

'Have I got to do everything myself?' he asked, impatiently.

When no response came, the Australian let out a sigh of frustration before climbing back on the bus. There was a toolbox tucked under the driver's seat. He opened it up and took out a screwdriver, which he turned over in his hands several times, mentally weighing up its effectiveness. After careful consideration, he replaced it and picked up a heavy wrench in its place. He then walked over to where the mortally wounded creature lay; making sure to approach it from the top end in order to steer clear of its deadly powerful legs.

Without further hesitation, he raised the wrench high above his head and then brought it crashing down against the skull of the lame and defenceless animal. The resulting impact sounded dull and wet. The backpackers turned away in disgust, but that which they could not see, could still clearly be heard. Two more blows followed, each eliciting a more sickening crunch than the last.

Once he had completed his grisly task Rhett calmly walked back to the bus where the backpackers were quick to clear out of his way. He then took hold of a water bottle and used it to rinse the blood from his wrench, wiped it down with a rag and returned it to the toolbox. He did not show one bit of emotion throughout.

'What about the carcass?' asked Matt. 'Are we just going to leave it?'

Rhett glanced skywards to where a wedge tailed eagle had already begun to circle. It was a formidable bird of almost prehistoric proportions. With a wingspan of up to seven feet, it would not be wise to be caught standing so close to the kangaroo carcass should the creature swoop down to feed.

'There is no need to do anything,' the Australian told them. 'Fresh meat never lasts long in the desert.'

With nothing more anyone could do they all got back on the bus. As Rhett drove them home the pickers huddled around the back seats to keep as far a distance from him as possible. They all wanted nothing more than to try and put the memory of the brutality that they had just witnessed as far towards the back of their minds as possible. Despite them having no influence or responsibility for what happened a feeling of guilt and shame prevailed throughout.

'I cannot believe we let that happen,' said Matt.

'There was nothing else we could have done,' replied Colin. 'Nature is cruel; that's just how it is.'

'I know, but here it all seems so amplified. Everything is preying on everything else. If it isn't eagles, there's always a spider or a snake looking for its next victim. Why does everything have to be so angry?'

'I don't think they have a choice. Life here exists in such an open and empty environment that there is nowhere to hide. There are no shadows in the outback except those we cast ourselves.'

Matt merely nodded in reply. Although he could see truth in what Colin told him he took no comfort in it. Nothing more was said for the remainder of the ride home.

Chapter 8

Over the following days talk around the caravan park centred mainly on the weekend's upcoming party. Although the backpackers would be spending Saturday night in much the same way that they did every week, having something to celebrate made this night stand apart from the others. Colin, however, still had more serious worries on his mind. He voiced his concerns during one of his regular smoking sessions with his countrymen.

'Do you think that Shawshank is likely to come sniffing around any time soon?' he asked.

'Shawshank?' queried Stephen.

'As in that prison movie; the *Shawshank Redemption*. I cannot use his real name and keep a straight face. Could you imagine that jerk in *Gone with the Wind*?'

'Oh, you mean Rhett?'

'Who else?' He placed his hands on his hips and squared his jaw, adopting what he believed to be a heroic pose. 'Frankly, my dear,' he began, before mimicking a pitch perfect Ocker-Aussie accent. 'I dain't give a damn yer facking cant!'

The impression seemed to strike a chord with his audience.

'So you're still fixed on this idea that your man's been to prison then?' asked Niall.

Colin took a long drag on the reefer.

'I have an uncle that's done time. What you'd call the black sheep of the family. It's easy to see how prison changes a man. After they have been released you soon start to notice little quirks in the character of an ex-con.'

'What sort of quirks?' asked Stephen.

'You've spent the last couple of days working closely with your man. Has he ever quoted scripture or made supposedly random references to the bible?'

'Now that you mention it, he may have said a few things, but that in itself doesn't prove anything. He may just have had a religious upbringing. For all we know he could even be second or third generation Irish.'

'My intuition's normally good on these things. Convicts have a lot of time on their hands and the one book that they all get access to is The Bible. Some of them take it literally too. Then there are the cigarettes.'

Stephen took possession of the joint.

'You mentioned that a few days back. What's it got to do with doing time?'

'Tobacco is really scarce inside. It's not only a source of pleasure, but a form of currency. They have to use it as sparingly as possible, hence the super tight roll ups that we have seen your man smoking.'

'So you're worried that he won't take too kindly to your own criminal activities.'

He nodded towards the joint, which he held in his hand.

'I just think that we should be careful,' said Colin. 'What did you say that he said to you the other day in the field?'

'He asked if we needed anything to help the nights pass a bit quicker. For all we know he may have been trying to flog us some pillows.'

Colin liked his friend's optimism, but he did not share in it. They were all a long way from home, which to all intents and purposes made Birribandi Rhett's town. The last thing that he wanted was to rub a local villain up the wrong way.

'I just think that we should play it cool until we find out a bit more information. Discovering what he was inside for would be a good start.'

'You never know,' said Niall. 'We may get lucky. Rather than being a drug dealer he may just be a murderer.'

He may have been joking, but neither of his friends was laughing.

M att sat on the edge of Jonas's bed talking to the German about Cairns. His younger colleague had yet to venture so far up the coast and was eager to hear the war stories of the more seasoned traveller. Hiro lay on the bed opposite on his belly, updating his journal. It was common for them to hang around the caravans in this way. Although there was rarely any socialising done in the girls' van, the other three were each mini communal meeting places where everyone felt free to drop in any time that they wanted to chat or just share in someone else's company.

'What are your plans for when you leave here?' Jonas asked.

The question was one to which Matt had given a lot of thought. He was determined to make the most of the extra year that he was working so hard for and planned on seeing as much of Australia as possible. What he wanted more than anything was to garner as much and as varied experience as he could.

'I may venture further inland; see the red centre. I suppose that Alice Springs would be the logical step as I could use it as a base for all the surrounding tours. How about you?'

'I'm heading up the east coast. If it is half as good as you say, I am in for a wild time, don't you think?'

'You will be right at home in Cairns. I'll give you the numbers for a few hostels that I've stayed in. I can't believe you haven't been already. Where have you spent all your time in this country?'

'Melbourne, mostly. That is where I flew in to. It is a really cool place. Did you know that the city was founded by Batman?'

Matt stared back, not quite sure how to respond. Jonas was never short of far out theories, but this seemed a little too random even for the German.

'It was founded by Batman; as in the Caped Crusader?' he asked.

'I guess so. They have many dedications about the city. I stayed at a hostel that was on Batman Avenue.'

'I'll just take your word for that,' Matt replied, sceptically.

He then turned to the opposite side of the van where Hiro was applying the finishing touches to a piece of art that he had been working on.

'How about you, Hiro?' he asked. 'Where do you plan on going after Birribandi?'

'I go Surfer's Paradise,' answered the Asian. 'There many Japanese there. Not so difficult for me.'

As Hiro spoke, Matt caught a glimpse of the notebook in front of him. He was instantly intrigued by the picture.

'Is that Rhett?'

'Ah, Rhett – yes. You rike?'

Hiro had captured the Australian's features in perfect caricature, even down to the miniscule cigarette, which the old man was always struggling to balance in the corner of his mouth.

'This is really good,' said Matt. 'Can I have a closer look?'

Hiro handed him the journal. As Matt scanned over the image he was amazed at how much detail had been rendered. The Asian clearly had some talent.

'Are you an artist?' asked Matt.

Hiro blushed.

'No, no – just for fun.'

'You could sell these. What else have you drawn?'

Matt started to turn the page over, but Hiro was quick to snatch it back from him.

'Personal,' the Japanese man said, as he reclaimed his property.

Matt was a little taken aback by the abruptness shown to him. Of course, he had been prying into the other man's business without any real cause. It was understandable that Hiro could be embarrassed if he was not used to sharing his art with people. Matt apologised before resuming his conversation with Jonas.

Later that evening when the two were by themselves, Matt brought up the subject of Hiro's reaction.

'Did you see the way that Hiro snapped at me earlier?' he asked.

'I saw him stop you from reading his diary,' replied Jonas. 'I think anyone would do the same.'

'He offered it to me. Besides, he must write it in Japanese so what could I possibly see in there?'

'You wanted to look at the pictures and he did not want you to. Do not worry about it. They are no big deal anyway.'

'You've seen them?'

'I've seen some. Mostly they are nonsense. He draws a lot of naked women, but with little detail. Sometimes he just draws the boobies. Hiro is a boob man, I think.'

Matt always liked to hear Jonas's unique perspective on things. The young German had a refreshingly simple brand of optimism, which he found to be invaluable at times, especially in the outback.

'Maybe we should find him a girl,' suggested Matt.

'When I find myself a girl, I can then start thinking about my friends. It is easy for you with the English girls here. It is a little difficult when you speak a different language.'

Matt was reassured by Jonas's assumption. Colin and Rose were now established as a couple and he hoped that Saturday's party would present the opportunity for him and Jenny as well. With the threat of competition now effectively removed, he was more positive than ever about the upcoming celebration.

Chapter 9

Saturday brought with it the prospect of a generous lie-in for everyone. For Matt especially this was a time to be savoured. In Cairns, he had often slept through to midday as he usually worked the late shifts at the bar. He could hardly believe that it had been just a week since he left, such was the extent to which his life had changed since then.

Neither he nor Colin had set an alarm, so he woke naturally as the morning heat forced him out of his bed. The caravan was poorly ventilated and the combination of sweat and dirty clothing was not a good mix. He sat on the step outside of the van to get some fresh air whilst he adjusted to the morning.

Jonas and Hiro occupied the van opposite and Matt was unable to tell if either of them had risen. With no books or television, the one thing that he dreaded above all else was being alone. The company of others was the only distraction offered in this kind of environment. Colin and Rose had made a connection on the first night and had grown closer to one another as the week progressed. Matt hoped that he would be given the opportunity to form a similar connection with Jenny at the party.

By noon everybody was awake and out of their beds. Rose and Jenny took the lead in organising Paul's party and were both keen on getting it all planned down to the smallest detail. They drew up a list of everything that would be needed and then coerced Colin and Matt into accompanying them to the shops to help carry it all back to camp.

The budding couples played it coyly as they followed the dusty trail into town, with the girls walking side by side several paces ahead of the boys. The distance was just enough that each pair was out of earshot of the other. The sisters giggled amongst themselves and every so often Rose would glance furtively over her shoulder.

'They're talking about us, you know,' said Colin.

'It's more likely that they're talking about you,' replied Matt.

'They probably think that we're talking about them too, but I wouldn't give them that pleasure.'

'You could have fooled me. So what are we talking about?'

Colin lit a cigarette.

'The party, obviously. Tonight is a chance for you and I to really let go. It's all too easy to grow accustomed to the lifestyle when you're travelling, but here we have to savour every chance that we get to have some fun.'

'I've had a lot of good nights since leaving home. Somehow I think tonight will suffer in comparison.'

Colin shook his head.

'That's precisely the attitude we need to change. You do realise that if all goes well tonight it could set us up for the rest of our stay here.'

Matt did not follow. He began to wonder if Colin had added some of his herbal flavour to the cigarette he was smoking.

'You've lost me. What's so great about tonight aside from

it being the birthday of someone that we hardly even know?'

'Have you met Pierro yet?'

Matt had only caught brief glimpses of the man in question, but having worked alongside Celeste he had heard more than he would like about the enigmatic chef.

'We've never been formally introduced, but I have heard a lot about him. He's supposed to be Italian, but Niall reckons he's a local. I'm not too sure how that works though.'

'Everyone here is descended from immigrants; except the Aboriginals, obviously. Some must cling on to their heritage more than others.'

'I suppose that makes sense. Do you think he has ever even been to Europe?'

'I wouldn't have a clue about that, but Celeste seems impressed. Then again, I suppose she's probably never been to Europe either.'

Matt often forgot that the girl was from Canada and not France. Her accent and mannerisms were so exaggeratedly Gallic that it was hard to think of her as anything else. One of the peculiarities of the backpacker circuit was that people tended to really play on their national identities, sometimes even bordering on self-caricature and Celeste was certainly no different in that respect.

'So what has all of this got to do with the party?' asked Matt.

Colin glanced towards the girls to make sure they were still out of earshot.

'Your man Pierro has the keys to the camp's stockroom. From what I gather, it's not only kitchen supplies that are in there, but everything for the bar too.'

'And you think that if we can get him onside he may siphon off a few freebies for us, is that it?'

'Not exactly. His bird's challenged me and the other lads to a drinking contest on his behalf. I say that we get him half cut and take the keys.'

'And what then? If you clean the place out, the theft is going to be obvious and if you don't, it won't be long before Pierro realises his keys are missing and has the locks changed.'

'Don't worry, I have it covered. Niall has found a place in town that cuts keys and it is open on Sundays. Pierro will find his "lost" keys long before he recuperates from his hangover.'

'Sounds like you have it all planned out. You're turning into quite the criminal kingpin in these parts.'

Colin appeared offended by the suggestion.

'What do you mean?'

'First you flood the market with free weed and now you're turning to bootlegging. You've only been here for a week and already you have a résumé that would make Al Capone envious.'

'I'm not profiting from any of this.'

'Robin Hood was still an outlaw.'

A broad smile appeared on the Irishman's face.

'Robin Hood; I like that.'

As Colin began to view himself in a more glamorous light, the four backpackers entered the outskirts of the town. Although small, there was still a section of suburban housing that had to be traversed before they reached the commercial main street. The area was clearly impoverished, with overgrown gardens and several boarded windows. If they had stumbled across this place at night they would not have felt quite so safe. A group of five Aboriginal youths were gathered on a street corner.

Matt thought that he recognised one of them as the boy whom he had seen shoplifting the previous week. The youth was a part of a group of five, all of them aged no more than sixteen or seventeen years old. They were chatting amongst themselves and paid little attention to the passing girls, but when Matt and Colin approached they began to disperse with only two of them remaining behind. One of these had an unlit cigarette in his hand.

'Could you spare a fella a light?' the youth asked.

Colin reached into his pocket and pulled out his lighter. He flicked the flame on with his thumb and extended it towards the youth, who lent forward with the cigarette in his mouth and took a deep inhalation to allow the flames to take hold.

'Thanks,' he said. 'You fellas are not from around here, are you?'

'Is it that obvious?' replied Colin. 'What gave it away?'

'Your shoes. They don't sell clobber like that in 'Bandi.'

Colin smiled to humour the boy.

'My shoes, eh? You're a funny guy. You know, I'd love to stay and chat, but we don't want to keep our lady friends waiting.'

He glanced back at Matt and nodded for him to start walking again.

'Not so fast,' said the youth, placing his free hand on Colin's chest. 'I said that I like your shoes.'

This time his tone had changed. It had become more demanding, more aggressive.

'You want me to give you my shoes – is that what you're saying?' asked Colin.

'I'm not saying man, I'm telling.'

'Well, I'm telling you to fuck off,' said Colin.

He grabbed hold of the boy's wrist and pulled it from his chest. He then turned to say something to Matt, briefly taking his eyes off the youth. The young would-be gangster took full advantage by removing the cigarette from his mouth and pressing the lit end firmly into the back of Colin's forearm

This Irishman shrieked in pain, but before he or Matt

could react the kids had already started running away. Instinctively, they both wanted to follow, but a far more pressing concern was developing further up the path. Rose and Jenny were coming under attack from the other three gang members.

'Shit!' Matt cried out.

Eager to intervene, he unconsciously shoved Colin out of the way so that he could run to help the girls. Though he sprinted as fast as he could, it was not quick enough. A few seconds was all the youths needed.

Rose, being the elder of the two sisters, naturally tried to protect her younger sibling by placing herself in between Jenny and the muggers. This left her dangerously exposed and one of the gang grabbed onto the base of her handbag; tugging at it violently. When she refused to let go, another of the kids slapped her across the cheek with the back of his hand.

This time she had no choice but to release her grip and her attackers were able to run away having successfully acquired what they wanted. Any pain Rose should have felt from the assault was supplanted by the shock. She became faint and when Matt caught up with her she fell into his arms, preventing him from giving chase. The other sister knelt down to help, with tears welling in her eyes.

'Jesus Christ – what happened?' he asked. 'Did they have a knife?'

'I don't think so,' Jenny replied. 'She hasn't been stabbed, they just hit her. Is she going to be okay?'

'She'll be fine,' Matt told her. 'I think we should get her checked out just in case though.'

Jenny nodded, her terror had not yet subsided and she flinched as a figure appeared just behind her, but luckily for her, it turned out to be a friend.

'What the fuck just happened?' Colin demanded, having

arrived late on the scene through having to deal with his own injury.

'Rose has been hit,' Matt told him. 'One of those cowards smacked her in the face. Obviously, the plan was for that little shit to distract us whilst his friends made off with the girls' bags. They played us for fools.'

'Those bastards!' Colin shouted, unable to contain his anger. 'I'll rip their fuckin' heads off!'

He turned around, scanning the area for signs of where the youths might have ran, but was unable to pick up a trail.

'COWARDS!' he screamed, unsure of where even to direct his rage.

'That's not helping,' said Jenny. 'We have to take care of Rose.'

Matt had managed to place the elder sister down onto the ground in a sitting position just as she was starting to come to. As her shock subsided, the pain increased, as if some sort of equilibrium needed to be maintained and she rubbed urgently at her face, trying to soothe away the agony. Colin crouched down and delicately pulled aside her hand so that he could inspect the damage. There was already a considerable bruise forming on her cheek, but fortunately, the thug had missed her eye and though painful, there would be no lasting effects. This did little to alleviate the Irishman's rage.

'This is a tiny town,' he said. 'I say that we leave no stone unturned until we find those scumbags and beat the living shite out of them.'

'What will that achieve?' asked a still tearful Jenny. 'All I care about is making sure my sister is okay.'

Matt recalled seeing a police station on his previous visit to the town. They would be sure to have medical supplies there and could also help with catching the muggers. It was a small town and chances were that there would not be too many kids matching the description of the ones behind the attack.

'The police station is only about a five minute walk from here,' he suggested. 'We should take her there.'

The others agreed and the three of them helped Rose back onto her feet. She could have walked unaided, but Colin in particular did not wish to take any chances. He placed his arm around her and supported her weight as they made the brief walk to the station. Matt led the way, all the time keeping a keen eye out should any of the youths return. Any thoughts of the planned celebration were now long forgotten.

Chapter 10

The station had just one officer on duty. If the laws of supply and demand were correct, this suggested that the town's criminal fraternity was not usually very active during the weekend. As the four backpackers entered, this sole upholder of law and order was hard at work stretching his detective skills to the limit, trying to solve one of the most difficult puzzles he had ever faced in almost thirty years on the job.

A bell was triggered by the opening of the front door, which alerted the policeman to the new presence in the room. He glanced up from the papers that had previously occupied his thoughts.

'Have any of you kids ever been to a place named Constantinople?' he asked.

Colin and Matt shared a look of incomprehension followed by suspicion. After their ordeal, they were naturally on the defensive. Colin in particular was quick to ensure he gave the policeman an alibi to prove he could not have been involved in whatever had happened at the place in question.

'We've been together at the caravan park all morning,' he

said. 'I can assure you that nobody here has been to Constanti-what's-it. Isn't that right, guys?'

He turned to the others for their reassurances.

'Don't be a cretin, Colin,' sneered Jenny. She then turned to the police officer. 'By Constantinople, I assume that you mean Istanbul. My sister and I visited there once on holiday as children, but I cannot see how that could possibly be of any relevance.'

'Istanbul, eh?' He scribbled something onto the paper in front of him. 'What is a word for someone who is bad tempered and irritable?'

'Angry.'

He briefly smiled, but his face dropped when he looked down at his paper.

'It can't be angry as this begins with a "T".'

'Tetchy, perhaps?'

'That's excellent.' He was completely unaware of the irony in the girl's answer. 'Now can you tell me what Japanese horseradish is?'

'No, I certainly cannot. Can you tell me who I need to speak to if I want to report a crime?'

The policeman was disappointed, but he was also a professional with a job to do. He threw his paper down onto the counter, revealing it to be a copy of the Brisbane Morning Herald. Local affairs did not warrant their own printing press so like many things in this town the news came imported from the city.

'How can I help?' he asked.

'My sister has been mugged,' replied Jenny. 'It happened when we were walking into town from the caravan park.'

The policeman looked Rose up and down. He was instantly drawn to the emerging bruise on her cheek.

'And did the perpetrator inflict that injury?'

This time Colin stepped forward to answer. He was inwardly reeling from the way Jenny had talked down to him a moment earlier and was determined to re-establish his authority.

'Yes, they did and they also burned my arm.'

He held out his scarred forearm for inspection. There was an opening in his skin equal in diameter to the cigarette that inflicted it, but it appeared larger due to the thickly congealed discharge of blood, which covered it like a wax seal.

'That looks nasty,' said the policeman. 'The first thing we need to do is to get that cleaned up.'

He briefly disappeared into a side room before returning with a small metal first aid tin. From inside, he removed some antiseptic cream and a roll of gauze. Rather than apply the medication himself, he handed it to Colin, who in turn passed it on to Rose to do the honours. All thoughts of the recent attack dissolved along with the pain as she tenderly dressed the damaged skin. He may not have received his injury as a conscious means of protecting her, but that did not matter. In her eyes he was a hero all the same. For the briefest of moments they were locked in one another's gaze until the policeman interrupted their intimacy.

'This will work best if I interview each of you separately. That way you can all give a clear, unbiased account without unduly influencing each other, either consciously or otherwise.'

Colin was not comfortable with the policeman's plan. He turned and looked him firmly in the eye.

'I have no objections to giving my statement alone, but I insist on being beside Rose when you talk to her. After what she's just been through there is no way that I'm going to let you put her in the dock like she's the criminal.'

'I assure you that I will not place her under any

unnecessary stress.'

'And I assure you that she is not going into any interrogation room without me.'

The policeman looked like he was about to object, but then seemed to think better of it. He lifted a cutaway section of the service counter to allow the couple through and then led them down a short corridor into a back office.

'The interrogation room is for suspects,' he told them. 'This is where we hold the public interviews.'

They entered a small, unimposing office. There were two desks that were both cluttered with files and stacks of paperwork. Although there were no computers, the rafts of printouts suggested that the station did, at least, have use of some twenty first century crime fighting aids. Community action posters lined the walls, urging vigilance and co-operation from the town's law abiding residents.

The officer beckoned the pair to take seats at one of the desks whilst he took his own seat opposite. He was middle aged and in the light of the office it could be seen that he had a friendly smile and kind eyes. He also sported the kind of handle bar moustache that was normally reserved only for those trying to raise sponsorship for charity, yet *Movember* was months away.

'This should not take too long,' he said. 'First of all, we will need to establish a few basic background facts.'

He retrieved a small stack of memo-like papers from a drawer of the desk. The sheets were 3-ply with white, pink and blue sheets respectively.

'I am Sheriff Norman Lee and I run this station. We are a small outfit. The only permanent policing staff that we have here are myself and my deputy, who has been with the department for seven years now. As you can probably guess, being a compact community there is not much criminal activity going on in this town. You folks have been extremely unfortunate to be in this position.'

Colin tried not to focus too intently on the man's moustache.

'It's good to know that we aren't keeping you from something serious like a murder investigation or anything,' said the Irishman.

The sheriff smiled.

'There has only ever been one murder in this town and that was thirty years ago, back when I was still a cadet. Thankfully such evil times have never been repeated. Now may I take your names please?'

'I'm Colin O'Meara and this is Rose Miller.'

The sheriff leaned across the desk to extend his hand to both of them in turn.

'Pleased to meet you,' he said. 'It's a shame that we could not have met under less formal circumstances. Are those your full names?'

'Anne is my middle name,' said Rose.

Colin merely nodded as the sheriff began to fill out the top of the reports. The pair were also asked to confirm their ages and nationalities.

'You said earlier that you are staying at the caravan park. I assume you mean Joe Wilson's place.'

Colin looked to Rose for guidance. She nodded.

'I guess so,' he replied. 'I was only ever introduced to him as Joe. He hasn't been around much. There's some other guy running things at the moment.'

The policeman put down his pen, indicating that the following part of the conversation was going to be off the record.

'I take it you are referring to Mr Butler.'

Colin shrugged.

'That's the guy's name,' he replied, 'but we know very little about him.'

The sheriff paused whilst trying to decide how much information he could divulge to the couple. He wanted to warn them, but not so much that it would cause them to worry unduly.

'Mr Butler has somewhat of a chequered past. Whilst I have no reason to believe that he has not reformed his character, I would recommend that you keep a good professional distance from him and let me know if you notice anything suspicious about his behaviour.'

'We just work for the guy so there's not a lot I can say about him.'

Colin was intrigued by the Policeman's unexpected line of questioning, but did not want to ask too many questions himself. The matter was soon laid to rest, however, as they went on to give their formal accounts of the attack. Colin went first and completed his statement swiftly. Rose, on the other hand, was interrupted by a buzzer from the reception shortly after beginning her account.

'I'm terribly sorry about this,' said the sheriff. 'I will be back as soon as possible.'

He stood and then left the office leaving the two of them unattended. The police station was small and a muffled conversation could soon be heard coming from the reception.

'What do you think that thing with Rhett was all about?' asked Rose.

'Isn't it obvious?' replied Colin. 'I said from the start that your man has form.'

The Irishman craned his neck to check the doorway before standing and making his way to a bank of filing cabinets lining the far wall. The concern in the sheriff's voice when Rhett was mentioned had heightened his suspicions regarding the old man. If their boss was known to the police then the chances were that they would have a record on him. He began looking over the filing cabinet.

'You can't do that,' protested Rose. 'What if you get caught?'

'Don't worry,' he assured her. 'I'll be as quick as I can.'

Colin estimated that he would have a window of no more than two to three minutes before the sheriff returned. All he wanted was to find out the reason behind the man's criminal record and he would never again be given a chance like this. It was an opportunity too good to miss.

The cabinets were labelled alphabetically and he went straight for A to E. He pulled on the drawer, tentatively at first, as he assumed it would be locked, but it slid open without resistance. Flicking through the dividers, it did not take long for him to find the file labelled *Butler, Rhett.*

'Hurry up,' urged Rose.

The file was thicker than Colin had anticipated and it was mostly handwritten. He reasoned that merely scanning through the pages would be too time consuming, so he instead took his mobile phone from his pocket and began capturing images of each page in turn. He did not have time to copy them all, but he thought that a half dozen or so would be a large enough sample to piece together Rhett's criminal past.

At the back of the file there was a mugshot, which must have been close to thirty years old at least. The features were not instantly recognisable, but the fire behind the eyes was unmistakable. Time may have drastically changed the way that Rhett looked over the years, but Colin could see that the same cold and bitter attitude was there from the beginning. He added a copy of the photograph to his illicit collection before replacing the file and dashing back to his seat.

Colin's heart was beating fast. Rarely had he felt such

excitement and he liked it. Just moments after re-joining Rose at the desk the sheriff returned to conclude their interview. If the lawman suspected what Colin had been up to, the young traveller would be in big trouble.

'I'm sorry about that,' the sheriff said. 'We will pick up where we left off and then I only need to take down an inventory of what was stolen before I can let you go.'

Rose did not dwell too long on her account of events. She was far more concerned that the sheriff would uncover Colin's recent misdemeanour. They had come to report a crime and she had no desire to be convicted of one herself. Matt and Jenny were still seated at the reception waiting for their turn to give statements when she and Colin came back out from the interview room. Colin told them that he would walk her home and that Matt should hang on to do the same for Jenny, who was the next to be called into the office.

Once they had left the station, the couple decided to skip the idea of carrying on with their shopping trip and instead headed straight back to the park. Rose was naturally nervous about anybody seeing her bruises so Colin distracted the group whilst she went back to her van to conceal them as best she could with make-up.

As soon as the news of the attack had been passed on, Stephen and Niall offered to go into town to pick up the shopping as they were all now more determined than ever to enjoy their party.

Jenny was not surprised in the least by the question with which the sheriff began his inquiry.

'Wasabi,' she answered.

Having to wait in the reception area whilst Colin and Rose were interviewed had given the girl ample time to calm down.

Despite missing some of the obvious home comforts she was beginning to feel at home in the outback. She liked the way the people were free from pretention and greed, but most of all it was the absence of unnecessary bureaucracy. If the sheriff had time to complete a crossword it meant that he was not bogged down with pointless paperwork. This in turn implied that he may actually take the necessary action to solve the crime rather than just write up a report about it.

After giving her statement, Jenny had a few questions of her own for the sheriff.

'What will happen to the kids if you find them?' she asked.

'The most important thing is to retrieve your sister's belongings. I know the majority of families in this town and what you have reported today is out of character for any of them. There won't be any need for formal charges to be brought, as the local elders do a much more effective job of bringing the youngsters into line than the law ever could.'

Jenny was intrigued. One of her reasons for coming to Birribandi was to experience indigenous culture away from the watered-down tourist offerings she had all too often found in the cities. She decided to press the sheriff further.

'So the Aboriginals have their own laws?' she asked.

'That's one way of putting it. Obviously, here in the town the same rules and regulations apply to everybody, but there is a protected indigenous settlement located about eighty kilometres away. It's a dry community so there is no alcohol, which means they've managed to stave off the majority of social problems that their people have had forced on them ever since the first colonials set foot on this rock.'

Jenny was pleasantly surprised by the open mindedness of the sheriff. It pleased her to see that a small town did not always breed small minds.

'We have a friend that works with us who comes from that

community. His name is Paul; we actually came into town today to pick up some supplies for a party we are throwing for him tonight; it's his birthday.'

'I know Paul well. He's a good kid. His father has helped us work on a number of projects designed to get this town's youth to take a more active role in their heritage. We work with kids just like those you had your unfortunate run-in with today.'

He stood and walked towards a set of framed pictures lining a wall. When he found the one he was looking for he beckoned her over to take a closer look for herself.

'This picture was taken about five years ago. Sam, you will no doubt recognise, along with myself - the other men are Paul's uncles.'

The photograph depicted a group of men standing amidst the wooden frame of some kind of structure, which she assumed they were helping to build at the time. Their smiles suggested they all shared a strong bond. There were several other pictures all showing similar scenes, but one in particular caught her attention.

'Tell me about this one.'

The sheriff knew at once what had drawn her to the picture in question. Like the previous photograph it showed a group of men at work together, but this time the face of one of the men was obscured by a small piece of black masking tape, which had been placed over the top of it.

'Traditional Aboriginal beliefs hold that a photograph captures not just the physical attributes of its subject, but the essence of the person as well. The man in that picture passed on not long ago. His spirit is now with the ancestor's, but to allow the transition to run smoothly it is important that nobody speak his name, otherwise he would not be able to rest in peace. To disrespect this tradition would be the cultural equivalent of not just treading on a freshly filled grave, but also vandalising the headstone.'

'And to display the picture would have the same effect as speaking the name,' added Jenny.

'Exactly,' replied the sheriff. 'The longer you stay here the more you will learn about these things.'

Jenny was once more pleasantly surprised by the policeman's broad view of local matters. She had also learnt something new into the bargain. The mugging was now nothing more than a mere memory that bore no influence whatsoever on her current mood. Matt would not be so quick to forget, however, as she discovered on their journey back to the caravan park.

'Do you think Rose will be okay?' he asked.

'Of course she will. My sister is a lot tougher than she appears. I would be surprised if she did not milk the situation to keep Colin fussing over her though.'

He was disappointed by her response.

'That's a little harsh. After all, she did suffer a blow to the face and she had her bag taken.'

'She did not have anything valuable in there, you know. Rose is much too irresponsible to be trusted with a credit card and she could not have had more than about $50 cash on her. I have all of our bank cards and passports with me, so there is no harm done.'

'What about the emotional wounds?'

'Are you serious?'

She thought it typical of a man that he believed because Rose had been a victim that she needed protecting in some way.

'If anything, Colin was the one who suffered the most.' she said. 'That was a nasty burn that he got. If he can cope with the mental anguish it inflicted then so can Rose.'

'But...' his voice trailed off.

She could guess at how that sentence may have ended and was glad that he had thought better of completing it. Rather than dig himself into a hole, he wisely chose to sidestep the issue.

'Maybe we should just try and put the whole sorry affair behind us,' he said.

That, she thought, was the smartest thing she had heard all day.

Chapter 11

Dinner was brought forward a couple of hours to allow more time for the evening's celebration. Once everyone had eaten, the mood in the camp became much more positive and nobody dwelled on the unfortunate events from earlier in the day. Pierro even made good on his promise and spent the afternoon baking a cake. The chef was also up for the drinking challenge for which Celeste had volunteered him.

Stephen and Niall, meanwhile, managed to purchase a range of party decorations, which they handed to the girls to decorate the camp. The pair also brought back a great deal of alcohol; far more, in fact, than either of the girls thought necessary.

'You do realise that Paul does not drink, don't you?' said Jenny.

'I know that,' replied Niall. 'We got your man a bottle of cola. All of this is for us.'

Not wishing to pay premium prices for alcohol at the park, the boys had bought in bulk from the bottle shop connected to the Tavern. They had four large crates of beer and two boxes of wine. It was the latter that caused the girls most concern.

'I hope you have something to mix with that goon,' said Rose. 'You know what happened the last time.'

Goon was an affectionate term given by backpackers to the lowest quality cask wine. Its dollar value worked out cheaper by the litre than water, but it carried more than double the kick of a premium lager. The only thing more legendary in traveller circles than the intoxicating effects of the drink were the momentous hangovers that inevitably followed. Sooner or later, as economic pressures tighten, everyone succumbs.

'You don't have to worry about us, ladies,' Stephen assured her. 'I don't think that we'll have any trouble keeping our heads tonight.'

He gave the girls a wink before the two of them disappeared into their van to get ready.

'They're up to something,' said Rose.

'Do you have any idea what?' replied her sister.

'No, but whatever it is, I am pretty sure that Colin will somehow be right at the centre of it all.'

Jenny shook her head disapprovingly.

'Are you sure you know what you are letting yourself in for with him? I mean, you do remember what happened the last time you got involved with a guy.'

Jenny did not share her sister's affection for the Irishman, but Rose shrugged away her younger sibling's concern.

'It's only a bit of fun. Anyway, he's really tight with the other guys so I cannot see history repeating itself with this one.'

'So long as you are sure you know what you are doing; I'm happy.'

'You're the best little sister I could have hoped for,' said Rose, as she gave her younger sister an affectionate hug. 'What about your own love life? Matt seems quite taken with you.'

'Oh, please,' said Jenny, pushing away her sister's arms. 'He's a nice guy, but you know that he is only interested in me for the lack of an alternative.'

'Don't put yourself down. Besides, I've seen you giving him the come on. Admit it; you like him too.'

Jenny rolled her eyes. She had never been wholly comfortable talking about boys with her friends and discussing it with her big sister just seemed wrong.

'Sometimes he can be sweet, but when it comes down to it he is only going to be interested in just one thing; they all are.'

'That's what makes boys so much fun.' Rose gave her younger sibling a playful push. 'You must have considered it.'

'Why must you always judge me by your standards, Rose? If Matt really likes me he will be prepared to wait.'

'He may be able to wait, but can you?'

'What do you mean?'

Rose glanced around to make sure that nobody else was within earshot.

'You have to look at it from the man's perspective. They will always take the easiest option.'

'Exactly,' interrupted Jenny. 'I am not easy.'

'That is not what I meant. It is not like the real world here. Every day we do the same things with the same people and there is no alternative to that. Men prefer to walk away after one night because it is easier for them to do that than to deal with all the things that come after. In an environment like this, that is simply not possible.'

'So you think that it would make no difference whatsoever whether I make him wait or not.'

'Ultimately, it is your decision, but you have to remember that you will most likely each go your separate ways once the three months are up anyway. Provided that you have realistic expectations, the situation could not be any less complicated.'

Jenny was starting to come around to her sister's way of thinking.

'So you think I should make the most of the time while it lasts?'

Rose shrugged.

'I think that is up to you to decide. You and I are not all that different you know, little sis. We can both be manipulative to get what we want; we just have different ways of going about it.'

Jenny did not argue. For one, when it came to Rose, disagreeing never got you far. And secondly, to a certain extent, what her sister said was true.

Elsewhere in Birribandi, preparations were underway for a much less celebratory evening. Rhett was getting ready to make his regular appearance at the local pub, but the visit would be about business as much as it was pleasure. A good night would mean that he would return from the bar with more money than what he set out with. Recently he had been having a lot of good nights and these were largely due to the steady stream of backpackers passing through the town. Rhett hoped the new bunch would not disappoint.

Before leaving, he had to make an important phone call. It was a while since Rhett had been in trouble with the law and he wanted to make sure that he continued to keep his nose clean. The voice at the other end of the line confirmed that the bar would be free of any unwanted interference from the sheriff, meaning that Rhett was ready to go. He grabbed his coat and made the familiar walk from his house to the pub.

The Birribandi Tavern was as busy as could be expected for a weekend. It was full of all the usual regulars; his regulars. Rhett was disappointed not to see the foreign kids, but he still had plenty of time to work on them. He had squeezed the previous bunch a little too strongly and would make sure not to repeat that mistake. His job meant that he would be able to study this new group more closely in order to find out what drove them and which buttons to press. Joe was paying these kids far too much money and Rhett was determined to make sure that he got a share of it. With three months at his disposal, he could afford to bide his time.

Chapter 12

The gang had just gotten the campfire going when Sam pulled into the park to drop off Paul. After saying goodbye to his father, the young Aboriginal approached them with a spring in his step. He was dressed in blue denim jeans and a smart short sleeved shirt. Away from the grime of the stick picking fields he looked considerably younger than his appearance at work suggested.

'Happy Birthday, Paul,' everybody declared in unison.

This was the first time they had received company in the caravan park and they were all grateful to have a fresh face around. Jenny got up from her seat and greeted her friend with a hug before handing him an envelope.

'This is from all of us,' she said.

He carefully tore across the seal and removed the card from inside. Its front depicted a traditional Aboriginal dot painting of a kangaroo. This was his favourite animal. As he opened the card, several notes fell out onto the dusty floor.

'This isn't money, is it?' he asked. 'I cannot accept this, guys.'

'Look closer,' urged Jenny.

Paul squatted down and picked the cash up from the floor. It was made up of Sterling, Euro's, Yen and even a Canadian Dollar. Each had a goodwill message written on it.

'We did not know what to get you, so we thought that we would each provide you with a memento from our own homes.'

The young Aboriginal was moved by the gesture, but the mood was soon broken as Colin interjected with his typical brand of lowbrow humour.

'The original idea was to get you a stripper, but none of the girls here would volunteer,' he said, with the dryness of sandpaper.

Paul was not sure how to respond to the Irishman's banter, but his blushes were spared as Colin was swiftly silenced by a sharp elbow to his ribcage from Rose.

'Don't be cruel,' she said.

Colin pretended to recoil in mock pain before getting the girl back by playfully tickling her under the arms. Their behaviour made Jenny cringe, but she managed to hold her tongue as Celeste quickly made sure that the spotlight switched to her.

'Pierro made cake,' she said.

Celeste already had a reputation for being an attention grabber and this did nothing to alter that perception. Her child-like enunciation only served to give everyone the impression that the exclamation was not in fact about Pierro or cake, but designed purely to get people to notice her. It was a strategy that she was capable of employing with humdrum regularity.

'I am yet to meet Pierro,' said Paul. 'Is he here?'

'I will go get him,' replied Celeste.

She got up and slowly walked toward the dining block. There was a confidence to her stride and a swing to her hips that suggested she was expecting all eyes to be on her. With the exception of those belonging to the two sisters, they were. Rose in particular found the girl's mannerisms distasteful.

'Pick your jaws up from the floor, boys,' she said. 'If you are not careful, spiders will get in.'

'Don't go getting jealous now,' replied Colin, who despite his attachment to Rose had been one of the most lustful eyed of the group.

It was not the smartest thing he could have said. Jenny giggled, before turning toward Matt and slowly running her index finger across the width of her neck, indicating a beheading action.

'You are not seriously suggesting I should be jealous of *that,* are you?' asked Rose.

She held him with a stare that could freeze napalm. Poor Colin did not know what he had let himself in for, but luckily the return of Celeste with the birthday cake was enough to defuse the situation. She was closely followed by her pseudo Italian boyfriend. This was the first chance the newer arrivals had to find out if the camp cook would live up to Celeste's inflated opinion of him.

Despite his girlfriend's best attempts to big him up, Pierro was not particularly tall. His height, when taken relative to the rest of the group, would place him at the lower end of average. Only Jenny, Celeste and Hiro were shorter. He was, however, well-built and wore a tightly fitted t-shirt to accentuate his muscular physique. With his olive coloured skin and slicked back hair as black as charcoal, he could have passed for a genuine Italian. That is, of course, until he opened his mouth and spoke.

'So which of you drongos thinks they can handle their grog better than I can?' he asked, in a broad Australian brogue.

His bravado was a little too robust for the occasion.

'First, we have cake,' insisted Celeste, silencing her lover.

She placed the cake stand onto one of the log benches and then bent down to cut it into segments. This time Colin had the good grace to look away as she put herself on display. Once done with the cutting, Celeste began handing the chocolate slices out amongst the group. The largest piece of cake was, of course, reserved for Paul. Pierro scanned the crowd intently to see how they liked his baking, but it was met with only muted acknowledgement.

When the last piece of cake had been dished out, people started to break away to form individual conversations between themselves. Rose went with the three Irishmen and they all headed in the direction of the dining room. Celeste and Pierro closely followed behind and the former was clearly massaging her boyfriend's ego after the disappointing reaction to his cake. Jonas and Hiro, meanwhile, were concentrating on building the fire. That left Matt and Jenny to play hosts to their guest.

'So how have you enjoyed your day so far?' asked Jenny.

After her earlier conversation with Sheriff Lee at the station she was eager to learn more about indigenous life, but did not want to be too direct for fear of appearing nosy.

'We do not celebrate birthdays as such,' Paul replied. 'In my culture, maturity is not defined by years. I have many relatives who do not even know their own age.'

'Really,' she said, with astonishment. 'How do you establish seniority?'

She glanced sideways toward Matt, whom she noticed had opened a bottle of beer and begun to drink. It was her hope that he would stay sober, as she thought Paul would feel more comfortable if not everyone was intoxicated.

'A man has to earn the right to call himself a man,' replied Paul. 'It is what is inside his head that counts. When you have the knowledge of the songs and the skills to protect your people, then you are a man.'

'Songs?' queried Jenny.

'That is how we pass down our knowledge; through song and dance. My people do not keep books, as ours is a spoken culture.'

'Are *you* a man?' interrupted Matt.

Jenny found his bluntness to be intrusive and inappropriate. Paul, on the other hand, took it in his stride. He welcomed people asking questions about his culture, rather than for them to take no interest at all. Inquisitiveness invited education, but indifference led only to ignorance.

'I am yet to undergo initiation, but that is not uncommon in this day and age,' he replied. 'With modern technology we are not so dependent on the old ways.'

'Around this place the measure of a man seems to be judged on how much alcohol he can consume in one night,' said Jenny. 'Pierro is being initiated as we speak.'

She turned to face Matt.

'I am surprised that you are not with them; helping perform the baptism.'

'That's Team Ireland's little project. I've got no part in what they have planned.'

'So they are up to something?'

'Like I said, I have no part in it.'

He was beginning to become cagey so she decided it was best not to push any further.

'Shall we take a seat around the fire?' she suggested. 'Jonas and Hiro seem to have gotten quite a blaze going.'

The three of them took seats on the rough logs that surrounded the fire. The glow of the flames projected an intimate beacon of light amidst the darkness. With a clear moonless sky above their heads, the entire galaxy was spread out before them.

'Remember when I told you that I would show you the stars, Matt?'

He nodded between sips of his beer.

'Well, there is no better night than tonight.'

'Higher,' said Stephen.

Niall reached out and overturned the card. It was the seven of clubs. He then picked up the box of goon and began filling a glass, which was placed in the centre of the table. He added roughly a centimetre to the level of the liquid. This took the contents to a little past a quarter full. After that, he took a swig from his beer.

'Lower,' he proclaimed confidently.

This time it was Colin's turn to flip the card. He revealed the four of hearts. Taking the box of goon, he filled the glass just past the halfway mark before downing his requisite two fingers of ale.

'Higher.'

Pierro turned over the six of Diamonds. The Irishman let out a sigh of relief. His plan was working.

'Place your bet,' he told Pierro.

The chef picked up the goon and filled the glass to its rim. He then finished off his bottle of beer before slamming it down onto the table top. He had already consumed double the amount of any of his opponents.

'Higher again,' he said.

Stephen slowly turned the card.

It was the two of spades.

'You lose – drink,' he ordered.

'Fuck it,' said Pierro, roughly grabbing the glass from the centre of the table.

He clumsily poured the liquid down his throat, but without urgency. After finishing, he wiped away the dregs from his mouth using the back of his hand.

'Too easy, although I don't see why we have to use this boxed shit. We may as well just piss in the pot and get done with.'

'You've gotta make the forfeit worthwhile,' said Stephen. 'It is called a drinking game for a reason.'

'And it seems like I am the only one drinking.'

He had a point. The game they were playing was supposed to be each man for his self, but a three to one divide was clearly visible. The Irish trio had earlier agreed that to avoid suspicion they would deliberately throw a few rounds.

When the contest resumed, Niall made an incorrect guess and paid the forfeit. Of course, with just his and Stephen's bets in the glass he drank only a fraction of what Pierro had. It was then once more Colin's turn to place a bet. He added a generous amount of goon to the glass before beckoning Pierro to turn the card over for him. What the Italian did not realise was that Colin already knew precisely what the outcome would be. His opponent was not able to count cards, but he did have a few tricks up his sleeve when it came to dealing them.

The stars shone like fireflies. They flickered like the distant embers of a celestial bonfire. It was not the density of the vast constellations that amazed Matt the most though, it was the colours. There were emeralds, rubies, sapphires and anything else that nature's spectrum could conjure up. For the first time, he truly felt like he was on *planet* Earth.

'It's beautiful, isn't it,' said Jenny. 'Did you know that if we were sitting on some alien world in the centre of the galaxy there would be so many stars surrounding us that the sky would sparkle like a never-ending sea of diamonds and there would never be darkness?'

She was clearly in her element. At times, Matt found her to be aloof or sometimes even frosty towards him. Not on this night. On this night, she was warm, relaxed and extremely alluring.

'A sky of diamonds, eh? Your parents should have named you Lucy.'

She smiled, seductively.

'They did. My full name is Jennifer Lucinda Miller.'

'Well then, Miss Miller, what else can you tell me about this amazing universe that we live in?'

She brushed some loose hairs behind her ear and then glanced around the circle before speaking. Much to Matt's annoyance, this served to remind him that they were not alone.

'I suppose we should start with the easy ones. Find the brightest star in the sky for me.'

He scanned the Heavens hoping that the answer would be obvious. After several passes of the visible skyline, he settled on a bright yellow star that possessed, without doubt, greater luminescence than those around it.

'That one there,' he said, indicating it with his outstretched finger.

Jenny laughed.

'Well done, but that is not actually a star. What we are looking at now is the planet Jupiter.'

'That's impossible,' said Matt. 'Jupiter doesn't glow and there is no way that it can be bigger than the stars around it.'

'It isn't bigger than the stars, but it is closer – many light years closer. That is why we can see it. We would need a powerful telescope to make it out clearly, as from here we can see only the glimmer of the sun's reflection across its surface.'

Matt was impressed. He had never before been able to identify a constellation let alone be able to spot a planet.

'What else is up there?' he asked.

He put his bottle down on the ground, as his head was now permanently craned upwards in awe. Drinking would be nothing more than a distraction.

'Do you see that thick band of stars over there?' she pointed high over his shoulder. 'That is the Milky Way. Well, technically all the stars around us are in the Milky Way, but that really dense bit is the centre. We are nestled within a spiral arm on the outer rim of the galaxy looking in.'

Matt was trying to mentally plot what the Earth's relative position within the galaxy must be, when Paul decided to add some elaboration of his own.

'If you look into the Milky Way really closely you can see the Great Emu,' he said.

Jenny was instantly curious.

'An emu in the sky – show me.'

Paul moved along the bench until their shoulders were touching. He pointed with his arm directly between the two of them, affording them both the same perspective on the direction of his fingertip. Matt was not best pleased about the close proximity of the pair, but he also knew that Paul posed no threat.

'That dark spot there is the head,' said the Aboriginal, tracing his arm across the sky. 'If you follow it along to the left you can see its body. The fact that it is so clear is because now is the time when the emu's lay their eggs.'

Jenny's brow furrowed. Matt was beginning to notice the subtleties of her facial expressions more and more.

'So you can keep track of the seasons by following the stars?' she asked.

Paul relaxed and much to Matt's relief, he also shuffled

back along the bench a little, putting more space between him and the girl.

'The stars tell us everything we need to know.'

'What do you mean everything?' asked Matt, determined to reassert himself in the conversation. 'Surely they can only help with plotting geography or as you already said; keeping track of the seasons. You cannot gain knowledge from them.'

'The stars hold many stories,' replied Paul. 'I think that in your country there are churches with painted windows; is that right?'

'Yes, they are called stained glass windows.'

'And what is the purpose of them?'

Matt had been drawn into the conversation and was not even aware of the apparent shift in tone.

'The paintings usually depict scenes from the bible. When you have a series of pictures together they can sometimes tell a story.'

Paul swept his arm across the sky.

'Well, what you see above you now is no different. To my people, these are our stained glass windows.'

'I don't understand,' said Matt. 'Do you mean the constellations?'

Jenny was not finding it so difficult to keep up and tried to explain it a little easier for Matt to understand.

'It is like Greek mythology,' she explained. 'Surely you know that the constellations take their names from ancient Gods and legends such as Andromeda and Orion.'

'Of course, I know all that,' he said. 'So what you're saying is that Aboriginal people have similar myths and legends that they tell based on the stars.'

Paul was not impressed by his choice of words.

'Not myths, the stories and songs that are passed on are not for entertainment, but contain truths and knowledge that are essential to our way of life.'

Matt did not intend to be disrespectful, but he found it impossible to accept what he was hearing.

'How can they be real? I mean, that doesn't make any sense. We know how the universe works from science and the fact that shapes in space resemble animals is just a coincidence.'

Paul had heard the arguments before.

'Our songs and stories have successfully helped my people and our ancestors to survive and prosper on these lands since the beginning of time. How much more real can you get?'

'He has a point,' said Jenny. 'The Aboriginal culture had not changed for over thirty thousand years before colonials arrived in this country. Even the great empires of Rome and Greece could manage only a fraction of that time before they were consigned to the history books.'

Matt looked to Jonas and Hiro for support, but received none. The German merely shrugged and it was unlikely that Hiro even knew what they were talking about. Matt was at a loss for words.

The contest in the dining room was starting to heat up. The drinking game had escalated into a more direct competition as Pierro insisted on taking on the three Irishmen in a straight race. Fortunately for his opponents, his judgement was not at its sharpest.

'So you think that you can neck a bottle of beer quicker than any of us, do you?' asked Colin.

'I don't think so, I know so. Any of you girls that think you are up for the challenge are welcome to bring it on,' Pierro sneered.

Colin turned to his compatriots.

'Did you hear that, lads?' he asked them. 'Who wants to go first?'

'I don't mind giving it a go,' said Niall, stepping forward to meet the challenge.

Niall was the lightest drinker of the three, but that did not matter. Winning was not something that he even considered. The two men unscrewed their bottle tops and eagerly waited for the signal to begin.

'On the count of three,' instructed Colin. 'One, two...'

Everybody leaned in to keep a closer eye on the pair.

'Three...'

Pierro did not even swallow as he emptied the liquid from the almost vertical bottle into his gullet. He then held aloft the upturned bottle to prove its contents had been completely drained before Niall was even half way.

'Too easy, mate; is that the best you've got?'

Colin passed the so-called Italian his second bottle and then opened one for himself. This contest went much the same way as the previous. As Pierro celebrated another victory, Colin turned towards Stephen.

'This is the dumbest ape that I've ever come across,' he said. 'If we keep him drinking at this rate he'll be out cold in no time.'

Stephen was too distracted to pay attention to his friend. He was staring across at Pierro and Celeste, who were embroiled in a passionate embrace. The drunken man lifted his girlfriend's petite frame up from the ground and was spinning her around as their lips locked.

'Maybe we shouldn't let his ego run away with itself,' he said.

As Pierro returned to the table, Stephen placed down two pint glasses and began to fill them from the bottles. He did this with all the precision of a professional barman, carefully producing the perfect head for each glass.

'Bottles are one thing; let's see how you can handle a man-sized drink.'

Stephen knew that the natives of Queensland, like New South Wales and the Northern Territory, preferred to drink from a schooner, which was substantially smaller than the traditional imperial pint glass. He thought it unlikely that the other man would be used to imbibing such a quantity at once.

'Ready when you are,' said Pierro.

This time they did not wait for a countdown. Instead, they stood facing each other like gunslingers in a Wild West stand-off. The silence lasted for a full minute before being broken. It was Pierro who made the first move. In doing so he clumsily tipped the glass too far and got a nostril full of beer, which sent him reeling backward gasping for air. Stephen, meanwhile, remained calm and collected as he swiftly downed the fluid in just seconds. It was an action that he had performed many times before.

Colin slapped his hands together.

'And Stephen pulls one back for the Irish!' he exclaimed.

'Fuckin' pricks,' shouted Pierro, wiping the froth from his face. 'You got lucky, that's all. Let's see how you handle the hard stuff.'

He removed a set of keys from his back pocket and headed into the kitchen. Colin followed. The kitchen was fairly sparse and was stocked with only the basics, but it was exceptionally clean. It was apparent that Pierro took some pride in his work. He unlocked a storage room and entered only to return moments later with a bottle of vodka. The store room door was left open behind him.

*

The evening was getting late and it was almost time for Paul to go home. The young Aboriginal had arranged for his father to pick him up at midnight.

'Thanks for inviting me over tonight,' he said. 'It has been good to finally see where you guys live.'

'I am sorry that the others were not more sociable tonight,' replied Jenny. 'It has been a smaller gathering than I anticipated.'

She felt most let down by Rose. She thought that her sister could at least have made an effort to spend more time with Paul on his birthday.

'No worries,' said Paul. 'I'm sure I will see them all at work on Monday and however they spent tonight, I expect they had fun.'

As if on cue, Paul had no sooner stopped speaking when they were all interrupted by the sight of a naked Pierro running across the park with his cupped hands barely containing his modesty. The camp's chef was clearly inebriated beyond the point where he would have any level of control over his own actions. The boys all cheered, but Jenny covered her face with her hands. Somehow, she just knew that the night was still far from over.

Chapter 13

Matt removed a beer from the crate and took a seat at the table. He was joined by both Colin and Niall, who were still revelling in their earlier triumph. It was half an hour since Pierro's streaking stunt and the Italian who had never been to Italy was now sleeping off his exertions alone in his bed.

'I take it that the evening went to plan,' said Matt.

Colin took a large swig of beer.

'It couldn't have gone any better,' he replied. 'Your man was dumber than we could have hoped.'

'Did you get what you wanted?'

Colin nodded over towards the end of the table where there was an empty bottle of vodka.

'Your man Pierro finished off that one, but there are half a dozen more that we stashed under the empty vans. We also got plenty of beer.'

Matt took a drink.

'And there's no danger of being found out?'

'That's the best part,' said Colin. 'The store was much more heavily stocked than we anticipated. Everything that we took was from crates at the back, so by the time it is noticed as missing we will all be long gone from this place.'

Rose and Jenny entered the dining room and sat down at the table. They had clearly been having a heated discussion between themselves, but seemed to have resolved whatever the conflict was. The elder sister took the seat next to Colin and placed her arm around his shoulders. She looked around the room.

'Someone's missing,' she said. 'Is Stephen with whom I think he is?'

'They both disappeared right after Pierro passed out,' replied Niall. 'We'll not be seeing those two again until morning.'

'There is no accounting for taste with some people,' said Rose.

This was not the first time that she had made a seemingly unprovoked and disparaging remark regarding the Canadian girl. Matt guessed there was some kind of history there that he did not know about.

'What is it with you two?' he asked. 'I mean, Celeste annoys all of us to varying degrees, but you seem to really hate her.'

'It's not natural to be cooped up indoors on a gorgeous night like this,' she said, pretending not to have heard the question. 'Who wants to go outside?'

Colin rose from his seat and accompanied her out of the door. Shortly afterwards, Niall followed them outside, leaving just Matt and Jenny at the table.

'Did I say something wrong?' he asked.

Jenny put a reassuring hand on his shoulder.

'There is history between her and Celeste, but it is a long story. I just had a heated conversation with Rose myself and now was probably not the best time to go asking her probing questions.'

'You had an argument; is that because of Paul?'

She reached out and poured herself a glass of goon.

'I thought that she should have made more of an effort with it being his birthday and all, but like an idiot, I had completely forgotten about everything she has been through today.'

Matt nodded. There was no need for him to vocalize his understanding as there could be only one thing to which Jenny was referring.

'Rose will stand up to anyone,' she continued, 'but getting assaulted like that has shaken her up more than I thought. It probably sounds pretentious of me, but things like that simply do not happen where we come from.' She touched the drink that she was holding to her lips before pulling it away in disgust. 'Please tell me that this vile concoction is not supposed to be wine.'

Matt smiled at her.

'Now you're sounding pretentious.'

The party had gradually fizzled out. After a few drinks, Rose's mask began to slip and a lot of suppressed feelings regarding the mugging surfaced. The last place she wanted to be was in a crowd of people and it was not long before she led Colin away from the group. As the two of them left, the Irishman pulled Matt to one side for a quiet word in his ear.

'Rose is going to stay with me tonight, so maybe you could, um, you know...' he struggled with his words, but Matt could guess what he was trying to tell him.

'You want a little privacy, is that it?'

'I knew you'd understand,' he looked over in the direction of Jenny, who was talking with Jonas and Hiro. 'You never know; tonight may be your night too.'

Matt waved his friend away without acknowledging the

insinuation. Things were going really well with Jenny and he was not about to blow all of his good work in a moment of drunken stupidity. He returned to the others who had come to a dilemma with regards to the firewood. Namely, there wasn't any.

'What's wrong, guys?' he asked.

Jenny turned from giving Jonas a ticking off to answer him.

'These two clowns have burnt up all of our wood. We only had a limited pile, which is why we always keep the campfire small. Niall has gone to check around camp to see if there are any more stocks.'

Matt could not see what the problem was.

'Surely it's only wood,' he said. 'I mean, doesn't it literally grow on trees?'

'Do you see any trees around here? Unless you want to go into town and explain to the locals why you are tearing up their garden shrubs.'

'Of course I don't. We can send in Jonas for that.'

Jenny smiled and Matt was glad to see that this latest setback had not dampened her spirits. They were soon rejoined by Niall, who was shaking his head as he returned from completing a circuit of the camp.

'There's nothing here,' he said. 'Maybe we can scrounge some from work on Monday.'

Matt felt stupid for not thinking of that himself.

'Of course, that's the obvious thing to do.'

'Don't get your hopes up just yet,' said Jenny. 'You still have to hope that Rhett will let us bring home a load of dead wood on the bus.'

'Why wouldn't he?'

Niall and Jenny both looked at him with their eyebrows raised.

'Because he's Rhett,' they answered in unison.

It was easy for Matt to see their point.

'What's the plan for now then?' he asked. 'Do you guys want to stay up a bit longer and use up what little firewood we have left?'

'Not me,' replied Jenny. 'I think it's time that we went to bed.'

She walked several steps before stopping and turning back around to face him.

'Well?' she said.

'Well what?' he replied.

She rolled her eyes.

'Are you coming?' she asked. 'I know what your wretched little roommate and my sister are getting up to right now, so I am guessing that you need a place to sleep. I must warn you though, that a place to sleep is all that I am offering.'

This was not exactly what Matt had been hoping for, but it did signal that he was making progress. He said goodnight to the others and was careful to make sure they did not see in which direction he was headed. The last thing he needed was for Jonas to offer him a high five, which the young German would almost certainly have done if he knew where Matt was going.

When they reached Jenny's van she led him up the steps. It was the first time that he had been inside and it was a lot cleaner than his own and the ones occupied by the other four guys in the camp. He guessed this was due to the girls own cleanliness and not because they had been given more favourable accommodation.

Jenny did not turn on the light when they entered the van. She needed to change out of her clothes and the starlight provided more discreet illumination than that of an electric bulb. Matt turned away as she undressed, but caught a fleeting glimpse of her back in the wardrobe mirror as she changed tops and slipped out of her jeans. He could see that her skin was flawless and tanned to perfection.

'You can turn around now,' she said.

He turned to face her. She had never looked more demure as she stood lit only by the pale glow of the starlight shimmering through the window. Her partially obscured silhouette only served to increase his frustrated desire.

'I guess it's time to say goodnight,' he said.

His manner was awkward, yet forcefully reserved. What he really wanted was to take her in his arms and to feel her warm body against his. As he looked deep into her eyes, she briefly glanced to the floor, betraying her own awkwardness with the moment.

'There is one more thing,' she began, before gingerly taking a couple of steps forward and taking a hold of his hands, which she used to lever herself in towards him. 'It would be selfish of me not to give you a goodnight kiss.'

She looked up into his eyes for a tantalizing moment, heightening his anticipation, before pressing her lips against his, to kiss him at first tenderly and then passionately as their grip on each other tightened. When their mouths finally broke apart, he ran the fingers of his right hand through her hair, whilst searching her deep brown eyes for the confirmation that he so desperately sought. She said nothing. She merely took him by the hand and led him across the room and to her bed.

Chapter 14

Rhett displayed all his usual charm when he picked up the team on the Monday morning following the party. They decided it best not to mention the firewood shortage to him. Instead, they thought that by discreetly taking just a few logs each day they could accumulate enough during the week to last them over the weekend.

The plan was successful to begin with. Every time that one of the group came across a log of the perfect shape and size, they would put it to one side to be retrieved later. Each of them was bringing a small rucksack to work, which had ample room to stash a handful of small logs inside.

It was on the fourth day that the plan started to go awry. Rhett unexpectedly decided to make a change to the way that he organised things by switching Niall with Colin on the clean-up duty. They assumed that this was just to give people a more varied job, but what they did not realise was that the Australian had a very different motive for bringing in Colin to work more closely with him.

'How are you both finding life at the caravan park?' Rhett asked.

The three of them were gathered around a large stump, the roots of which extended a good distance into the ground and therefore required digging out with shovels. Rhett did not usually attempt small talk and both Colin and Stephen were instantly suspicious.

'It's bearable,' replied Colin. 'After finishing work, we eat, sleep and then the next day we repeat the whole process again.'

'You must find some time for a bit of fun though.'

The old man was acting increasingly out of character, which the pair found most unsettling.

'We maybe enjoy the occasional drink every now and then, but who doesn't, eh?'

'I didn't see any of you in the pub at the weekend.'

'We just stick to the beer that we can get at the caravan park. We're all on pretty tight budgets, so the pub is a luxury we can't always afford.'

'Is it just a drink that you enjoy, because if you wanted more than that I may be able to help out?'

The two backpackers exchanged nervous glances.

'I don't know what you mean,' replied Colin, trying to concentrate more fervently on his digging.

'There's no need to play coy with me,' said Rhett. 'I know that your friend here likes a good smoke. Everyone in that camp does. That pommie guy, who left, couldn't get enough weed and I know he was passing it on.'

Stephen rammed his shovel into the ground, where he then left it before wiping the sweat from his brow with the back of his gloved hand.

'You were Ben's dealer?' he asked.

'There's no need to put a name on it. I simply supplied him with what he needed. I'd be happy to offer the same courtesy to you. Just let me know how much you require and I can guarantee a better price than either of you will ever have paid in the city.'

'We're okay for the time being,' replied Colin. He then looked to Stephen for support. 'Don't you still have a bit left over from when Ben was here?'

'Yeah, when the others left they gave us all their weed as they said they could replace it more easily when they got to the coast,' confirmed Stephen.

Rhett did not seem wholly convinced, but he did not push the matter.

'Fair dinkum, just remember that the offer stands for when you do need something. I'd hate to think that you were stupid enough to let yourselves get ripped off by one of my rivals.'

'Don't worry,' assured Colin. 'Yours will be the first door that we knock on.'

'*I'm* not worried.'

The emphasis Rhett placed on his words gave the pair the distinct impression that they were the ones who should be worried and they were. Their supervisor did not seem like the kind of man that either of them would wish to cross.

'They are all shit today,' announced Jonas.

The group had worked their way towards the far end of the field and the amount of wood to be cleared was sparser than in the centre. It was also composed mainly of simple twigs and leafy branches. There was little to nothing that would be of any use as firewood.

'It's no big deal,' said Jenny. 'We have a small stock at the camp now.'

The German was frustrated.

'I feel like it is my fault that we ran out,' he said. 'I will find some more for us today.'

The dedication and the determination that Jonas showed to right what he perceived as being his wrong made Jenny smile. She had been smiling a lot recently. This was owed in no small part to Matt. He had been placed on wide duty for the day, but she did not mind as they would be able to spend plenty of time together in the evening.

'You seem very cheerful today,' commented Rose. 'Let me guess; you are thinking of lover boy over there.'

'I am not.' She blushed. Then after a short pause; she added, 'it is good though, isn't it? I mean, being able to find someone out here in the bush. Surely you must feel the same with Colin.'

'Colin makes me feel a lot of things, but I am under no illusion over where our relationship is heading. Once he gets back to civilisation he will soon forget about me. Your boy Matt will be exactly the same; trust me.'

She heard the words that her sister was speaking, but Jenny attached no importance to them. Right now was all that mattered and that was going very well indeed. As long as her thoughts kept her occupied at work, she was happy. When they all broke for the end of the day, she saw Jonas run off to the side of the field. He spent a few moments scrabbling about in the bushes before re-emerging with his hands full.

'What is that lunatic up to now?' asked Rose.

'Don't be cruel,' replied Jenny. 'He is just getting us some more firewood. Look what he has in his hands.'

The German was cradling a veritable log in his arms. He slowly hauled it back towards the bus, as running with such a burden would be nigh on impossible. Once he got there he began to haul his prize through the retractable doors. This soon garnered attention from an unwanted quarter. Rhett was quick to pick up on what the young backpacker was doing and he marched towards the bus with menace in his stride.

'What the fuck do you think you're doing?' he snarled.

Jonas was taken aback with shock, as was everybody. They had all been in no doubt that their boss would possess a mean temper, but this was the first time that any of them had witnessed it first-hand.

'What's the problem?' asked Stephen, who was the largest and most strongly built of the group and therefore had no hesitation in standing up to the malevolent Australian.

'What's the problem?' Rhett echoed. 'This bloody idiot dumping waste on my bus is the problem. Where exactly do you think you are taking this trophy of yours anyway?'

'It's j-just for f-f-firewood,' stammered Jonas, who turned a deathly shade of pale with the threat of Rhett looming over him.

'Firewood?' Rhett pushed past Jonas and snatched hold of the offending log. 'I'll show you what the fucking problem is with firewood.'

He raised the wood high in the air before swinging it forcefully down to the ground. Jonas instinctively drew back from the path of the log, but he was not the intended target. The wood came to a crashing halt against the hard step of the bus doorway. As it did so, it broke in two, revealing a brittle centre. The step was covered in what appeared to be tiny white ants.

'Now can you all see what the problem is?' asked Rhett, who was more composed, but still visibly angry.

'What are they?' asked Niall.

'Termites,' answered a voice from behind.

The speaker was Sam. The group had not noticed him arrive, but the moment that Rhett lost his cool, the Aboriginal elder had lent his presence to prevent things from getting out of hand.

'Exactly,' said Rhett, somewhat frustrated by the

indigenous man's presence. 'They're fucking termites. Anyone dumb enough to introduce those little bastards to the caravan park is going to have a lot of explaining for Joe when he comes back. There'll also be a hefty fumigation and repair bill, which I will most definitely not be paying, do you understand?'

'S-sorry,' said Jonas.

The rest of the group nodded to indicate their understanding.

'Is this the first time or have you been taking wood before today?' asked Rhett.

Nobody answered him and the lack of a response from the dumbstruck backpackers told him everything that he needed to know. He picked up the broken pieces of timber and threw them to the side of the field before brushing the insects from the steps of the bus.

The inside of the vehicle was silent on the way back to the park, but not for a lack of people having things to say. Everyone had an opinion on what had just happened, but none were brave or suicidal enough to air those opinions in front of Rhett. Not one word was uttered throughout the duration of the journey home.

Once the backpackers had disembarked from the bus it would be usual for Rhett to leave. Instead of doing so, he turned the engine off and dismounted from the driver's cab.

'I want you to gather up all of the wood and dump it in the field outside,' he demanded

They were made to remove everything and not just what had been taken from the harvest site during the week, as an infestation could spread quickly. Once they had piled up the wood, Rhett doused it in petrol from one of the canisters that they used at work and set it ablaze. In spite of his foul mood, the old man still elicited a gleeful smirk as he watched the wood disintegrate amongst the flames.

'Where's the monkey that's supposed to be looking after this place?' he then demanded.

Heads turned towards Celeste.

'I think he means Pierro,' said Niall.

'What are you saying?' she asked. 'Pierro is no monkey.'

'Never mind that now. Can you just get him, please?'

Colin and Matt were both laughing at her reaction, but Stephen was solemn. He had no sense of humour when it came to his rival. Celeste indignantly stamped off to the dining block. She knew that Pierro would either be in the kitchen preparing dinner or relaxing in his attached bedroom. When the Canadian returned with her boyfriend in tow, Rhett had quite a few things to say to him.

After scolding him for allowing the others to do something so stupid right under his nose, Rhett ordered the chef to spray the exterior of the caravan against which the log pile had rested to stave off any threat of infestation.

Pierro did not offer any protest no matter how humiliating and demeaning the dressing down he received. He may not have mixed socially with the group, but he did have the courtesy to allow them enough space to do as they wished. He did not view himself as an authority figure as to do so would imply responsibility, which was something that he could most definitely do without.

Before getting back on the bus and leaving, Rhett turned to address the group one more time.

'It's quite clear that bozo here is not capable of looking after you lot, so from now on I will call in every so often to make sure that you haven't destroyed the place. Do not let me find anything like this again.'

After issuing his orders the Australian was gone. He had, however, made one thing perfectly clear; the camp would no longer be the safe haven from work and place of relaxation that it had once been. Just after things had been starting to look up, life in Birribandi had taken a sharp turn for the worse.

Chapter 15

Morale amongst the park residents had hit an all time low. Even dinner was not its usual celebratory affair, with nobody bothering to hang around for socialising afterwards. There was a definite mood of despair in the camp and it was affecting everybody. The idea that Rhett could turn up unannounced at any time had them all on edge. For Colin though, there were even more pressing troubles to be contended with. He sat in his van with Rose discussing the worst of those potential problems.

'Rhett tried to sell you drugs; are you sure?' she asked.

'He left no room for doubt; trust me.'

The Irishman lay on his bed, whilst Rose sat cross legged on the floor plucking her eyebrows. Seeing the concern in her boyfriend's features, she put her beauty regime on hold.

'And he also claimed that he was supplying Ben and the others?' she asked.

'That's what he said.'

She got up from the floor and started to rummage through Colin's personal effects on the bedside cabinet. After several moments fumbling, she took hold of his mobile phone.

'How do you check the pictures on this thing?' she asked.

He took the device from her.

'The police reports; I totally forgot about those. They should be able to tell us what we are dealing with.'

He scrolled through the pictures, but the reports were unreadable. It was a cheap, basic model of phone. The display was too small and the handset lacked adequate zooming capabilities.

'It's no good,' he said. 'I'll have to upload them onto a computer and have a closer look then. I'll take it to the library at the weekend.'

She sat down next to him on the bed and placed her arm around his shoulders.

'You aren't worried by this, are you?'

'Maybe, I dunno. The way he was talking seemed really creepy, like there was an underlying threat to it. He definitely made it clear that he won't stand for us buying from anyone else.'

She lent her head on his shoulder.

'You aren't though, are you? You had your stash with you when you came, so he isn't exactly losing out on business, is he?'

'I wish it were that simple. The problem is that Rhett is not only in charge of us at work, but he is now going to start poking his nose into this place. If he wants to make things tough for us, he will.'

There was a knock at the door.

'Who is it?' Colin called out.

'It's me; Stephen. Are the pair of you decent or should I come back later?'

'Very funny,' replied Colin, getting up to let his friend in.

Stephen did not take a seat, but remained standing in the doorway.

'I was wondering if you fancied a smoke,' he said.

Colin looked to Rose and she merely waved him on.

'You two boys go and feed your sordid little habit. I'll still be here when you get back.'

He exited the van and the pair met up with Niall outside. They went to the far side of the park amidst the empty vans where they hoped that they would not be disturbed.

'Is there any word on Pierro?' asked Colin.

'According to Celeste, he is seriously pissed off,' replied Stephen. 'There is no love lost between him and Rhett, but he's still blaming us for what happened.'

'Do you think he'll give us any trouble?'

Stephen shrugged.

'Who knows? I wouldn't be surprised if he was still smarting from his humiliation at the party. After this second incident, he's likely to be baying for blood.'

'Brilliant,' said Colin. 'If having Shawshank on our backs was not enough, he now has his own mini-me.'

The comparison was enough to elicit a smile from Stephen.

'Thankfully, I don't think that Pierro is quite in the old man's league when it comes to intimidation. Although in terms of physical proportion, you may be onto something with the mini-me idea. He is a short arse.'

Colin detected something more personal than mere dislike in his friend's words. He discreetly glanced to Niall to see if he had picked up on this too. The third man returned Colin's look with an equal measure of concern.

'That isn't jealousy I'm hearing, is it?' asked Colin.

'What do you mean?' replied Stephen.

'It's just an observation,' said Colin, holding up his hands to indicate that he meant no offence. 'I'm just a little concerned that you may be getting attached to a certain someone in the camp.'

Stephen screwed up his face to show that he found the suggestion ridiculous.

'Who me?' he asked. 'The way I see it - if anyone here is getting too attached, you should be taking a long, hard look at yourself.'

'Okay, okay,' replied Colin. 'Forget I said anything.'

The Irishman knew that he had hit a raw nerve, but he decided to leave it at that. Stephen was smart enough to take care of himself and who he chose to get involved with was nobody's business but his own. Colin had enough to worry about as it was. No matter what anybody said he knew that the Rhett problem was not about to go away anytime soon.

Matt had just been in the shower and was on his way to Jenny's van when he passed Hiro. It was often hard for him to gauge the Asian's mood and he was keen to find out what the Japanese man made of Rhett's behaviour towards Jonas earlier.

'I hope the old man didn't worry you today,' he said.

Hiro pulled a confused face.

'Worry; me?'

'I mean Rhett; when he threatened Jonas. That was pretty scary, eh?'

'Ah, Rhett - yes; very scary,' Hiro agreed. He then added, 'Facking termites,' in a remarkably accurate imitation of the curmudgeonly Australian.

Humour and music were the only two ladders that Hiro seemed able to communicate with his fellow travellers and Matt thought it ironic that after struggling with the basics of English for so long the Asian had mastered the intricate subtleties of the Ocker Aussie accent. He shared a laugh with his eccentric friend before carrying on and entering Jenny's van. She was lying on the bed waiting for him. Whatever trouble was brewing with Rhett, neither of these two saw themselves as being in the firing line and they were determined to make the most of their precious time together.

Chapter 16

The wood problem was finally solved early on Saturday morning when Sam and Paul dropped by with a large quantity of termite-free timber from their settlement. They explained that they had no problem in keeping the caravan park stocked right through the season and that should supplies run low, everyone knew where to ask. It was agreed by all that to be on the safe side, neither Jonas nor Hiro would be placed in charge of the campfire again.

Colin, meanwhile, spent the morning in the library printing off a copy of the pictures that he had of Rhett's police file. He suspected that the information he was to garner from it would serve him in good stead for the duration of his employment alongside the Australian. He even ran off a print of the mug shot as a keepsake. It would serve to remind him of the arcane spirit that was lurking behind the aged exterior of this habitual criminal.

The bulk of the file yielded few surprises. Rhett had been busted for possession numerous times and had also served a stint in prison for possessing with intent to sell. His most recent arrest was a little over seven years previous, but the fact he supplied other backpackers with weed and then offered the same to Colin and his friends proved that he was far from retired.

There was one report amongst the printouts that predated all the others, stretching back thirty years to when Rhett was in his early twenties. The information that this document revealed was far more disturbing than anything in the remainder of the file and Colin decided that it would be best to keep it from the girls in the camp. At least until he had more of the facts at his disposal.

He was not at first sure how best to use the information that he had on the old man. He supposed that if Rhett were to start and push the drugs more strongly, he had some leverage in that he now knew of the other man's past and the threat of talking to the police could be enough to scare him away. Whatever the case, he was certain that the rest of the guys should know what their gaffer had been up to over the years.

'That was a long time ago, surely you don't think he could still be a threat to anyone?' asked Matt.

Colin had the reproduction mug shot in his hands. The longer he looked into those predatory eyes, the more he could see the familiar Rhett with whom he worked each day. He did not so much think that the Australian had not changed, but more that the old man was incapable of changing.

'Probably not, but we can't afford to take any chances,' he replied. 'The guy's a career criminal. If he cannot profit out of us then we're merely a liability to him.'

'I don't understand,' said Matt. 'Surely you can just choose not to deal with him. It's not like any of you are pedalling your own drugs behind his back.'

'I wish it were that simple,' said Colin. 'Rhett sells weed, and some of us here are smoking a hell of a lot of that stuff. He's going to want to see some of that action.'

'He isn't losing anything by that though, is he? You already had a supply when you arrived, so it's not like you went behind his back, is it?'

'That won't make any difference. The fact is that both Stephen and Niall here were his customers, even if they didn't know it, and now they are getting their fix from me. If he cannot get the money from us by one means, he may resort to another. He might threaten to grass us up to the authorities and exhort the cash from us instead.'

'This is bullshit.'

'I agree, but like I said; we cannot take any chances.'

Colin took a sheet of paper from his pocket and unfolded it.

'Before you pass judgement, you should take a look at this,' he said. 'I separated it from the rest of the file, because I don't want Rose to see it.'

He handed the piece of paper to Matt. The report stated that Rhett had been taken in for questioning in relation to an allegation of sexual assault. No charges were brought against him for the crime, but it did bring a worrying new dimension to his past.

'Where's the rest of the report?' asked Matt. 'This is incomplete; it only refers to the allegations not being pursued. What about the actual interview?'

Colin shrugged.

'That was all I could get hold of,' he said. 'I didn't want to risk getting caught, but surely that's enough?'

Matt was not as easily swayed as his friend.

'Without proof of a conviction, this doesn't mean a thing. Besides, it doesn't have any bearing on your current predicament anyway. I doubt the old git could even get it up, let alone rape someone. All this report proves is what we already knew. Rhett is nothing but a small-time loser and you would be crazy to let him get to you.'

When the news of Rhett's criminal record spread, it surprised nobody and actually served to diminish the fear that the old man held over the group. With the cloak of mystery removed he no longer seemed quite so intimidating and the next couple of weeks passed more easily than the previous.

Time was also proving to be a healer following the mugging on the day of Paul's birthday. Just three weeks on and Rose's confidence was fully restored. She no longer feared going into town, although if she ever suggested venturing in alone, Colin would be quick to forbid it. He did, after all, know of a more serious threat than that of teenage muggers and he was taking no chances with his girlfriend's safety.

On the harvest front, the first field had been cleared and the group was now working on the second. For Stephen, Niall and the girls, this signalled the halfway point for the time they needed to put in for them to qualify for the visa extension. The two men were eager to move on, but the girls were reluctant about leaving their respective beaus; particularly Jenny.

What none of them realised was that their world was about to change sooner than any one of them could ever have predicted.

Chapter 17

The week did not begin well. Since moving to the new field the workers were beset with one setback after another. They were making slower than anticipated progress and this was largely down to a series of sandstorms that would strike with next to no warning whatsoever.

The common perception of seasons being divided neatly into spring, summer, autumn and winter had no bearing at all on how the weather behaved in the outback. Even the simplified idea of a wet season and a dry season, which commonly applied to Queensland, proved hopelessly inadequate. In the Aboriginal calendar there were as many as six distinct weather cycles that were observed.

What the group were currently experiencing was the windy season. This consisted primarily of a series of mini tornados, which peppered the landscape with next to no warning. Whilst these scaled down whirling dervishes were to an actual cyclone what newts were to crocodiles, they still proved highly disruptive.

The biggest problem facing the backpackers was in the composition of the terrain. Unlike the first muddy field that the group had cleared, they were now working in an actual desert. The loose sand was easily whipped up in the wind and in the space of less than a minute all visibility could be lost in a cloud of swirling sand.

Sometimes the storms would blow themselves out within half an hour, but at other times they would rage long enough to put paid to an entire day's work. Over the course of the week two afternoons had to be written off as completely unprofitable. Because of these wasted days the group were advised that if any more time was lost they would have to work the following Saturday.

The early forecast had not been good for Friday and sure enough, midway between the morning break and lunch, the weather took a turn for the worse. It always started with a sudden drop in temperature of roughly ten degrees. When that happened, the gang knew that they had fifteen minutes at best before conditions would become intolerable, but sometimes the Aboriginal men could pre-empt even that.

After bringing the tractor to rest, Sam climbed down from the driver's cab and slowly walked over to his son. They talked amongst themselves for a few moments before Rhett went over to intervene. The Australian would not tolerate slacking off work for any reason.

'Why have you stopped?' he demanded.

'Storm headed this way,' answered Sam, in a slow and deep cadence, which exerted a great deal of authority without being domineering.

Rhett glanced around and above his head.

'Looks clear enough to me,' he told them. 'Keep working and if it does come, then we stop only when we have to.'

The Aboriginal men did not argue and Sam simply got back into his cab and restarted the tractor. Paul offered a shrug to the group, indicating that they may as well follow orders.

Everyone knew that it was not wise to ignore Sam's instincts and sure enough, not more than three minutes after they had returned to work, the tell-tale drop in temperature occurred. As it did so, Jenny shivered.

'What are we supposed to do now?' she asked.

'The boss says we gotta keep working, so that is what we have to do,' answered Paul.

She could tell that he did not agree with these orders, but he was also powerless to do anything about it.

'This is ridiculous,' she told him. 'We all know what is about to happen.'

She looked to her gaffer for any sign of common sense or logic, but he remained oblivious to the natural warning signs that were all around. A twister formed not far from where he stood and he even tracked its passage with his eyes, but said nothing. The first twister was soon joined by others and the sands began to rise with them. It was less than ten minutes since Sam had predicted a storm amidst the calm serenity of the field and they were hopelessly trapped in its ferocious grip. It was a scenario that could so easily and should have been avoided.

'Everybody onto the trailer,' instructed Sam.

Fortunately, the vehicle bore only a light load and there was room for everyone to safely take shelter from the surrounding tempest. Rhett was the last to climb aboard and he did not acknowledge his lack of foresight in not calling off the shift sooner, as Sam cautiously drove everybody back to the side of the field where the bus was parked.

Once everyone had transferred over to the bus, Rhett did not wait for the storm to subside before heading back to the highway. Nerves were tense as the Australian pulled blindly onto the road, but visibility did eventually improve as the caravan park was located well beyond the catchment area of the storm.

'Who wants to go to the pub?' asked Colin.
The Irishman was frustrated that he would be losing his Saturday lie in and was determined to compensate in the only way he knew how.

'The Birribandi Tavern?' replied Rose. 'Are you certain that is wise? Surely you have heard the rumours.'

Colin had a mischievous glint in his eye, which had previously been lacking due to his worries over the Rhett situation. He sensed the opportunity to escape from his troubles, if only for one night.

'That is precisely why I want to go,' he said. 'Who can resist the thought of this town's most beautiful daughters serving cold beer in their under-crackers.'

'If you are planning on eyeing up other ladies then I may just have to come along to keep you from misbehaving,' said Rose.

The rest of the backpackers did not require much persuading to join the excursion. After weeks of being cooped up in the caravan park, everybody was eager to experience a change of scenery and the timing could not be better. The only person not to go along was Celeste. She claimed that she wanted to spend more time with Pierro, but some among the group suspected that the real reason was something different. The Irishmen, in particular, believed that the Italian was tightening the grip he had on his young lover and did not want to let her out of his sight.

Since this was to be the first night out for everyone in several weeks they each made an extra effort when getting ready. Smart clothes, perfume and aftershave were removed from backpacks for the first time since being packed. There was to be no taxi service to the venue though. As usual, they had to walk the dusty road into town.

It was still early when they arrived, so they had no trouble in putting two tables together to accommodate all eight of their bodies. Much to the chagrin of Colin and Matt, as they went to collect the first round, the bar staff was not only fully clothed, but entirely male.

'You two look a little disappointed,' Rose commented as the boys returned with the drinks. 'Is this place not quite what you were expecting?'

She stole a cheeky sideways glance to her sister, who was also looking forward to seeing how the two were going to try and cover up their obvious interest in witnessing the full delights of Skimpies Night.

'Why would we be disappointed?' asked Colin. 'This seems like a fine establishment.'

'How about the staff?' retorted Rose.

'They're capable enough and pull a decent pint. What more could I ask for?' he replied.

Matt just shook his head at the futility of it all. He knew that the girls were just as curious to see what actually went on at this bar as they were and he therefore saw no point in denying it as steadfastly as Colin had. Sometimes his friend just did not know when to remain quiet.

The bar filled up as the evening progressed and in doing so the table drew several curious glances from the locals. These were mostly directed towards Rose, which unsettled Colin. He did not find it easy to contain his disdain for such attitudes.

'Jesus Christ,' he exclaimed. 'You would think that they'd never seen a blonde before.'

'They probably haven't,' replied Stephen, before taking a sip of his Guinness. 'Peroxide's a twentieth century invention.

They're too busy trying to get to grips with those new fangled mechanical chariots to worry about modern hair dyeing techniques.'

'Just one minute,' interrupted Rose. 'I will have you know that my hair is one hundred percent natural. There is no peroxide in these locks.'

'So how come little sister here has brown hair?'

The Irishman was clearly gearing up for a bit of mischief.

'Swedish milkman,' suggested Niall.

'Will you two cut that out,' she protested. 'I assure you that I am as naturally blonde as you two are dumb.'

'Well, that just proves my point,' said Stephen. 'You see, we weren't born idiots. It took years of carefully metered alcohol to reduce our brains cells this much.'

'He's telling the truth,' added Niall. 'Our dim-wittedness is definitely a product of nurture rather than nature.'

Rose scowled at them; her combative countenance demanding an apology.

'Maybe your man Colin can settle this,' suggested Stephen. He then turned to wait for his friend's response. 'Well?'

'Well what?' asked Colin.

'Is she a natural blonde? If anybody here is in a position to verify her claim, it's you.'

Colin shifted awkwardly in his seat. It was not the easiest question for him to answer. He was torn between joining in with the teasing and being one of the lads, or siding with his girlfriend. After a short deliberation, he opted for the latter since it was better to share a bed than to share a joint.

'A gentleman never tells,' was his simple response.

'Are you thinking what I am?' asked Stephen, turning to his partner in crime.

'I think so,' replied Niall. 'He doesn't know.'

'Exactly; I bet she's a Sphynx.'

'What do you mean by that?' Rose asked, suspiciously.

'He means like the cat,' Colin explained.

'I don't get it,' she said.

'Furless,' the pair laughed in unison.

'Are you going to let them speak to me like that?' she asked Colin.

Colin glanced towards the exit, plotting his escape route.

'I'm staying out of this one,' he said. 'Besides which, it's time that I got some fresh air.'

He nodded to Stephen who in turn stood up from his seat.

'Fresh air sounds good to me too,' replied Stephen. 'Are you coming, Niall.'

'No thanks, I've spent enough time outdoors this week.'

Colin and Stephen exchanged a brief look of confusion.

'Are you sure that you wouldn't like some *fresh air*?'

Their friend still failed to cotton on to the implied meaning.

'I've already said that I'm fine here. Are you two okay?'

They remained standing, not quite sure what action to take next, but they were soon to be given assistance from across the table.

'For Christ's sake, Niall, will you not just go outside with your buddies and smoke a joint with them!' shouted Jenny.

She had started to loosen up considerably since getting together with Matt and was showing a much less inhibited side to her character, especially after a glass of wine. Colin hid his face in embarrassment, but luckily for him none of the locals picked up on the girl's unwitting testimony.

'Why don't you climb up on the bar and announce it next time,' he said.

Suddenly aware of her gaffe, Jenny tried hard to suppress a giggle.

'Sorry, I didn't realise,' she timidly offered.

'Well, try and be more subtle next time. For all we know there could be friends of Joe within earshot or even worse - Shawshank.'

At once everyone started to look around, nervously, just in case the old man had slipped into the bar without them knowing. The backpackers shared many common bonds and a dread of their belligerent foreman was just one of them. Even in his absence Rhett projected a foreboding shadow wherever his name was mentioned.

Seeing that the coast was clear the three Irishmen departed to go and enjoy their smoke whilst Jonas exhibited a restlessness of a different sort. Jenny noticed that he had been eyeing up a pair of girls by the bar for some time. She urged him to make a move.

'Go and introduce yourself,' she said. 'I bet they'll just love your accent.'

'Do you really think?'

'Of course, just do not overdo it.'

'What she means is try not to be *too* German,' added Matt.

'*Too* German?'

Jonas was puzzled.

'Don't listen to him,' said Jenny. 'Just be yourself; trust me.'

'Wish me luck,' he said, before leaving in the direction of the girls at the bar.

Jonas did not immediately return, but instead seemed to strike up a promising conversation with the local pair. When the three Irishmen got back from their smoke they were impressed by his confidence to go it alone.

'Quite the dark horse, isn't he,' commented Stephen. 'How come you didn't go with him?' he then asked Hiro.

The Japanese man tucked his head between his shoulder blades. He had a very slender, wiry frame that gave him an almost contortionist appearance, like a posable wireframe model.

'Too shy,' he explained.

Before they could embarrass the Asian further they were briefly interrupted by Jonas returning from the girls at the bar.

'What are you doing back here so soon?' asked Matt. 'You didn't scare them away, did you?'

'No, no,' he said. 'I need to speak to Colin.'

He turned to the Irishman.

'Do you have much weed left?' he asked.

Colin was instantly sceptical.

'A little; why?'

'The girls wanted to know. They said that all backpackers were stoners and asked me if I could get them any weed.'

'What did you tell them?'

He looked for Stephen's reaction, but his friend's expression gave nothing away.

'I said that I could get them a joint; just the one to take back to their place.'

Colin was extremely apprehensive, but he also did not want to disappoint his friend. He was torn between risking word of his stash spreading through town on the one hand and letting Jonas down on the other. So long as it was to be a one off and no money changed hands, he reasoned that he could probably get away with it.

'Okay,' he agreed. 'But on one condition.'

'What's that?'

'Promise me that you're going to get laid tonight.'

'I'll try my best,' Jonas promised.

Whilst his campmate's excited libido spread laughter throughout the group, Colin silently wondered if he had done the right thing.

It was not long before Jonas left the bar with the two girls in tow and it was widely assumed that none of them would be seeing him again that night. Their assumption was to be proven true regarding the German, but one of the girls who earlier left with Jonas returned after about an hour with a group of young locals. These newcomers glanced over to the table where the backpackers sat several times before one of them, who appeared to be the girl's boyfriend, came over to speak to them.

'Excuse me,' he began. 'Are you the friends of that Dutch guy who is with Libby?'

Colin looked the man up and down. His instincts told him to expect trouble.

'We don't know any Dutch guy,' he answered, a tad puzzled by the question.

'I think he means Jonas,' said Rose. 'He must have told those girls that he was Deutsch when he was trying to impress them. He probably thinks it sounds more sophisticated than German. The two words are similar so I can see how they made the mistake.'

Colin gave a nod and then turned to answer the stranger.

'Yeah, we know him. What of it?'

The stranger stole a cautious glance over his shoulder before carrying on. He appeared nervous and his manner was awkward and uncomfortable.

'The girls said that you had some weed. I was wondering if maybe you could sell us a bit.'

Colin felt his stomach tighten. This was exactly the situation that he had been hoping to avoid. He knew that he should have trusted his gut and not given in to Jonas so easily.

'Not us, sorry.'

He turned back to face his friends at the table, but the local was not willing to give up so easily.

'Aw, c'mon, mate,' the man pleaded. 'It's not like I'm on the scrounge or anything. I'll pay you a fair price for it.'

Colin began to feel like he was being watched. In fact, he knew that he was being watched. People had not stopped staring at the backpackers since they sat down. He needed to get rid of the potentially troublesome local and he reasoned the quickest way to do that would be to just go ahead and make the deal. It was against his better judgement, but he could tell that the local was not going to give up and he did not want to risk creating a scene.

'Okay,' he conceded. 'But not here. We'll go outside.'

Stephen followed them out to keep watch. When they returned, they urged the others to drink up quickly as they thought it would be best not to stick around for too long, in case other prospective buyers made themselves known. Colin insisted that the buyer had understood that the deal was strictly a one off, but he also knew that now people knew he had weed, there would always be somebody wanting to make a deal with him. He simply could not chance hanging around the bar any longer.

'Have I at least got time to powder my nose?' asked Rose, barely able to contain her frustration.

'Make it quick,' replied Colin.

The Irishman was anxious. To make matters worse, shortly after Rose left, he heard a familiar, yet most unwelcome voice from behind where he stood.

'Should you children be in here on a school night?' asked Rhett.

The old man sounded alert and Colin guessed that he could not have been in the bar long, but he was nervous as to what he may or may not have seen. Stephen was facing Rhett and had to answer, whilst Colin and Matt tried their best to pretend they had not heard. Colin mouthed "get rid of him" to his friend.

'We're actually just on our way out,' said Stephen. 'We only called in for the one, to check this place out.'

'That's a shame,' replied Rhett. 'The girls will be out soon. Things usually start to pick up after that.'

He eyed the trio suspiciously. Niall and Hiro had managed to slip away unnoticed, but Colin and Matt could not leave without passing Rhett, so they were forced to remain. All the while, they prayed that they would not be pulled into the conversation.

'Maybe you can tell us all about it in the morning,' said Stephen. 'Like you said; tonight's a school night.'

The communal door leading onto the respective toilets opened, but it was not Rose or Jenny that stepped out. It was the local that had earlier bought the weed from Colin. Stephen put his head down, hoping that he would not be recognised. The man walked past without acknowledgement, but when he came to Colin, he gave the backpacker an enthusiastic pat on the back.

'Fuckin' legend,' the man said to him.

They all knew that it was too much to hope that Rhett did not notice this and they were right.

'Friend of yours?' the old man asked.

Stephen made a show of looking over to the guy, who was now walking back to join his friends at the bar.

'Don't know the fella,' he said, then turning to Colin he added; 'how about you?'

His friend shrugged.

'I know him,' said Rhett.

He did not elaborate further. He did not need to as the tone of his voice said it all. The tense silence that followed was broken only when the girls returned from the bathroom. Neither of the sisters attempted to disguise their revulsion upon seeing Rhett. Colin and Matt put their arms around their respective partners and along with Stephen, the five of them walked past the Australian to the exit. No farewells were exchanged and the three men in particular knew that the tension was likely to extend into work the following morning.

They all left quietly, but the silence was quickly broken when they got outside.

'What was he doing there?' asked Jenny.

'It's his town,' answered Matt. 'I imagine he's a regular in that place.'

'Well, thank God that we left when we did. It is bad enough having to tolerate him at work. I could not stand having to see any more of that man than is absolutely necessary.'

'I think that his seeing us was more of a problem,' said Colin.

'What do you mean?' Jenny asked.

The night air had a sobering chill to it and she shivered as it pierced the flimsy material of her blouse.

'It's just a hunch,' replied the Irishman, 'but I think that Rhett may not be his usual cheery self at work tomorrow morning.'

Chapter 18

A slightly later start of seven o'clock was scant consolation for having to work on a Saturday. Jonas was the only member of camp smiling as the backpackers waited for the bus to arrive. He had returned to the park several hours after the others the previous evening after ending his night on a high, both metaphorically and literally.

The youngest member of the group was eager to boast of his exploits, but nobody was in the mood for listening. Neither were they particularly talkative themselves. The entire camp was eerily silent but for the maniacal laugh of a kookaburra bird high in the branches of a nearby tree. The creature summed up the prevailing mood perfectly.

The lull was eventually broken by the drone of an approaching engine. The familiar white bus pulled in to the park, but Rhett was not seated behind the wheel as expected. It was being driven by Sam with an ever-smiling Paul by his side. As it came to rest, the younger man stepped off to greet his friends.

'Where's Rhett?' asked Jonas, who was glad of the chance to speak to someone.

'He phoned up earlier to say that he's running late,' replied Paul. 'He won't be in until lunchtime, so we have an easy morning ahead of us.'

'Did he say why?' asked Stephen.

'Nah, the old man never gives anything away. My guess is a hangover, so he's likely to be extra cranky when he does show up.'

'Well, his loss is our gain.'

They all climbed onto the bus and set off on the hour long drive to the field. As the sun rose, it revealed a pure, cloudless sky without hint of any impending storms that could shorten their day.

When the bus arrived at its destination everybody could see that the previous day's sandstorm had done a thorough job of covering up the wood that had to be cleared. It was apparent that shifting it would be a slow process, which was something Rhett would never tolerate, making his absence a timely one.

They soon got started, but with less rigidity to the formation that people took up around the tractor. Nobody had the responsibility of having to police their own section as the work was distributed and shared equally among all. The only constant carried through from previous days was that Celeste, as usual, was to do absolutely nothing.

Without the pressure of a strict supervisor watching the group's every move the morning passed swiftly and pleasantly. It could even have been considered fun. There were certainly worse places to be than outside in that field on a sunny day. Of course, everything would change shortly before midday when Rhett was due to arrive.

Matt was the first to spot the old man's ute as it approached the field. He expected trouble immediately and called out to warn Colin, but much to his surprise, the Australian remained in the vehicle after parking up.

'How long has he been here?' asked Colin, joining his friend at the side of the trailer.

'He just turned up.'

Colin took another look in the direction of the ute.

'What do you think he's waiting for?'

'I don't know,' replied Matt. 'I don't think that he has even looked at us yet. It's like he's in some sort of trance.'

Rhett remained motionless behind the wheel. It looked to the pair like he was sleeping.

'The old git's too hung over to even get out of the car,' said Colin. 'I've probably been worrying for nothing. I bet he got so wasted last night that he doesn't even remember seeing us.'

The boys were preparing to go back to work when they were startled by a sudden scream. The sound had originated from behind the trailer where the girls were working. When the two men looked at one another, they each read the concern in the other's face. Chances were that it was one of their girlfriend's whom had cried out.

'What's wrong? Matt called out, jogging to the scene with Colin following closely behind.

Jonas and Hiro were standing with their backs to him and blocked his view. As he passed them he began to feel a sickly sensation in the pit of his stomach. Somehow, he just knew that Jenny was going to be the one in trouble. Everything had been going far too well between them. He was never this lucky.

Sure enough, it was the younger of the two sisters who knelt on the ground, her face contorted in agony.

'My hand,' she whimpered. 'I think I cut it on something.'

'Let me see,' said Matt. 'It's probably just a splinter.'

At least he *hoped* that it was just a splinter. Tenderly taking her hand, he checked over the stricken area. He was immediately drawn to a rash-like red circle about an inch in diameter, which blemished the soft, fleshy area between her forefinger and thumb. At the centre of the wound were two tiny pin pricks.

'That's not a splinter, she's been bitten,' declared Paul, who was standing over Matt's shoulder.

'I can't have,' Jenny protested. 'I would have seen a snake. There's nothing there.'

'Not a snake,' replied Paul. 'You've been bitten by a spider.'

The Aboriginal called for his father and then ordered the others to search around for the spider. Matt wanted to stay and comfort Jenny, but he knew that it would be best not to interrupt Sam whilst he administered first aid. His time would be better spent looking for the creature responsible. Until he knew what they were dealing with it would be impossible for him to rest easy.

He overturned the scattered pieces of timber in a frantic search for any signs of movement, whilst silently praying that when the culprit revealed itself it would not have a red back.

'I've found something,' called Niall. 'I don't know if this is the one that bit Jenny though. It looks far too small to have caused so much pain.'

'That's our man,' confirmed Paul, squatting down to inspect the guilty arachnid.

Matt took a look at the creature at the centre of the drama. It was no bigger than a thumbnail and to his great relief displayed no tell-tale red stripe. The only marking it bore was a small white dot at the base of its abdomen.

'This is good, isn't it?' he asked. 'As long as it's not a red back she'll be okay, won't she?'

'It's a white tip,' said Paul.

The Aboriginal's features were entrenched in dread.

'I don't understand,' said Matt. 'I've never heard of a white tip. They aren't deadly, are they?'

'No, they won't kill you,' replied Paul. 'These little buggers do a lot worse than that.'

Rhett was feeling more than a little frustrated. An early morning shot of vodka had failed to improve his mood. Neither had a second. Nor even a third. In the end he had imbibed almost half of the bottle, but still he felt no better.

Those kids were causing him no end of trouble. It was bad enough that they were refusing to deal with him, but now they were muscling in on his business. They had not just cost him that one sale last night either. Because they had undercut his price by so much his regulars were sure to now accuse him of ripping them off.

What he needed more than anything was time to cool down, but missing work was not an option. He suspected that the two Abo's had it in for him. If he failed to turn up due to a hangover, even on a Saturday, those two would delight in reporting it back to Joe in Brisbane. The pom would not give him a second chance.

When he arrived at the field he could see that the tractor had barely moved from the previous day. It was obvious that those foreign layabouts had been slacking without him. This really pissed him off, but he was in no position to reprimand them in the state he was in. All he could do was park up and try to get some rest. Before he knew it, he had fallen asleep.

His slumber did not last. He had no idea how long he slept, but it could not have been for too long as the sun was not far into the West of the sky when he was woken by a loud hammering on the side of his car door. It was the old Abo and he looked agitated.

'Christ, Sam, go easy, will you.' He looked the big man up and down and then his eyes turned to the weeping girl behind.

Whatever the trouble was, it was the last thing that he needed. 'Why've you stopped working?'

'The girl needs medical attention. Got bitten by a white tip.'

Rhett knew he would be expected to take the girl into town. Given that the nearest antivenin was stored at the police station, this was not an idea that appealed. That bastard Sheriff Lee would know he'd been drinking and slap him with a DUI charge for sure. An even greater worry was the matter of what he had stashed under the tarpaulin in the back of his ute. He would sooner let the girl's arm rot off than face the law.

'You take her on the bus,' he instructed. 'I'll look after things here.'

'The sister is coming too,' insisted Sam. 'She cannot be expected to stay whilst worrying about the girl's safety.'

Rhett did not offer an objection, but he drew the line at anyone else leaving early. He should have just called it a day then and there, but he did not want to give the others the satisfaction of finishing early, even if it meant punishing himself further. He decided that he would drive the tractor himself in Sam's place. With hindsight, it would become a decision that everyone would regret.

Chapter 19

A fate worse than death. That is what Paul had implied when he told Matt of the toxic properties of the white tip spider. The Aboriginal went on to explain that the arachnid's venom, if left untreated, would eventually spread throughout its victim's entire system, causing their body to rot away from the outside in like a living corpse.

Matt hoped that his friend's concern was nothing more than mere superstition. The idea of turning into a zombie was, of course, a fantasy, but the symptoms did not sound too far from that of a flesh-eating virus. If the toxins were allowed to spread then the only feasible way to treat the infection would be through amputation. The thought that Jenny could lose her hand because of something as seemingly trivial as an insect bite was too much to bear.

All the remaining backpackers were in varying degrees of shock, but since the chances of lightning striking twice were remote they all kept on working regardless of the newly discovered danger. Of course, with Rhett helming the tractor they had little choice in the matter.

The Australian was driving at almost double the pace his predecessor had, ensuring that everybody was kept busy. Even with the sisters gone, all the positions around the vehicle were covered. Jonas and Hiro were working the flanks, with Stephen and Niall as catchers. This left Matt and Colin to walk behind the trailer with Paul helping out where needed. As usual, Celeste merely made up the numbers.

'I should've gone with them,' said Matt, as he bent to pick wood from the ground.

He was struggling to keep positive, because since Sam left he was completely in the dark regarding Jenny's condition.

'Don't beat yourself up over it,' advised Colin. 'There's nothing you could have done. She has Rose with her and the speed that this old crank has us working will soon take your mind off it.'

Despite his friend's best intentions, Matt could not keep from dwelling on the potentially life threatening injury that his girlfriend had sustained. He did not think it was right to carry on as if nothing had happened while Jenny was in such danger.

'It just seems silly to me that we didn't just call it a day and leave with Sam and the girls.'

'You know why that is, don't you?' Colin used his head to signal in the direction of the old man on the tractor. 'He's punishing us for last night.'

'Do you think he talked to that crowd Jonas was mixing with?'

Although Matt shared his friend's concern over Rhett, he did not let it enter his thoughts nearly as often.

'I'm certain of it,' replied Colin.

The Irishman deposited a stack of timber just as the tractor came to rest. Noticing that Stephen and Niall were struggling to keep up and Paul was doing his best to help them, he decided to unhook the trailer himself.

'I'll get this one,' he said to Matt, whilst signalling for the others to remain in their positions.

Matt stayed behind the trailer, but took several steps away

from it to ensure he would not find himself in its path when it lurched backwards. He then heard Colin's signal that the locking mechanism had been released and was soon joined by his friend who jogged back to help him brush away the last pieces of timber from the trailer.

Once they had cleared everything from the back they pulled down on the side of the upraised trailer to return it to its original horizontal position. Paul took the petrol canister from the rear of the tractor and began using it to prepare the fire, whilst Colin walked around to reattach the trailer.

He had locked down the mechanism and was moving out from between the two sections of the vehicle, when suddenly, it lurched forward, catching him completely off guard. Matt could do nothing but look on in horror as he saw his friend's face contort in agony and then drop away from view behind the deadly bulk of machinery.

He screamed out for Rhett to stop the tractor. It came to rest immediately, but if Colin had been pulled under one of the wheels it would already be too late. The trailer had to weigh at least a ton and could crush human bones like they were egg shells. Matt held his breath as he waited to see exactly how much damage had been inflicted.

Incredibly, Colin walked away from the accident. He did not stay on his feet for long though. After scrambling away from the trailer, he only made it a few feet before falling to the ground. Matt again feared the worst, but his friend had just bent down to grab a handful of broken timber.

'You fucking maniac!' Colin screamed, as he threw the wood at Rhett's cab. 'Are you trying to kill me?'

The Australian did not respond to the younger man's furious questions. He just sat patiently still in the driver's seat. Even his usual scowl was missing, leaving him completely devoid of all expression or emotion.

'Arsehole!' screamed Colin, who had now turned his back to the tractor.

He began to walk away, but kept shouting back as he did so.

'You can stick your job, you fucking criminal. They should put you back inside and throw away the fucking key.'

Still the Australian ignored him.

'Fucking rapist!'

This time the words struck their mark. Rhett leapt from the tractor cab with unfathomable speed and caught up with Colin almost instantly. The drone of the vehicle's engine masked his movements completely. Matt called out to warn his friend, but he was too late. Rhett reached out with his left hand and planted it firmly onto Colin's right shoulder. He yanked the Irishman around with one sharp tug and followed this up with a powerful right uppercut to the chin. The action was completed in one fluid motion and carried enough force to knock his victim to the ground.

No sooner had Colin hit the floor and Rhett began to capitalize on his attack by unleashing a series of kicks to his ribs. Matt ran towards them straight after the first blow had been struck and once he was within range, he leapt headlong into the aggressor, sending the two of them crashing to the ground. The way that they landed favoured the younger man and he thought he had everything under control.

With the initial onslaught neutered, Matt turned to check on his friend. In doing so he lowered his guard just long enough for Rhett to shake free of his grasp. Rather than attempt another assault the Australian instead ran in the direction of the tractor. Reaching up into the cab, he withdrew something from under the driver's seat. It was a crowbar.

Matt could feel the adrenaline rushing through his body, but he knew that no matter how invigorated this made him feel, he would not fare well against such a crude weapon. He cautiously stepped back a few paces, but kept himself between the old man and his stricken friend. By this time everyone else had been alerted by the commotion and it was not long before he had the other two Irishmen by his side.

'Stay back,' warned Rhett.

He brandished the weapon in his right hand and held it high, ready to unleash a deadly downward strike on anyone foolhardy enough to go near him. For the backpackers, this brought memories of the lame kangaroo on Rhett's first day in charge flooding back. They all knew perfectly well that the man stood before them had experience in breaking skulls with blunt objects and that he would not hesitate to do so again.

'Come on, Rhett, put the rod down,' said Matt, hoping to placate him. 'We only care about making sure that Colin is okay.'

'D'ya think I'm stupid?' Rhett snarled back at him. 'You bastards will never get the satisfaction.'

'What satisfaction? Just give us the keys to your ute so we can get Colin some help.'

'Over my dead body.'

Stephen took a step forward.

'That could be arranged, you know,' he said. 'There are six of us and even a crowbar is not going to beat those odds.'

The old man's heavily creased features gave nothing away. It was impossible to discern whether he was contemplating backing down or merely deciding who he wanted to kill first.

'You count six, eh? Those two foreign kids ain't gonna help you. They probably shit their pants already and the Abo's a pussy just like his old man. You bunch of fags have nothing.' He briefly turned downwards and spat on the ground. When he raised his head, he was grinning maliciously. 'Or were you referring to the girly back there? I bet she would put up one hell of a fight.'

'Monster!' cried Celeste, who until that moment had teetered anonymously by the back of the group.

Paul put his hand on the girl's shoulder to try to calm her, but she shrugged it off and strode purposefully toward the bonfire that had just been created. Once there, she reached down and picked up a piece of timber that was roughly thirty centimetres long. The tip of the wood was ablaze with fire.

'What are you doing, Celeste?' asked Stephen, switching his concern from the old man to the girl.

Ignoring the question, she proceeded to throw the flaming projectile towards the malignant farmer. It hung in the air for a tantalizing moment before crashing down to the ground in front of him. Her aim was a good few feet off target, but she had clearly expressed her intent as she reached for a second missile.

'Celeste stop!' cried Stephen.

Before he could intervene, his worst fears were realised. Celeste did not have the opportunity to throw a second projectile. Instead, she started to convulse wildly, but it was not with anger or rage. She was having an epileptic fit.

'Everybody, stand back,' Stephen instructed.

He took off his shirt and balled it up to form a crude pillow. Fortunately for Celeste, the soft sand, which covered so much of the field, cushioned her fall and Stephen was able to keep her airways clear as he waited for the seizure to run its course. It was the first time he had witnessed one of her attacks, but his protective instincts kicked in as he realised that he cared for her a great deal more than he was previously willing to admit.

Rhett could not have come up with a better distraction had he planned it himself. As Stephen nursed the stricken girl back to consciousness, the Australian climbed into the tractor cab.

With the engine already running, he was able to pull away quickly.

Despite being such a cumbersome vehicle to drive, the tractor could accelerate when required. The empty trailer offered little resistance and served as an extra barrier between its driver and any would be pursuers. It lurched dangerously from side to side, creating a possibly fatal hazard for anyone attempting to run alongside, but it was not actually necessary. Nobody followed, as helping the injured took precedence.

'Shit,' cursed Stephen, realising that Rhett was getting away.

Along with the others he could only watch on defeated as their enemy made a hasty exit. Colin, meanwhile, was now beginning to regain consciousness. He winced with pain as he attempted to sit upright.

'Take it easy,' advised Matt. 'You took quite a bit of punishment from that arsehole. It would be best not to exert yourself too much before we can get you checked out.'

'I don't need to see no doctor.'

His declaration was akin to a man emerging from a week spent lost in a desert only to turn down the first glass of water offered to him.

'That's not your choice, I'm afraid. When we leave here we're heading straight to the hospital. Unless you'd prefer to walk home.'

They were joined by Niall who had previously been tending to Celeste.

'We're all going to be walking home now that creep's gotten away.'

Matt looked along past the edge of the field to where the tractor was now clumsily parked. Rhett's ute was nowhere to be seen. For the time being they were essentially stranded.

'Sam will be back soon. We'll just have to wait.' He then added; 'how is Celeste?'

'The convulsions have stopped so she's no longer in any immediate danger. I was hoping that one of you had some water that we could give to her.'

Paul stepped up and handed a bottle over.

'Here, take this,' offered the Aboriginal. 'It fell from the tractor as Rhett made his getaway.'

'Thanks,' said Niall, taking possession of the receptacle.

He then quickly jogged back to where Celeste was now sitting upright with Stephen's help. The seizure had not lasted long, but it would take at least an hour before she would regain all of her strength and be back to normal. She gratefully accepted the water and took a sip.

Although no permanent damage had been done, there was simply no way that any of the backpackers could continue to work alongside Rhett after this. Things could have gone so much worse and everybody knew it. The old creep had now made it perfectly clear of what he was capable.

Chapter 20

Those worthless little bastards had ruined everything. He could not even attempt to argue it as his word against theirs since that sanctimonious Abo kid had witnessed it all. There was simply no way of getting out of this one. He guessed that he had at best three hours before they reported him to the authorities. Three hours before that bastard Sheriff Lee would come knocking at his door.

He yanked open the glove compartment and reached inside. His fingers fumbled over some loose papers that he stored there. That would be the time sheets and payslips that he had neglected to complete. Of course, none of that mattered at all now. He had certainly forfeited his own wage and had no concern whatsoever for that of the scum who had gotten him into this fix.

After more fumbling, he finally found what he was looking for. He retrieved the bottle and weighed it in his hand. He figured that it was about half empty. That would barely be enough to whet his appetite, but there would always be more waiting for him when he got home.

He placed the bottle in his lap and then gripped it firmly

between his thighs, whilst unscrewing the cap with his left hand. He then casually threw the screw top out through the side window and took a large gulp from the bottle. The warm liquid was like a panacea, revitalising and sharpening his senses. It restored his confidence and gave added power to his convictions. The stronger he felt, the weaker the world around him became. He shook the last drops from the bottle and then recklessly discarded it through the open window of his ute. The glass vessel shattered unceremoniously on the hard surface of the tarmac, leaving a hazardous covering of dangerous shards for the next vehicle to pass by.

Just five minutes after he had finished off the bottle he began to feel the shakes returning. He needed more. Although he was temporarily out of booze, he did have another quick fix at his disposal. Reaching into the breast pocket of his shirt, he retrieved his rolling papers and tobacco tin.

Even he was not foolhardy enough to attempt to roll a joint whilst driving at high speed, so he downshifted into third gear and lowered his speed to a more manageable level. The highway was perfectly straight, allowing him to temporarily take his hands off the steering wheel. As he began mixing tobacco and marijuana in the centre of the paper, he noticed a faraway dot appear on the horizon ahead of him.

'Fuckers,' he mumbled.

Not wanting to draw unnecessary attention to himself, he accelerated back into fifth gear. The only thing that would alert the suspicions of a traffic cop more than a reckless driver was an overly cautious one. However, as the opposing vehicle neared, he could see that it was not a patrol car. It was the one thing that he despised even more. The sight of the white bus brought his seething anger back to the surface.

Sam must have dropped the girls off at the station and then headed back immediately, as it had been barely ninety minutes since they left work. If their roles were reversed he would have been tempted to run the other man off the road, but there was no chance of doing that against a bus so he kept to his lane. He did, however, hope to get a reaction as he drove past and the old Aboriginal did not disappoint. The surprise in Sam's eyes displayed not only shock, but also fear. Rhett thought that there was not a more positive reaction he could elicit from anyone. He met the fool's dumbfounded gaze with his own best sneer to remind himself of what weaklings he was dealing with.

Over the next few kilometres he intermittently glanced into the rear view mirror until the bus disappeared from sight altogether. Once he was sure that the highway was clear, he slowed back down to resume the construction of his roll-up. He dispensed with his usual frugality and stuffed as much weed inside it as he could. The alcohol in his system had increased his appetite for inebriation and he was determined to get wasted. After lighting the bespoke cigarette, he began to toke on it impatiently.

He wound up the window of the ute in an attempt to retain more of the intoxicating smoke within the vehicle. As the haze descended over him, the world around began to slow down to a crawl. In order to compensate for this perceived drag, he accelerated the vehicle further to bring his motion into line with that of his excited brainwaves.

Still he needed more.

Each drag on the joint became more prolonged as he attempted to draw back the blissful fog deeper into his lungs. The more he consumed, the more he craved. He had the appetite of an imploding star, where not even light can escape the gravity of its insatiable desire. With every toke his actions became ever more lackadaisical. The highway was reduced to nothing more than a blur, resembling the smeared strokes of an abstract canvas, as he lapsed into a state of almost complete oblivion.

It was at that moment that he saw the Angel of Death approach. The monster filled the sky in front of him. Its wings were beating powerfully as they propelled it headlong towards him. It was a giant pterodactyl, swooping in for the kill with the scent of blood in its nostrils and murder in its eyes. Like a heat seeking missile it had locked onto its target and nothing could stop its impending impact.

There was a catastrophic crash as the world around him exploded into a shower of diamonds. Rhett raised his arms over his face to protect it from the onslaught of razor sharp talons that clawed from the growing abyss in front. Then there was a brief moment of calm as the world began to spin. He saw the ground tumble and fall as if the Earth had been somehow plucked from its orbit and sent spiralling through space into the far reaches of the cosmos. And then all became still.

The battered and crumpled framework of the vehicle had travelled twenty metres since careening off the road. The limp and bloodied form of the wedge tailed eagle that had hit the windscreen lay impaled amidst the debris of the shattered glass. Rhett was still alive within the confines of this twisted mess of metal and rubber. He was unconscious and therefore unable to detect the distinct smell of petrol vapour as the spillage from the ruptured tank pooled all around him.

Overhead, the sun burned brightly in the sky. Its rays were intensified as they passed through the warped glass of the wreckage. The concentrated beams of light bore into the spilled petrol heating and exciting its atoms as they strived relentlessly towards ignition. Sooner or later, that one killer spark was inevitable.

Chapter 21

The backpackers were relieved to see Sam return to the field. Matt in particular was eager to hear news of Jenny's condition and he met the bus before it had even parked up. He noticed at once the distress in Sam's features and expected the worst.

'How is she?' he asked, as soon as the automatic door slid open.

Sam looked at first confused by the question, but then realisation dawned.

'Your friend is doing just fine,' he replied. 'She will make a full recovery, but right now I am more concerned by what has happened here. I passed Rhett on my way in.'

'That's a long story. First we need to get Colin to a doctor. Paul can fill you in on the way.'

Sam refused to be harried.

'Slow down there, fella. We ain't going nowhere yet. I picked up a flat on the drive back. You boys can help me get it changed.'

'But...' his voice trailed off as he thought better of it.

Although Matt was frustrated, it would have been pointless

to complain about what was beyond anybody's control. He took the jack from Sam and then he and Stephen set about removing the damaged tyre, whilst the elder man retrieved the spare from the underside of the bus's rear. By the time they had finished, Colin had regained much of his strength. He was able to walk unaided, but let out a wince as he climbed the step onto the bus.

'You should save the theatrics for when you see Rose,' said Stephen. 'Nothing turns on a woman more than getting the chance to play nurse.'

For once, Colin did not have a sarcastic retort. All he wanted was a pillow and time to recuperate. Since his condition was not as urgent as Jenny's, but required more specialised attention, Sam decided to take him to the hospital, which was a two hour drive away at a town named Cooper's Creek.

The bus pulled out onto the highway and turned left. This took them in the opposite direction from that which they had come earlier in the day. By the time they were to return later in the evening it would be past nightfall and the road bordered by complete darkness.

Cooper's Creek had a modest population of just over three thousand. Compared to Birribandi this made it a veritable metropolis. Whilst Sam took Colin into the hospital for an x-ray on the Irishman's bruised ribs, the others decided to explore the town. Those who had their mobile phones with them heard the familiar jingle that indicated network coverage as they arrived. Celeste had made a full recovery by this time and was eager to phone Pierro on the caravan park's landline to advise him that she was going to be home late.

'Well?' asked Matt.

'Well what?' replied Celeste.

'Did he mention Jenny?'

She looked put out by the question.

'Why would he mention her? I called because I did not want him to worry about me being late.'

Matt could not believe how self-centred the girl was.

'Never mind,' he told her.

He supposed that he had probably been worrying too much anyway. After all, Sam assured him that Jenny was going to make a full recovery and he trusted the Aboriginal elder's word. There was no use in dwelling any further on the matter and it made sense to try and enjoy this rare opportunity to sample life in rural Australia away from Birribandi.

'What does everyone want to do?' asked Stephen. 'We may as well enjoy the freedom whilst we have it. They have a fast food joint here or we could check out one of the local pubs.'

The decision was unanimous.

'Pub!' they all exclaimed in unison.

The inside of the bar could not have contrasted more heavily with that of the Birribandi Tavern. It was stocked with a full range of international beers as well as offering the usual local fare on tap. There was a full menu available for ordering food at any time of the day and the walls were lined with flat screen televisions, which showed all the major sporting events. They even offered a backpacker discount on the drinks.

'I've really missed this,' said Matt, as the group took their seats in a booth by the window.

'I know what you mean,' agreed Niall. 'Nothing beats a civilised drink in a civilised bar.'

'Since when have you been civilised?' asked Stephen.

The Irishman was sitting next to Celeste and even had his arm around her. This was the first time that Matt had noticed them show any kind of familiarity in front of the group.

'You know what I mean,' said Niall. 'Today has really put things into perspective for me. Maybe it's time for me to move on.'

Despite harbouring a similar thought himself, Matt was surprised by Niall's admission.

'Surely you aren't thinking of leaving because of what that creep did today, are you? Once word of what Rhett did to Colin gets back to Joe, he'll be gone in no time. In fact, I doubt that we'll ever see him again as it is.'

'It's not just Rhett. I've been thinking of leaving for a while now. There are other places where I can complete the three months to get my extension. It makes sense to see a bit more of the country whilst I do it. It's easier for you lot as you all have somebody to share the experience with.'

Stephen had clearly been included in his friend's summation, but he did nothing to refute the insinuation. Matt wondered if he was more open about his involvement with Celeste because the other two girls were not there or if something had changed since the attack in the field, which had escalated their relationship. As they continued the conversation, Paul entered the bar. The Aboriginal had been along to the hospital to let his father know where they all were. After buying a cola, he joined his friends in the booth.

'Dad said that they should not take too long. The A&E was almost empty. Colin should be in and out within the hour provided the doctors do not ask too many questions.'

The last part of this speech was directed towards Matt, which did not go unnoticed by the others in the group.

'Why would the doctor ask too many questions?' queried Niall.

'Maybe you should ask our friend here,' replied Paul.

Matt immediately became the centre of attention and tried his best to play down the situation. He hated it when his actions were scrutinised in this way.

'I just gave Colin a little help, that's all; something to ease his burden a little.'

'Don't tell me that you are distributing drugs now as well,' said Niall.

'It's nothing like that.' He was annoyed at Paul for putting him on the spot like this. Now it had been built up they were sure to make more of a fuss than necessary. 'I just gave him my Medicare card. I thought it was bad enough that he had to take a beating. It's hardly fair that he should have to fork out hundreds of dollars on top.'

Being foreign nationals, most backpackers were excluded from the country's free health care system. Matt being from the UK was the only one of those present that had eligibility to the scheme courtesy of a reciprocal agreement between his home and host nations. By passing on his card to Colin he was breaking the law.

'You do realise that is fraud,' said Niall.

'It's no big deal. I'm just passing on one of the benefits of the former empire. I thought you'd be glad to see the British giving something back for a change.'

Niall shook his head, disapprovingly.

'You do realise that if you get caught they could suspend your visa extension,' he said.

Matt had not considered the consequences and was eager to change the subject.

'Give it a rest, will you. You're starting to sound like Jenny.'

Stephen laughed out loud.

'You're in there, Niall,' he said. 'He thinks that you're his girlfriend. After all his talk about the British Empire giving something back, you may see some action after all. It won't be the first time that the British have screwed the Irish, will it?'

'Very funny,' said Matt. 'All I do is try to help a friend and this is the thanks I get.'

'He's only pulling your leg,' said Niall. 'Besides, the only way you would be found out is if Colin slipped up somehow. There's more chance of us all being invited round to Rhett's house for Christmas lunch than that happening.'

Mention of the Australian sent a shudder through the group.

They finished their drinks, but did not get more as Paul spotted Sam and Colin across the road. The latter had a plaster just above his left eyebrow and the surrounding tissue was heavily bruised, but he appeared to be walking much more freely and comfortably.

After fussing over their friend, they all got back on the bus for the long drive back to Birribandi just as the sun was beginning to set. When they traversed the dark and lonely highway they passed within twenty yards of the wreckage of their supervisor's car. With the night sky overcast and empty, the crash site had been completely swallowed up by the void. Not one of them suspected a thing.

Chapter 22

'He did what?'

The news of Colin's run in with the old man came as a complete shock to Rose. Pierro had let her know that the bus was running late, but that was the only part of the message he passed on. When she heard about the attack, she was livid.

'It's not that big of a deal,' insisted Colin, hoping to placate her by playing it down. 'We've talked it over with Sam and he is going to speak to Joe. There is no way that Rhett will be coming back to work after this.'

'Of course it is a big deal,' she told him. 'You have to report it to the police. We already know that he has a criminal record and with those bruises he's given you it isn't going to be hard to convince a jury to convict him.'

'That's exactly what I don't want. I'm not wasting my time getting involved in trials. This is supposed to be a holiday.'

Colin was loath to admit it, but he was more concerned that his own misdemeanours may come to light than he was in seeing the old man brought to justice. There was no telling how much weight Rhett had in the town and the Australian could certainly make some allegations of his own. If it became known that the beating had been sparked by Colin potentially muscling in on Rhett's drug dealing, then he himself may not emerge from the resulting investigation with a clean record.

'So you are happy for him to get away with it?' she asked.

Once Rose set her mind to something she would rarely give up. This had been one of the things that attracted Colin to her, but not on this day.

'I didn't say that I was happy and it's not like he is getting off totally scot-free, is it? He's lost the last job that anyone will ever be dumb enough to give him, which means that he's going to spend the rest of his miserable life rotting away at the bottom of a bottle.'

Before Rose could respond she was interrupted by a knock on the caravan door. Colin got up and opened it.

'It's just us,' said Matt, who was standing on the step with Jenny. 'We aren't interrupting anything, are we?'

'Not at all,' replied Colin, who offered a condescending sideways glance to Rose. 'We were just discussing the pros and cons of getting involved with the Australian legal system.'

'Colin thinks that we should do nothing and let the thug who beat him get away with attempted murder,' said Rose, from the bed.

Matt knew that his friend would be looking to him for solidarity and he therefore tried to dismiss the girl's concerns.

'I wouldn't go so far as to say that it was attempted murder,' he said. 'The old man stank of booze from the moment he turned up at work. Come the morning, he probably won't even remember what he did.'

'So would you work with him again?' asked Rose.

'Well, that's a different question entirely,' replied Matt.

Jenny crossed the van and took a seat on the bed next to her sister.

'Nobody is going to have to work with him again,' she said.

'Matt and I have talked it over and we think that so long as we all stick together there is no way that Joe will consider giving Rhett another chance.'

Rose was not convinced.

'It isn't about the work. It's the principle. Do you seriously expect me to stay knowing that he is out there? I've already been attacked once in this town and that was before we had an actual enemy.'

Jenny offered Matt a brief glance of concern before continuing the conversation with her sister.

'You want to leave Birribandi, don't you?'

'Well, why is that such a big deal?' Rose looked over toward Matt as well. 'The four of us could get a campervan and go together. It's about time that we did some actual travelling, after all.'

Matt shifted restlessly in the doorway.

'I can't afford to leave now. My visa has almost expired and I don't have the time to look around for another harvest job. This is now or never for me, I'm afraid.'

'Well, I'm sorry,' said Rose, 'but I cannot stay; not now.'

'Maybe we should wait and see what happens over the next few days,' offered Jenny.

The younger girl was torn between leaving with her sister and staying with her boyfriend. She had come travelling with Rose and she knew that it was the familial bond that would ultimately win through.

'She's right,' said Matt. 'You won't be able to get a bus back to the city until next weekend anyway. It makes sense to use that time to think things through a bit more.'

'Okay,' agreed Rose. 'I will give it one more week, but do not expect me to change my mind. As far as I am concerned, my time in the outback is over.'

*

On Sunday, Sam visited the caravan park. He had spoken with Joe and they both agreed that Rhett's contract should be terminated immediately. The only problem was that neither Sam nor the man in Brisbane had been able to get in contact with their rogue foreman. It was as if he had disappeared from the face of the Earth.

'So where is he?' asked Matt.

'No one knows,' replied Sam. 'I've driven past his house twice now and his ute is not outside. His neighbours said that he didn't come home last night, which means he could be anywhere.'

'He's probably in the pub drowning his sorrows,' said Colin.

'That was the first place I looked. Joe has been trying to call him non-stop and he's had no luck either.'

Colin lit a cigarette.

'Good riddance is what I say. He probably thinks we'll have gotten the law onto him so will most likely have split town. He must be halfway to Alice Springs by now.'

'Could we be that lucky?' asked Matt.

'Who cares? So long as he doesn't come back, I'm happy to stick around.' He turned to address Sam, 'So where do we stand with work? None of us was ever entirely sure what contribution Shawshank actually made, so his disappearance shouldn't be a problem, should it?'

'That is for Joe to decide. He is coming back in a few days and we will have to see whether he can find a replacement, otherwise he may have to stay on himself.'

'Surely he'll let you run things. From what I've seen you were practically in charge anyway.'

The Irishman took a drag on his cigarette before turning his head and exhaling deeply. There was no breeze, causing the smoke to be left hanging in the air.

'It ain't that simple,' said Sam, who was beginning to feel uncomfortable.

'Of course it is. All you have to do is make sure that we get our pay at the end of the week. Surely the books can't be that hard to balance. Or has Joe been fiddling us all of this time?'

Sam did not answer.

'If you want, we can put in a word for you when Joe gets back,' offered Colin. 'The way I see it, you should have been given this job already anyway.'

'That won't be necessary,' replied Sam. 'Joe will find somebody who is more suited to the job.'

Colin was about to argue, but Matt intervened by shaking his head at his friend. He sensed something in the way Sam spoke that told him the matter was not as clear cut as Colin believed. The Aboriginal's body language was clearly resigned and Matt did not want to push him further.

'Does this mean that we will all get the next few days off?' asked Matt.

Sam relaxed.

'Joe thinks it is best if we call off the next couple of days' work. He is worried that Rhett may show up at the field and try something stupid.'

'Let him,' said Colin. 'He caught me off guard yesterday, but if he ever thinks he will get the better of me again, he has another thing coming.'

The Irishman's bravado, though false, was understandable. It was not the first time he had been the victim of an assault since coming to Birribandi and on each occasion he had been unable to successfully stand up to his assailant.

'Well, we are not going to take any chances this time,' said Sam. 'I have notified the sheriff of what happened and he will have a discreet word with Rhett when he returns from wherever he is. If he hasn't already left, then he soon will.

There is nothing for him in this town after what he did to you.'

'So the Police are gonna run him out of town; is that it?' asked Colin.

'Not quite, but they can make sure that he does not bother you again.'

Once Sam had returned home, it left it to Matt and Colin to update the girls with the latest developments. They both hoped that the news would be enough for Rose to reconsider her decision to leave prematurely. Her reaction would not quite be what they were expecting.

'This is even worse!'

Colin had been hoping for a more positive response, but the more he thought about it, the less surprised he was by his girlfriend's reaction to the news of Rhett's apparent disappearance. Knowing that the Australian was out there was frightening enough, but not knowing where he was, was simply terrifying

'Sam thinks that he may have done a runner,' said Colin. 'There's little chance that he'll try any kind of reprisal. With his previous record he'd be setting himself up for a return to prison for sure.'

Rose wrapped her cardigan around herself as if the mere mention of a man so cold hearted as Rhett was enough to lower the temperature of the room.

'Well, I will feel a lot better when I know for sure that there is a great distance between him and us. As far as I am concerned, this changes nothing.'

Colin hoped that she just needed more time. She was still feeling vulnerable after the mugging and had grown more insecure as a result. He passed on news of her reaction to Matt later that night. The Englishman was understandably disappointed, but like Colin he was still hopeful that she would change her mind. Jenny, on the other hand, took the news more positively. She agreed with the idea that Rhett had most likely done a runner and would not dare return to the town.

'Did Sam say that there was definitely no chance of him showing up at work?' she asked.

'Pretty much,' replied Matt. 'We asked him how it would affect the work that we do, but the answer that he us gave was a little confusing.'

'How do you mean?'

'Well, Colin suggested that Sam himself should step forward to replace Rhett. It seemed like the obvious solution to me too, but he became agitated when we put it to him. I personally do not see the problem; he was pretty much running the operation as it was, just without having to fill in the paperwork that went with it.'

Jenny winced when Matt mentioned the paperwork part of the job.

'You do realise that Sam cannot read or write, don't you?'

He stared back at her, blankly.

'I will take that as a no. Paul told me shortly after I started working here. You may have embarrassed Sam a little when you brought up the subject of doing the paperwork. He will not hold it against you, but you should probably be careful not to mention it again.'

'Thanks, I just wish that I had known sooner.'

'There are a lot of things that I wish I had known sooner; things that could have saved us a lot of trouble these past few weeks.'

He took her hand in his.

'Do you think that Rose will stay a little longer?' he asked.

'I hope so. She maybe just needs more time to come to

terms with everything. I'll do my best to talk her round, because I know that I am not yet ready to leave.'

They hugged. Matt really hoped that Jenny was right, because the thought of completing his time without her was not something that he even wished to consider.

Chapter 23

Boredom quickly descended upon the caravan park without the necessary distraction that work brought with it. The backpackers spent the morning lazing in their vans with neither the impulse nor the energy to make the day their own. Only with the arrival of an unscheduled visitor to the camp did they rouse from their slumber.

The sound of the car engine alerted those inside to the outside presence. Colin's van, which he was sharing more and more with Rose rather than Matt, was the closest to the entrance of the park. He became aware of his own heart beating as he pulled back the curtain to view this new arrival. Despite him going to great lengths to convince Rose that Rhett would not dare come to the park, the old man was the first person that came to mind when Colin thought of who the visitor could possibly be.

'Who is it?' asked Rose, who was strewn lazily across the bed.

The window was small and offered only a restricted view. By the time that Colin had reacted, the vehicle had already passed into a blind spot. He heard a car door slam, but could see neither the driver nor the vehicle.

'I can't see. Maybe you should run and get Matt and the others.'

This aroused her suspicions immediately.

'Why would you need the others? You don't think that...' Her voice trailed off.

'It's probably just Sam or a friend of Pierro. I would rather not take any chance, that's all.'

Rose got up from the bed and slipped on her sandals before rushing toward the door.

'Wait!' he called out, but she had already gone.

Colin fumbled into his sandals and then went out after Rose. As he rounded the van he could see that she was now a lot more relaxed as she stood cross armed in the driveway. She turned to him as he approached.

'It's nothing to worry about,' she said. 'It's only Sheriff Lee. I guess he must have retrieved my purse.'

'How can we help you, officer?' Colin asked, with unconscious sarcasm, as he caught up with Rose. 'You've got some good news for us, I hope.'

The policeman did not respond immediately. He instead waited until he had narrowed the gap between him and the couple to a more personable distance. When the gulf had been reduced to no more than a metre he removed his sunglasses and held them in his hands, which he then crossed solemnly in front of his waist.

'Unfortunately, we still have no word on the items that Miss Miller had stolen. I am actually here today regarding a different matter.'

Colin could feel his muscles tense. The policeman seemed much more business-like than he had during their previous meeting. He immediately suspected that this visit had something to do with their missing foreman. His stash was sitting unguarded, just metres away, and would not be hard to discover should the policeman have received a tip off regarding his recreational habits.

'Anything that happens in town doesn't really concern us, officer. Whatever the problem, I doubt that anyone here would be able to help you much.'

Rose nudged her boyfriend in the side. Whilst Colin was not short of charm, she had noticed that he tended to come across as arrogant and smug when on the defensive. She hoped that he had not inadvertently given himself away.

'This is a rather delicate matter,' said the policeman. 'Perhaps we could discuss it indoors.'

Colin was eager to lead the lawman away from his van.

'Let's go to the dining hall,' he suggested. 'There's more room in there and we'll be able to put a brew on.'

Matt was on his way back from the shower block when he saw the policeman follow the other couple into the dining room. He immediately called for Jenny to join him in finding out what was going on. Rose was making coffee when they entered, whilst Colin was sitting opposite the policeman in silence. Matt pretended not to notice the seated pair as he took a clean cup from the table and joined Rose at the kettle.

'It makes a nice change not to be spending Monday morning in the field, doesn't it?' he said.

'It's wonderful,' she replied. 'The longer we have off, the harder it will be to go back to work though.'

She used a subtle movement of her head to indicate the alien presence in the room. Matt offered a delicate nod in return. He wanted to offer his support without making it look like he was offering his support.

'Maybe we should warn Joe to start looking for

replacements,' he said.

He then filled two cups; one for himself and one for Jenny. The aforementioned was still standing in the doorway and he beckoned her in to take her cup. Rose, meanwhile, had filled three cups.

'Could you give me a hand?' she asked.

After passing Jenny her cup, Matt took one of the three mugs from Rose and carried it along with his own to where the two men were seated at the table.

'Good morning, officer,' he said, pretending to have noticed the policeman for the first time. 'I hope you've brought us good news.'

The policeman took his cup and placed it on the table top to cool down.

'Unfortunately not, but it is news that concerns all of you, so I would be grateful if you and Miss Miller would join us.'

Matt glanced towards Colin seeking a clue, but all he received in return was a shrug. The Irishman appeared nervous and was using the cover of blowing into his mug to take deep, calming breaths of air.

'Is this to do with the mugging?' asked Matt, but he had already deduced the answer.

'No,' replied the policeman. 'Unfortunately, we have been busier than usual these past few weeks. First there was the mugging, and then there have been a spate of break-ins, and we've also had two reported missing person cases to deal with; one of which has now been solved.' He glanced to each of the girls in turn as if what he was about to say would affect them more. 'The news is not pleasant so I will get straight to the point.' After a protracted pause he added, 'Rhett Butler is dead.'

Chapter 24

'**G**ood riddance to the old git is what I say.'

The group had all gathered in the dining area to discuss the news that Sheriff Lee had delivered just a half hour earlier. After an uncomfortable silence, Colin had been the first to vocalise his opinion.

'There is no need to be like that,' Jenny told him. 'Rhett may not have been a very nice person, but he was still a human being all the same.'

Colin was unmoved by her reasoning.

'I can say whatever I like. That scumbag gets no sympathy from me; not even in the grave. In fact, I think it's a shame he didn't kill himself a couple of months sooner and save us all a load of misery.'

Jenny was disgusted by what she was hearing.

'I can understand why you feel that way; I just think that it is disrespectful to be so flippant about it. It is as if you are getting pleasure out of another man's death.'

'What about the pleasure that old Shawshank got out of beating me in the field? You weren't there so you don't know what he was capable of. He practically threatened to rape

Celeste for Christ's sake!' He stood and walked away from his seat, choosing to sit on top of an adjacent table, which placed him in a more elevated position than the rest of the group. 'What if he had threatened either Rose or yourself? I bet that you would not be so quick to defend him then.'

Jenny looked around for support, but found nobody willing to back her up against Colin. Everyone had their head bowed as if they were reflecting on the conversation without wishing to actively participate in it. There was not one of them who had not been affected by the old man's malice at some point. The dominant emotions felt by all were relief coupled with guilt. Nobody could truthfully say that they were not glad to have seen the last of Rhett Butler.

'I am well aware of the potential danger that he posed,' said Jenny, 'but I would much rather have seen him in a prison cell than the grave.'

'He got what was coming to him,' replied Colin.

Jenny was horrified.

'That is a terrible thing to say. It almost sounds like you would have wanted to kill him yourself had he not died.'

'Maybe I would have. If he'd been stupid enough to try and attack me again, who knows what I might have done?'

She knew it was obviously just meaningless macho nonsense the Irishman was spouting, but Jenny still felt that someone should argue on the side of logic. She bit down on her bottom lip to compose herself before speaking.

'If you had killed him, you would be a murderer and even he never stooped that low.'

'Do any of us even know that?' replied Colin, who was relishing his role as preacher and seemed happy to sit and moralize for as long as required. 'For all we are aware, there could be a dozen bodies buried under his porch.'

'I cannot listen to any more of this.'

Jenny got up and left through the front door. She had been incensed by Colin's attitude and needed to walk off some of the tension. After a brief moment, Matt joined her outside.

'You shouldn't be too harsh on him, you know. We have no idea what's going through his head right now. Imagine if a man had drunk himself into a stupor and then killed himself in a car crash just hours after you'd been in a fight with him. How would you feel?'

'You think Colin blames himself for Rhett's death?' This was not a conclusion she would have reached herself, but she was able to follow Matt's line of reasoning. 'If that is the case then he may think of himself as...'

'...a killer.'

Jenny at once regretted her own stupidity.

'I should never have said those things to him. Do you think I should go back and apologise?'

Matt put his hands on her shoulders.

'It is probably best to leave things as they are for the time being. He knows that you didn't mean what you said. Just give him a little time to come to terms with what's happened.'

'Are you sure? I mean, somebody should talk to him and let him know that it wasn't his fault.'

'And you think that you are the best person for that? Trust me; Colin will be fine. Me and the guys will have a drink with him later and help him to put everything into perspective.'

'You mean get drunk.'

He offered her his most reassuring smile.

'Like I said; we'll help him put everything into perspective.'

Matt picked up a six pack of beer and took it back to the van with him to help begin Colin's rehabilitation. If his friend needed to let off some steam; then so be it. After the beating that Colin had taken just days earlier he was entitled to say whatever he liked about the man who had done it to him.

Matt found his friend sat on his bed looking over the police report, which he had previously stolen, whilst the pungent odour of marijuana permeated the small van. He did not take this as a good sign. He was hoping to keep Colin away from the weed as it was a much more unpredictable drug than alcohol. At least with beer he would be better equipped to second guess what his friend would be thinking.

'I thought you might like a drink,' Matt said, as he twisted a bottle out of the plastic mesh and handed it to the seated man.

Colin accepted the offering, but did not reply. He remained rapt in his study of the illegitimate files, which sat in his lap. If Rhett had occupied a great deal of his thoughts in life, he had become an obsession in death. The Irishman could not stop thinking about what had happened, as well as what might have been.

'You were right with what you said earlier,' Matt told him.

He was sitting on the edge of his own bed and did not wish to get too relaxed as he was hoping to coax Colin outside. His friend glanced up, only appearing half interested in the conversation.

'Rhett certainly had it coming,' Matt continued. 'It's all there in that report you're reading. Looking at the way he lived his life, it's a wonder he didn't kill himself sooner, eh?'

Colin continued to flick through the pages in front of him.

'What do you think he would have been like before it all went wrong?' he asked.

The question seemed vague and almost rhetorical, making Matt unsure if he was expected to reply.

'You mean before the first arrest?' he asked.

'It says here that he was just twenty one when he was first taken into custody.' Colin was finally beginning to connect.

'There must have been a time when the old git had some kind of dreams or aspirations. Do you think he would have been much different to us?'

'Yes, I do. I think he would have been nothing like us.'

'You cannot be sure of that.'

Colin paused, briefly lost in his own thoughts. 'What's the best you've ever hoped for?' he then asked.

Matt shrugged away the question. He was not sure where his friend was leading him on this.

'I mean in life,' the Irishman elaborated. 'What do you hope to gain from it all?'

'I can't say that I've really given it that much thought. I suppose I just take each day as it comes and hope for the best. Life will sort itself out sooner or later.'

Colin laughed, but it was a laugh of the most condescending kind.

'Life will sort itself out. That's a brilliant philosophy. Life certainly sorted itself out for Rhett, didn't it?'

He tilted his bottle vertical as he finished off the last of the liquid inside and then took a replacement from the pack. Matt was barely halfway through his own beverage.

'You can't compare us to him,' said Matt. 'He chose his path and paid the consequences.'

'How do you know that you won't make the same mistakes? We don't know what it was that triggered his descent. One moment of stupidity and your entire future could be flushed down the pan.'

The conversation was beginning to make Matt uneasy.

'There is a line that I would never cross. That's what the difference is. Rhett had that inside of him from the start, but I don't.'

'All I am saying is that you never know what will happen in life.' He passed the picture across to Matt. 'Are you religious at all?'

Matt was distracted by being handed the photograph and struggled to see what relevance religion had to the conversation. As he glanced down at the picture, Colin started taking increasingly large gulps from his beer.

'I was dragged along to church a few times when I was younger,' said Matt. 'My mother had a habit of rediscovering God following any family bereavement. My brothers and I were normally made to attend for about three weeks after the funeral, but then she would give up on it all again.'

'So you believe in salvation then?'

'Well, my mother obviously did. As for me; I'm happy to be an agnostic. You'll never know the answer until you die anyway; so why let it bother you?'

'Agnostic; antagonistic more like. At least atheists have the balls to take a stance. Where I'm from we don't have the luxury of simply ignoring the big questions. We have Christ the Redeemer thrust upon us from birth.'

Matt finally saw the point that his friend was trying to make.

'Redemption; that's what this is about, isn't it? You are wondering if Rhett repented for his wrongdoings.'

'Oh, I'm sure Shawshank repented all right. During those last excruciating seconds when the flesh melted from his bones, I'm pretty sure that he did nothing but repent. It would be just like the old man to live a life without conscience or remorse and the moment that it all ended, he was a born again believer.'

Matt finished his first bottle. As he reached for a second, Colin beckoned him to pass over his third.

'Isn't everyone entitled to forgiveness?'

Colin's fingers rested on the screw top. There was a hiss as he loosened the cap, but he did not remove it immediately.

'It's just that with men like Shawshank you always expect that one day they will get their just desserts.'

'And he did. Would you have preferred him to spend his last years leaching off the state in some rest home?'

'That's not what I mean.' He finally removed the cap, discarding it onto the bedside table. 'People like him should be held accountable for what they've done. He should have been made to confront the misery that he caused.'

'I think that you are reading far too much into this. Rhett was not some cartoon super villain; he was just some miserable old criminal who died as a result of his own negligence. These things happen every day.'

'It shouldn't have happened to Shawshank though. Not before somebody had the chance to confront him over what he did.'

Colin had become agitated and started to drink even more fervently than before. It did not take long for him to finish off the bottle.

'Someone like you, you mean?' asked Matt.

Colin did not reply. His eyes were contemplating the final beer bottle, but he did not reach for it.

'It's not Rhett redeeming himself that we're talking about, but you, isn't it?'

'I don't know what you mean. Why do I need redemption?'

Matt finished his drink and then took the final bottle. He was determined not to let his friend get a lead on him.

'You never got closure after he attacked you. When you talk about just desserts, you are talking about Rhett being punished for what he did to you specifically. Now that he's gone, you have all of this anger building up inside you and no way to release it.'

'So what do you suggest? How do I take out my frustrations on a dead man; desecrate his grave?'

Colin's words got Matt thinking.

'It's not a bad idea.'

'I was taking the piss,' the Irishman scoffed.

'At least hear me out,' urged Matt, whilst he wracked his brains trying to remember something that he had been told earlier. 'After you and Rose left the police station that time, Jenny told me something on the way home. She had some story about a face being covered on one of the photographs on the wall of the interview room.'

'Was that the picture frame with a bit of duct tape on it? I noticed that when we were being interviewed. I thought it was just covering a crack in the glass.'

'No; there was more to it than that. You know what Jenny's like when it comes to culture. She recounted this whole story about Aboriginal superstitions. If only I could remember it.'

Colin was becoming restless. It had been too long since his last drink and watching Matt with a bottle in his hand made him thirsty.

'Just give me a moment,' said Matt. 'I cannot remember the ins and outs of the story, but basically it was something to do with photographs containing a part of the spirit of the person they depicted. Whenever someone dies in these parts, the pictures have to be covered in order for the deceased to successfully crossover or something.'

'Sounds like superstitious nonsense to me,' said Colin.

Matt finished his drink.

'It probably is, but it may help to exorcise some of your demons. Let's stick this picture up in the centre of the park for everyone to see. If we are lucky, each time someone looks at that ugly mug of his it will add to his torment in the afterlife.'

'Do you realise how ridiculous that sounds?' asked Colin.

'Have you got a better idea?' countered Matt.

Colin got up and retrieved the photograph from his friend.

'Let's do it now. We need to go out there to get more beer anyway.'

Chapter 25

Rhett looked down on the gathering below with his usual contempt. His countenance bearing the trademark scowl, frozen in time for over thirty years since the moment the flash bulb had captured it on that morning of his first arrest. Only one lonely face returned his gaze. Hiro had been the last to learn of the old man's demise. The others rarely attempted to communicate with the Japanese man, other than through superficial pleasantries and even now he had simply been told only that Rhett had died. The details he had to try and piece together himself through snatched pockets of conversation.

Words like "speeding", "crash" and "fireball", he understood. Others such as "degenerate", "intoxicated" and "comeuppance", he did not. So far as he could ascertain, his former master had left this life in a blaze of glory. It was a fitting end for an outlaw. That is how Hiro saw it. Whenever the others spoke of their late supervisor, their stories had always pertained to mystery, violence and a life lived on the edge. How could Rhett be anything but an outlaw?

'I don't think that you're going to beat your man in a staring contest.'

Hiro was aware only of a voice.

'I'll give you fifty bucks if you can make him blink first.'

The Japanese man turned to see if the speaker was addressing him.

It was the bald Irish one. Of them all, this was the one he understood the least. He offered a forced smile in return and held up his bottle of beer. The bald one always seemed to approve when Hiro had a beer in his hand.

'That's the spirit,' said Colin.

Rose and Jenny were seated opposite Hiro with their backs to the photograph. Neither of the girls had been able to stand the old pervert gawping at them in life and saw no reason why they should be subjected to the same indignation now that he was gone.

'Is it not time that you took that awful picture down,' said Rose.

'Aw, come on now,' pleaded Colin. 'Not long ago everybody said that I was being harsh on old Shawshank. We should all cut the guy a break; after all - this is his wake.'

Jenny directed her most frosty stare at her sister's boyfriend.

'A wake celebrates the life that is lost,' she told him. 'This is just a bunch of people getting drunk because they are happy that someone died.'

'That's not fair,' protested Colin, who was not altogether steady on his feet. 'I genuinely miss the old man. I had a lot of affection for him.'

He looked to Matt to back him up and there was a brief pause before they both burst out laughing.

'You encouraging him is not helping either,' said Jenny.

Matt offered her his best attempt at open mouthed astonishment. He looked like an incompetent mime artist attempting to convey Edvard Munch's *the Scream*.

'Matt's been a great help to me today,' said Colin. 'It was his idea to stick that picture up in the first place.'

'Is that so?'

Jenny half scowled, half sighed toward her lover, but she allowed Colin to go on.

'He said that the more people see the picture, the more Rhett will suffer in the afterlife,' explained Colin. 'That'll teach the bastard for kicking me when I'm on the floor.'

Jenny shook her head, despairingly, but she was not angry. Everyone had been through a lot and some were able to cope a bit better than others.

'Explain to me how that works, will you?' she asked him.

'Matt said that you were the expert. Surely you don't need me telling you what you already know. Shawshank's soul is in that photograph and as long as it is on display he cannot rest. Look,' he staggered and almost fell on top of the girls as he turned to point at Hiro. 'The old git is being tormented as we speak. Hiro has him fixed with that narrow-eyed stare of his, stopping him from crossing over to the afterlife.'

She moved along her log seat to stay out of Colin's likely line of descent should his legs give way.

'The only thing that Hiro is doing is corrupting his eyes with a most unpleasant image. I don't know what little fantasy you and Matt have dreamed up, but it has nothing to do with anything I have told him. Photographs cannot be cursed and as far as I am aware there is no Aboriginal belief that states that they can.' She turned to Matt. 'What you are doing is disrespecting not only yourselves, but also an entire race of people.'

The pair dropped their heads to the floor like a couple of naughty children.

'Now, for the love of God, will one of you please get rid of that picture.'

211

Colin reached up and grabbed the bottom of the photograph. He tore it down with a sharp tug and then threw it onto the campfire. The flames took hold quickly, turning the image to nothing but hot ash and embers.

'It's not the first time that Shawshank has burned this week,' he joked.

He nudged Matt in the side to coax a reaction, but the Englishman was all too aware of his girlfriend's disapproval to offer the response that his friend desired of him.

'Finally, we can move on,' said Jenny. 'As far as I am concerned, the shadow of Rhett is well and truly out of our lives.'

The party continued into the night and much to Jenny's relief, the topic of Rhett was not broached again. There was, however, still one seed of discord in the camp and it was named Celeste. She spent the majority of the night sat on Stephen's lap, but as the approaching sound of a car engine heralded the arrival of her boyfriend, she was quick to move herself. It was not long before she disappeared behind the door to the dining room with her official lover.

'What do you men see in a girl like that?' Rose asked Colin and Matt.

'You're asking the wrong people,' replied Matt. 'I think you already know what our taste in women is.'

'Oh please,' said Rose, but her sister was now smiling.

'Maybe we should go and have a word,' suggested Colin, who in his present state was the least qualified to offer advice to anyone.

He walked away rather than wait for a reply and Matt followed him across to where Stephen was seated. They each picked up fresh beers, as well as a third for their friend.

'Get this down you and you'll feel a lot better,' Colin said, as he handed a bottle to the jilted man.

'Thanks.' Stephen gladly accepted the bottle, but turned it over several times in his hands as if doubting whether drinking really was the answer. 'You two probably think that I'm an idiot, don't you?'

'Not at all,' replied Colin. 'Sooner or later they get the better of us all.'

Stephen sighed before finally undoing the screw top to his beer.

'I've always known that she was with him and never had any expectations to the contrary,' he said. 'It's just that these last few days she's really opened up a lot more. You guys probably don't see it, but the confrontation in the field has really brought out her vulnerable side.'

'Have you tried talking to her about this?' asked Matt.

'Any mention of Pierro and it stops the conversation dead.'

Colin knocked back a large gulp of his beer.

'Perhaps you should try talking to him then. Warn him off like.'

Stephen shook his head.

'If I did that then one of us would almost certainly have to leave and he works here, remember? Don't you guys want to eat?'

'Then you have to tell her how you feel whether she wants to listen or not. Otherwise just put up with it.'

Colin often had an answer for everything and these views became even more forthright when he was drunk. His words had the desired effect on Stephen, as the Irishman was re-energised in his thirst. He knocked back the beer as if it were a shot. After recklessly discarding the empty bottle, he walked towards the open crate to pick up a replacement. When he got there his attention was quickly drawn by a noise coming from the dining hall. He was not the only one to notice as there was quite a commotion coming from inside.

Pierro stormed out, slamming the door behind him as he left. The Italian did not even stop to acknowledge the group around the campfire. He simply got into his car and sped away in a cloud of orange dust.

'It looks like you may have been caught out after all,' said Colin, but his compatriot was not listening to him.

Celeste did not emerge from the dining hall until the sound of Pierro's car had died down. When she did walk out there were tears streaming down her cheeks and a complete lack of her usual brazenness. Stephen was quick to go to her side. She at first shrugged away his offer of help, but soon relented and allowed him into her caravan. Half an hour later, he returned to the campfire, but his mood showed little improvement.

'Well?' asked Matt, as Stephen approached.

'She says that she needs time to herself "*to get her head together*",' he replied.

The emphasis that had been placed when quoting the girl was indicative of the level of frustration he was feeling.

'Did she say why Pierro stormed out like that?'

'She ended it with him. Apparently, he was already suspicious that she was cheating on him and confronted her about it.'

'Does he know that it was you?'

'I don't think so. She never told, but it won't be long before he figures it out anyway.'

'Well, if he tries anything we will back you up,' said Colin.

Stephen gave a slight nod to acknowledge his friend's good intentions, but he was far too lost in his own thoughts to pay it much heed. Although he did not say it, he was more concerned for Celeste than for himself.

Chapter 26

Due to the excessive amount of alcohol that they had consumed the evening before, both Matt and Colin had been made to spend the night in their own beds, alone. Therefore, when Rose arrived at the shower block for her morning wash to find a stream of overflowing water, she assumed one of the boys had passed out in there and left the shower running all night. Her intuition told her that it would most likely be Colin who she would find.

When she entered the building, she did indeed find an unconsciousness form lying on the saturated tiles, but it was not that of her lover. He was fast asleep in his bed and blissfully unaware of the violent and bloody scene that confronted Rose. The limp and naked body that she had found stretched out before her was female and it had not found itself in this position as a result of too much alcohol.

It took almost an hour for the emergency services to arrive. Celeste was taken to the casualty ward at Cooper's Creek Hospital where she remained in a critical, but stable condition. She did not regain consciousness. Her entire body was laced with bruises; there was a deep laceration on her forehead and she had suffered a considerable loss of blood. The doctors said that she was lucky to be alive.

A feeling of complete and utter disbelief descended on the camp. Many of the backpackers had previously witnessed Celeste's convulsions in the field, but none could have imagined the violent and devastating impact of this most recent seizure. With nobody around to have helped and due to the hard tiled surfaces of the shower room, her latest epileptic attack had been close to fatal. Because of the seriousness of her injuries, the doctors had refused her any visitors until further notice, which left the backpackers waiting anxiously to be updated on her condition. Stephen in particular took the news badly and very few in the camp felt in the mood for socialising. Only the two couples felt secure enough to talk about what had happened.

'It would not surprise me if she had this planned,' said Rose, 'a stunt to get attention that backfired.'

Her views were not shared by the others.

'That is the most inconsiderate thing I have ever heard,' said Jenny. 'How can you be so heartless? No epileptic would purposefully induce a seizure.'

'Jenny's right,' said Colin. 'Celeste has an illness and there is no way that even she would stoop so low as to try and use it to her advantage. She could have died last night, for Christ's sake.'

Rose shrugged, but did not take back her words. The four of them were seated in the boys' caravan away from the eyes and ears of the rest of the group. In light of Rose's bold accusations, this was just as well.

'I don't understand this deep rooted hatred you have for her,' said Matt. 'What aren't you telling us, because as far as I can tell she has done nothing to you?'

'Nothing; her? Do not try and tell me that little bitch is all sweetness and innocence. She may be able to wrap anyone with a penis around her little finger, but I know what that girl's true face is and it is not pretty, believe me.'

'So what did she do?'

Rose did not respond. She just sat with her arms and legs crossed in unwavering defiance. Matt turned to Jenny for the answer. The younger sibling looked to her sister, who offered no objections to her telling the story for her.

'It all goes back to before the two of you arrived in Birribandi,' Jenny began. 'There were four English guys here and they got along really well with everyone. It was a really tight group, not unlike what we had before all this trouble kicked off. One of them, whose name was Ben, had a...' She stopped for a moment to try and rephrase what she was about to say. 'Well, he and Rose were...' Again she struggled to find the appropriate words to convey her story.

'I get the point,' interrupted Colin. 'I'm not stupid. I know that your sister wasn't a virgin when I met her.'

Jenny was abashed, but carried on with her story regardless.

'Like I said, everything was going really well. Then one night Celeste decided that she wanted Ben too. She was already with Pierro, but as you know; that is not enough to stop her.'

'So Ben slept with Celeste whilst he was still with Rose,' interrupted Colin.

The Irishman's assumption was motivated more through a desire to belittle Rose's former lover than to deduce the outcome of the story.

'We do not know for sure whether he did or he didn't,' said Jenny. 'All I can say is that there was a marked change in Ben shortly after Celeste's intentions were revealed. He became nervous and was always looking over his shoulder and then one day he and his three friends just up and left. I must admit that it did seem like they were running away from something.'

'Pierro!' exclaimed both Colin and Matt in unison.

'Exactly,' confirmed Jenny. 'Whether Ben slept with her or not, we think that she planned on telling Pierro that he did.'

'And you think that's why he left?' asked Colin. 'This Ben character cannot have been much of a man if he was running away from Pierro.'

Rose finally stirred from her silence.

'Pierro may come across as a dim-witted fool, but he has a lot of friends in this town. There is no way that Ben slept with that little floozy, which is why she would have made sure that he was punished for it. She'd have had no trouble convincing Pierro and his apish friends to form a lynch mob.'

'Lynch mob?' scoffed Colin. 'This isn't the Wild West, you know. I think that you girls have read far too much into this. From the sound of it, this Ben had a guilty conscience and took the coward's way out.'

He paused for a moment whilst considering another possibility.

'Or maybe he was running away,' he said. 'Just not from what you thought.'

'I don't understand,' said Rose. 'What else could he have been running away from?'

'Shortly after I arrived here, Stephen told me that Ben was buying weed from some guy that he met in the local pub. Perhaps that had something to do with it.'

'You think that he had run into trouble with some local criminals?' asked Jenny.

'Well, we all know who was running the drugs trade around here, don't we? I did a deal behind Rhett's back and he tried to kill me for it. It makes sense that your friend Ben could have made the same mistake.'

'He has a point,' said Jenny, but Rose was not interested.

'I get accused of unfairly blaming Celeste for everything and then you all go and do the same thing with Rhett. Now that vile man has passed away, you could easily make him a scapegoat for anything, but I'm not buying it. I don't care what anybody says, Celeste was bad news and I for one will not be shedding a tear over her.'

Jenny sighed with resignation and then got up to return to her own caravan. Matt rose with her, but before he left he had one final piece of advice for Rose.

'Think what you will about the girl, but for Stephen's sake try to keep it to yourself in future. He's pretty torn up right now and badmouthing Celeste is not going to help anyone.'

He hoped that Rose would take heed of his words. Tensions were running high and sooner or later, he feared that somebody was going to snap. After all that they had been through during the past week, he did not feel that any of them were equipped to cope with any more conflict.

In what was quickly becoming a familiar sight at the caravan park, a police car pulled into the driveway in the early hours of the afternoon. Unlike the previous visit, this time the sheriff had come not out of courtesy, but on official business.

'How can we help you, officer?' asked Colin, who as always, was the closest to the entrance of the camp. 'You aren't bringing us more bad news, I hope.'

The sheriff stepped out of his car and at the same time a second policeman exited from the passenger side. Whatever the reason for the visit, the lawman had deemed it necessary to bring back up. The second officer was a good deal younger than the sheriff and did not look much older than some of the backpackers.

'Could you direct me to the van occupied by a Mr Stephen

Kenny, please.'

It was an order not a question. The sheriff offered none of his usual niceties and Colin immediately suspected that something was not right. If his friend was about to receive some distressing news then he wanted to be there to offer his support.

'Stephen's in number one. It's right by the reception.'

The two policemen began to walk and Colin stayed alongside of them, eager to find out what was going on.

'You may wish to return to your own van,' said the sheriff. 'This is a private matter between Mr Kenny and the police.'

'Stephen's a friend of mine and we have no secrets here. If this is what I think it is and it's about Celeste, then he's going to need all of the support he can get.'

The second policeman, who looked familiar to Colin despite this being their first meeting, offered an undisguised look of contempt. If the man had not been in uniform, Colin would be fearful an assault on him was about to take place such was the vehemence that the man held.

It did not take long for them to arrive at the door to caravan number one, and such was the tranquillity of the park that they did not need to knock. Stephen had heard them coming and opened his door as they approached.

'Mr Kenny?' asked the sheriff's deputy, who seemed to have a real relish for his job.

'Yes, that's me,' replied the Irishman.

That was the opening that the policeman had been waiting for, but the sheriff placed an arm across his deputy's chest to prevent the man from overstepping his authority. The more senior of the two then took control of the situation in the way that it should be handled professionally.

'Mr Kenny, I would like you to accompany my partner and I to the station, if you may.'

'I don't understand,' said Stephen, who harboured a similar fear to Colin. 'Has Celeste woken up; is she okay?'

Again, the deputy looked like he could barely keep his blood from boiling over, but he somehow managed to control himself.

'Mr Kenny, I ask you once again. Will you please accompany my partner and I back to the police station, where we need to ask you a few questions.'

The authority in his voice was not lost on either Stephen or his friend.

'Am I under arrest?' he asked.

'You are not being charged with anything yet, but if you refuse to co-operate, I am authorised to take you into custody by force if necessary.'

'This is crazy,' said Colin. 'Exactly what is he supposed to have done?'

Seeing that Colin was not going to give up, the sheriff decided to drop the charade and just come out with the truth of the reason behind his visit.

'We are investigating the assault and rape of one Miss Celeste Espuche,' he said. 'Whilst we are yet to finalise our list of suspects, you, Mr Kenny, we have been informed were having an illicit relationship with the victim. As such, we believe that you have information that would be vital to our enquiries.'

Stephen could not believe what he was hearing.

'There has obviously been some mistake,' he said. 'Celeste had a fit and banged her head on the bathroom tiles. How could she possibly have been raped?'

The sheriff was unmoved by the emotion in the young man's voice.

'That, Mr Kenny, is what we hope to find out.'

*

The remaining backpackers gathered in the dining hall. They had no means of communicating with their two friends at the police station so all they could do was wait. Colin had insisted on accompanying Stephen, but the police drew a line against anybody else tagging along. The boys returned at five o'clock, three hours after they had left. Colin was the first through the door as Stephen went straight to his van to be alone.

'Thank God you're back,' said Rose, rising to greet her boyfriend. 'Where's Stephen? They aren't keeping him there, are they?'

'No, he's back in his van. I think it's best if we allow him some time to himself for a while.'

'So what exactly happened; is it true that Celeste was raped?' she asked.

He beckoned her to take a seat and the couple joined the others at the table.

'The short answer is yes; she was raped.'

Everyone around the table began to shuffle uncomfortably. Niall, who was closest to Stephen, put his head in his hands, fearful of the implications for his friend.

'Is this for definite?' asked Rose. 'I mean, I found her and those wounds cannot have been inflicted by rape. She clearly had a fit and hit her head against those hard tiles. Are you sure that she isn't just making it up?'

'Will you stop with the accusations,' snapped Colin, who had been through a stressful time waiting for Stephen at the police station and was finding it hard to keep his temper in check. 'She was raped, okay. Her seizure occurred after the assault. The doctors who examined her at the hospital alerted the police after checking her wounds. She isn't even conscious yet.'

Rose put her head down. She was humiliated, but also

penitent for her callous and false accusations.

'Is Stephen the only suspect?' asked Niall, 'because if the police are looking for the culprit, I could certainly offer up a more likely candidate.'

'He's right,' interjected Matt. 'This had to have been done by Pierro. We all saw his reaction when he walked out last night.'

'Pierro has an alibi,' said Colin.

'And so does Stephen.' Niall's frustration was starting to penetrate his usually relaxed demeanour. 'He never left the van once during the night. I'm a light sleeper and I would definitely have noticed if he had.'

'That is why both of them have been released without charge while the police carry out their investigation.' Colin took a deep breath to keep composed. Despite agreeing wholeheartedly with Matt and Niall, he was trying to be as diplomatic as possible in relating what little information he had. 'Hopefully, Celeste will regain consciousness soon and she can put the matter to bed once and for all.'

After the group had adjourned their meeting, they went back to doing the only thing that they could. They returned to their caravans and they waited.

Chapter 27

Joe returned to Birribandi as soon as he had received the news of Celeste's ordeal. He arrived back at the town late on the Tuesday evening and so as not to disturb his employees too much, he waited until the following morning before paying them a visit. When he did turn up at the caravan park, he brought with him a most unwelcome passenger.

'What's he doing here?'

Colin was barely able to control his temper upon seeing the man exit from the passenger side of Joe's car and he knew that Stephen would not exercise such restraint when he learned of Pierro's return.

'I don't want to see any trouble,' warned Joe. 'Pierro has been through enough in the last twenty four hours and he has as much right to be here as you.'

The camp's chef was not in good shape. He had dark rings around his bloodshot eyes and had gone without more than just sleep, as he was also unwashed and unshaven. His condition conveyed a state of extreme stress that could be attributed to either grief or guilt. Colin put it down to the latter.

'Do you really think that bringing him back here is wise...or even safe?' Colin asked.

Joe did not like the thinly veiled threat in the Irishman's words. However, before he could remonstrate with the younger man he became distracted by a far greater concern. Colin turned to see what had caught Joe's attention, but he already had a good idea what it would be. Joe attempted to step around Colin to intercept Stephen before he could start any trouble, but Colin prevented him by placing a hand on his boss' chest.

'Don't go blaming Stephen for anything,' said Colin. 'Not when you are standing by that monster over there.'

With Joe briefly distracted, Stephen took full advantage of the opportunity presented to him. He had not only Colin, but also the car between himself and Joe, which provided him ample time to make his move. Pierro was expecting the onslaught, but had little fight in him. He merely shielded his face as Stephen unleashed a flurry of punches to his torso.

The Irishman was not the type to punish a defenceless opponent and the longer that Pierro refused to strike back, the less frenzied his attack became until Stephen was simply pushing the other man against the side of the vehicle, hoping to provoke a combative response.

'Why won't you fight me, you coward?' he cried.

Joe brushed Colin aside and approached the frustrated man, but he knew that the threat had already passed.

'Let it go, Stephen,' he said. 'You know this is not the answer.'

'He needs to pay for what he's done.'

Stephen lowered his guard, but his arms were still tensed and ready to react at a moment's notice.

'Pierro has been neither charged with nor found guilty of any crime,' said Joe. 'Like you, he is grieving and like you, he is a free man until such a day that a court decides otherwise.'

The point had been made. Both men had suffered an equal heartbreak and both men had equal cause should either have perpetrated the horrendous crime that had torn apart the harmony of the camp in just twenty four short hours. The only lesson learned from the morning was that both of the hospitalised girl's lovers could not be trusted to be kept close together. Joe decided that it was best for everybody if Pierro left the camp and stayed at his house until Celeste's attacker was found, whether it be one of the two rivals to her affections or somebody completely different.

Everybody rallied around Stephen once Joe had left along with his much despised passenger. Not one of the backpackers doubted their friend's innocence and they ensured that he knew that he could count on their unwavering support. In a way, the caravan park was a community of outcasts; every one of them an outsider. If they were to get through the hard times ahead, it was imperative that they all stuck together.

Chapter 28

Pierro returned to the caravan park after nightfall. He parked his car just before the entrance to the driveway and turned off the engine. He did not want to alert the residents to his presence and so walked the rest of the way into the park. No noise came from within the unlit vans and the only sound that could be heard was from the repetitive croak of cane toads. The only light was from the pale glow of the moon.

The interloper did not plan on staying for long. All he wanted was to get to his room and pick up an important item to take back to Joe's. It was a simple task that he would never get to complete. Unbeknownst to him, his entrance had not gone unnoticed.

The door to his bedroom gave way at a gentle push. Although it had been left unlocked, there were no signs of any disturbance. He had expected Stephen and his friends to have turned the place upside down in a vain search to find anything incriminating that they could use against him. Perhaps he had underestimated them, or maybe they simply did not expect the room to be left so invitingly unlocked. A break-in would certainly arouse suspicion and be very difficult for them to explain.

He had filled a small rucksack with clothes and toiletries earlier in the day. Frustratingly, Joe stood and watched over him whilst he packed. This was supposedly for his own protection, but it prevented him from taking what he needed the most. That is what he had returned for now.

The bottom drawer of the cabinet slid out easily and the bundle was safely where he had left it. He reached down and picked it up. Unable to resist the temptation, he briefly flicked through the crisp wad of notes. He had not saved as much as he would have liked, but it was enough for him to make a clean break from that God forsaken town. He carefully slipped the cash into his bag and crept out the same way that he had entered, all the while careful not to make a sound.

As he strode silently through the kitchen and back to the dining hall, he found the doorway now blocked by a shadowy silhouette. To be caught snooping around at night in light of the crime that some were accusing him of would not bode well in his defence. He tried desperately to think up an excuse for his being there at that late hour, when the figure took a step forward, exposing his physiognomy to the defining beams of moonlight.

At once Pierro knew what he had to do. Earlier in the day he had been caught out in a state of shock and despair. He had been weak and not stood up for himself. There was no way that he would make that mistake again. He lurched forward with brutal determination. Once within range, he grabbed the other man by the throat with his left hand, shoving him into a side wall. He then held him firm whilst drawing back with his right to administer the first blow. He only became aware of the knife as he felt its blade pierce just beneath his rib cage.

The burning agony increased as the cold steel passed

through cartilage, bone and finally into his heart, completing its deadly diagonal ascent. At that final moment, the pain stopped. It had become so sharply focused that it withdrew into a singularity and then it was gone. It took with it, the feeling, the air and the life from Pierro's now limp body.

The killer withdrew his weapon with as much care as he had used when delivering the fatal insertion. He displayed the precision and skill of a seasoned butcher, killing not with malice or rage, but with carefully executed efficiency. Without making a sound, he calmly laid the body to rest on the tiled floor.

Pierro's bag had been left at the other end of the dining room. The killer picked it up and examined the contents. It was not long before he came across the cash, which he then shoved into the inside pocket of his overcoat. Killing the Italian had been a necessity, but finding the money made the task all the more worthwhile. He took one last look around to make sure that he had left no trace of his presence and then he disappeared back into the night.

Chapter 29

'I didn't do anything!'

'Save it for the Judge, kid. We have close to a dozen witnesses that saw you assault the deceased just hours before his death. We also know that you were sleeping with his girlfriend, who is at this moment fighting for her life in a hospital bed. Let me guess; she said that she was going to leave him and then changed her mind at the last minute; is that why you wanted to kill them both?'

'I'm telling you that it wasn't me. You have the wrong man.'

The deputy did not listen as he roughly manhandled Stephen into the back of the squad car. His superior would never tolerate such callous treatment of a prisoner, but Sheriff Lee was within neither sight nor earshot of the incident. He was inside the dining block with Joe, trying to restore calm and order to this shocked community of backpackers.

Birribandi had a small police department with limited resources and as such the crime scene had been cleared quickly. There were no spacesuit-clad forensic scientists swamping the area for minute biological clues invisible to the human eye or any intrusive reporters looking to capture their big break. The body was removed by ambulance to the local mortuary where it now sat beside the charred remains of the week's earlier casualty.

'This cannot be true,' protested Niall. 'I know Stephen and he is not capable of murder.'

The sheriff was unmoved.

'A week ago, I would have thought that nobody in this town was capable of such an act. In all of this town's history there has only ever been one other crime of this magnitude and that was over thirty years ago.'

'That's right,' said Colin. 'When Rose and I were at the station to report the mugging, you told us that there had been a murder in this town before. How do you know that it wasn't the same killer this time?'

'I can understand your frustration, but it is not possible for the crimes to be related. Although there are startling similarities; both cases involved a rape and a murder, I can safely rule out any connection. The previous crime was solved thirty years ago and has no bearing whatsoever on today.'

Colin was frustrated, but determined not to give up on fighting for his friend's freedom.

'It could be a copycat killer that you need to be looking for.'

'I will decide who needs to be investigated,' said the sheriff, 'and right now we have the most promising suspect in custody.'

The policeman did not take kindly to being told how he should be doing his job, but still Colin refused to give up.

'What about the rape? Just because Pierro got murdered doesn't mean that he didn't attack Celeste. If you ask me, he got what he deserved.'

The policeman did not want to be drawn into an argument,

but Colin was starting to test his patience.

'I hope that you are not condoning murder, Mr O'Meara.'

'No more than you are condoning rape. How is Celeste, by the way?'

The sheriff paused in the same way he had before raising the subject of Rhett's past in the mugging interview. He hoped that by divulging some information about the injured girl it may take the backpackers minds away from making unhelpful speculation regarding the murder.

'Miss Espuche has regained consciousness,' he said. 'And she is expected to make a full recovery, although it will take a lot longer for her emotional wounds to heal.'

This news, though not as shocking as the murder and subsequent arrest, was enough to garner the anxious attention of the group. It even managed to distract Colin. The questions came thick and fast.

'Celeste's awake?' 'Has she talked yet?' 'Did she name her attacker?'

The sheriff had neither the time nor the inclination to address each of the questions individually. He was willing to give them nothing more than the facts and had no desire to encourage idle gossip.

'We have taken a statement from the victim, but we are yet to receive any leads as to the identity of her attacker. Miss Espuche is currently suffering from post-traumatic shock.'

'Shock or not, she must have given you a name,' said Colin. 'Who attacked her; was it Stephen or was it Pierro?'

The Irishman was letting his frustrations get the better of him once more and Rose put a reassuring hand on his shoulder to help calm him down.

'We have been given a name, but it makes no sense to us,' the sheriff replied. 'The victim has a confused recollection of events and it will take a lot more time and considerable counselling before we believe she can give us an accurate account of what happened to her.'

'What do you mean the name makes no sense?' demanded Colin. 'If she fingered the culprit then he is your man. That's a first-person testimony from the victim. Surely the case could not be any clearer cut.'

'I wish it were that simple, I really do, but there is just no way that we can act on the information she has given to us.'

'That is ridiculous!' Colin was starting to lose his cool again. 'Who is it? Who did she say attacked her?'

The policeman drew in a large breath as if he himself could not believe what he was about to say. He had hoped to avoid having to disclose the name, but he could now see that more harm would be done by keeping it a secret.

'She said that the man who assaulted her was Rhett Butler.'

The revelation was met with astonished silence.

'Like I said; it makes no sense whatsoever,' added the sheriff. 'Rhett Butler is dead. I have seen his body myself. It may have been charred beyond all recognition, but it was definitely him. We have a coroner's report to prove this; the DNA was a match so he is one suspect that we can definitely rule out.'

'So how could she think that he had attacked her?' asked Colin. 'Did she get a clear look at the guy who did it?'

'That is another reason why we cannot take her testimony too seriously. She never actually saw her attacker, she only heard his voice. According to her, that voice belonged to Mr Butler.'

Colin's eyes narrowed.

'In that case, Pierro is your man. He had the same accent as Rhett. It had to be him.'

The sheriff would not be moved.

'This is Australia; most folks in this town have an accent

similar to Mr Butler's.'

'Stephen doesn't,' said Colin.

The policeman was well aware of what the young backpacker was implying, but he had been drawn into this conversation for far too long. He had spent too much time with these kids as it was and there was more pressing business for him to attend to.

'That is all the information that I can give you at this time,' he said. 'I have talked it over with Mr Wilson and we have both agreed that it will be for the best if we allow you all to keep working. A solid routine is what everyone needs right now to help them get through these hard times. As a precaution, I will be taking all of your passports with me when I leave here today as the investigation is far from over, but you will still have the freedom of the town.'

'Taking our passports; why?' asked Jenny. 'Surely none of us are suspects.'

'You have each said that you think that Stephen is innocent of the murder. If that is the case then the killer could be sat among us right now. Until this case is closed, I am not taking any chances.'

To emphasise that he had spoken the final word, the sheriff stood and walked out the door. As far as he was concerned, he had found the guilty party and all he had to do was prove it, but if he had thought that his talk would allay the fear within the camp, he was very much mistaken.

'This stinks.'

Colin had been the most reluctant to hand over his passport and had done so only when Joe threatened to search the caravan for it. He still had a considerable stash of illegal drugs hidden in there and did not wish to be joining Stephen in jail.

'I'm more concerned about being stuck here whilst there's a killer on the loose,' said Matt. 'Who knows which one of us could be next? From this moment onwards we need to make sure that nobody is left alone; especially the girls.'

The possibility of a continuing threat got Colin's attention.

'Do you really think that we could be in danger?' he asked.

'We both know that Stephen couldn't kill anyone. Whoever murdered Pierro is still out there. It could be that the Italian had enemies, but we cannot afford to let our guard down for a moment.'

Colin nodded his agreement, but he did have another concern that he wanted to get off his chest.

'What do you think about the other thing?' His voice trailed off as if he was embarrassed to even bring up the subject.

'I think that we can safely rule out Rhett as a possible suspect,' Matt replied flatly.

'Are you sure? What if there was something in that superstition of yours and we brought him back?'

Matt could not believe what he was hearing.

'What do you mean "brought him back"? We didn't do anything, remember? All we had was a photograph and if that could raise the dead then the whole planet would be crawling with zombies. When my Nan died nobody covered her pictures and she didn't come back to haunt us all.'

'Yeah, well I'm going to go along to the library and do a little research of my own. I'm not prepared to just sit around and wait for some madman to either rape or kill again. The sheriff said that this town has suffered these crimes before and they may be connected. We know that thirty years ago Rhett was questioned over a rape and the fact that his name has been mentioned again has to be more than just coincidence.'

'Rhett is dead,' said Matt. 'How can a dead man rape somebody?'

'That,' said Colin, 'is what I intend to find out.'

Matt accompanied Colin to the library purely in keeping with his vow not to leave anyone alone. He saw no merit or sense in digging up the past and he hoped that the sooner Colin got such crazy ideas out of his system the better. The library had two terminals dedicated to internet access and the pair booked one of these to aid them in their amateur investigation.

'Here we go,' said Colin, 'I've logged onto the newspaper archives. All we have to do is search under certain key words and see what we get.'

'I didn't think this town had a local newspaper,' said Matt.

'It doesn't, but in a country this small the story was bound to have been picked up by one of the nationals. Especially thirty years ago. What else have they got to report on?'

Matt could see his friend's point. During his stay in Australia he had noticed that seemingly trivial incidents and events that would never leave the regionalised locality they occurred in back in Britain could pass from one side of the continent to the other in this vast, yet sparsely populated nation.

'Where do you plan to start?' asked Matt.

'We know that there's only been one murder in this town before last night, so let's start with the obvious.'

Colin keyed in the words "Birribandi" and "murder". The search brought back just one result. The Irishman highlighted the header and then left-clicked the mouse to bring it up. The story was five years old and related to a memorial service that the townsfolk had held to mark the twenty fifth anniversary of the killing. There was no mention of Rhett and it only said that the murdered man was a then twenty two year old footballer named John Warwick, who was killed by a woman he was alleged to have assaulted.

Colin tried going back and putting in different keywords, but they all brought up nothing. The crime far pre-dated the internet and the original news stories had not been deemed worthy enough to have made the archive. The pair had reached a dead end.

'Well, that's that then,' said Matt.

Colin was speechless. He really thought that he was going to dig up some dirt on his old foreman. He stood up and roughly shoved his chair back under the desk, causing an elderly library attendant to glance up, but she did not say anything. As he tried to compose his thoughts, he briefly scanned over a series of framed photographs that lined one wall of the library. There were three in total and one in particular caught his attention.

'You better take a look at this, Matt,' he said.

'Look at what?' replied the Englishman, who despite his earlier reservations was also disappointed by the lack of a result in their search.

'This picture on the wall,' said Colin.

Matt glanced over. The first picture was of a farmer posing with a prize winning goat. This was next to a certificate awarded to Birribandi for reaching the final shortlist of ten for the title of Australia's tidiest town in 1981. Matt assumed that Colin was referring to the third picture, which was of a sports team.

'What about it?' asked Matt.

'Who's that sitting third from the left in the front row?'

Matt squinted as he perused the image.

'It can't be,' he said.

'It is,' replied Colin. 'It says R Butler underneath and look at who is sitting beside him.'

Matt scanned through the names until he found Rhett's. Beside it was the name J Warwick.

'That's the man who was murdered,' he said.

'And he knew Rhett,' added Colin. 'I told you that we would find a connection.'

As they talked, they were approached by the librarian who had come to investigate after the earlier disturbance when Colin had slammed his chair.

'Is there a problem, gentlemen?' she asked.

'No problem,' said Colin. 'We were just looking at the photographs, that's all.'

The librarian was wearing reading glasses that were attached to a cord around her neck. She removed these, which left them hanging over her chest like a necklace.

'You two boys are from the caravan park, aren't you?' she asked.

They briefly looked at one another.

'Yes, we are,' replied Colin. 'I take it that you have heard about the recent tragedies.'

The librarian nodded gravely, but sympathetically.

'The whole town is in mourning,' she replied. 'My prayers are with the girl and that poor boy's family.'

Matt was only half interested in the conversation as he was ready to leave, but his friend had other ideas.

'Have you always lived in Birribandi?' Colin asked the woman.

'Yes,' she replied, 'ever since I was a little girl.'

Colin nodded in what he hoped was a thoughtful way.

'You must remember the first time that crimes such as these happened,' he said. 'Wasn't that thirty years ago now?'

'Yes, it was,' she confirmed. 'I had two young children at

the time. You just don't expect such horrific acts to take place on your own doorstep.'

Again, Colin nodded.

'Did you know any of the people involved?' he asked.

'Did I know them?' she echoed. 'In a town like this there are no strangers. Especially thirty years ago.'

The librarian looked past Colin to the framed photograph.

'Are you interested in local history?' she asked him.

Colin tried to muster as much enthusiasm as he could.

'If it's to do with sport, I am. I take it that this team were quite successful?'

The librarian's face seemed to drop a little as if suddenly reminded of an even greater tragedy than the one that they had been discussing.

'They could have been,' she said. 'It's funny that you ask, because the same man who was murdered all those years ago played for that very team.' She pointed to John Warwick in the picture. 'They made it all the way to the state final. One of the players was even being courted by some of the professional clubs from the national league.'

'It wasn't the one who was murdered, was it?' asked Colin, who was trying his best to keep the conversation going.

'No, it wasn't John,' she replied. 'It was this man here.' She pointed to Rhett. 'His name is Rhett Butler, like the character from *Gone with the Wind.* And like his namesake, he was also a hit with the ladies.'

The two backpackers glanced at one another. This time they were more amused than surprised. They each made a conscious effort to suppress the urge to giggle.

'What happened to him?' asked Colin.

The librarian looked up into the corner of her eye as she retrieved the requisite memory.

'Drink and drugs soon put an end to his career,' she said,

rather sternly. 'After the murder investigation the big teams cooled their interest in him and he turned to the bottle.'

'He was involved?' asked Colin, innocently.

'He was,' she confirmed. 'The girl did not name John as her attacker until after she had killed him.'

'I don't understand,' said Matt. 'How does Rhett fit into this?'

'Well, like I said; the girl was late coming forward about the attack. It was actually her parents who reported it, but she refused to say anything herself. Witnesses confirmed that on the night of the alleged assault she had gone home with the two boys in question. They were roommates, you see; so the police interviewed both of them.'

'So it could have been Rhett?' asked Colin.

'No,' she replied flatly, 'just days after the assault, she stabbed John to death at his home and told the police that he had been the one who attacked her. Rhett was cleared of any blame, but the scandal affected his performance in the cup final. After blowing his one chance at the big time, he fell apart. He eventually progressed from alcohol to the stronger stuff and then just last week he died behind the wheel of his car whilst drunk. You must have heard about it.'

Colin and Matt both nodded, but said nothing more. They assumed that the woman had no knowledge of Rhett working for Joe and did not want to arouse her suspicions by telling her.

'What about the girl?' Colin asked. 'Is she still in prison?'

'Oh, she didn't go to prison,' said the librarian. 'She pleaded insanity and was instead sent to the psychiatric hospital at Cooper's Creek. As far as I know, she's still there.'

'Fascinating,' said Colin. 'Just out of interest; what was her name?'

'Naomi Green,' replied the librarian.

Colin again performed his pseudo intellectual nod for the woman's benefit.

'It's been very interesting talking with you,' he said, 'but it is time that we got back to the park.'

'Well, don't let me keep you,' she said. 'Hopefully, I'll see you both again sometime.'

They thanked her for her time and then left to return to the park. Colin was very animated on the walk back.

'Did you hear what she said?' he asked. 'The killer is at the hospital in Cooper's Creek. The psychiatric ward is to the rear of the main building; I passed a sign for it when I had my x-ray.'

'So she's at Cooper's Creek,' replied Matt. 'That means we can safely rule her out as Pierro's killer.'

'Don't you see?' said Colin. 'Cooper's Creek is where Celeste is. Do you think that this Naomi Green is still there?'

Matt could guess where his friend was leading him and he did not approve.

'You aren't seriously suggesting that we pay her a visit, are you?'

'Why not? It couldn't do any harm and we may even find out what part Rhett had to play in the crimes.'

'This is crazy. I'm not going to quiz a patient in a mental home about a rape that took place thirty years ago. Besides which, we can probably guess how it happened. The pair will have taken the girl back to their house and whilst Rhett slept in his bed, his friend assaulted her on the couch. Then she goes crazy and stabs him for it; end of story.'

Colin was not interested in random speculation when he could get the true story directly from the source.

'I'm sure if we tell Joe that we want to go and visit Celeste, he will take us. Once we are there, we just need to slip away for a few moments as the psychiatric wing is just next door.'

'I have a bad feeling about this,' said Matt, but he reluctantly agreed to the plan.

Deep down the Englishman knew that his friend would get into much more trouble if he was not with him.

Chapter 30

Niall and Jonas insisted on accompanying the two men on their visit to see their hospitalized colleague. They left early on the Thursday morning with Joe giving them all a lift to Cooper's Creek. Their boss agreed only after imposing several strict rules regarding what the men could and could not tell the injured girl. He wanted to make sure that Celeste was spared further trauma unless absolutely necessary. Naturally, this meant that both Stephen and Pierro were taboo subjects.

'She is going to be suspicious as to why Stephen isn't with us,' said Niall.

'Tell her that he is ill and confined to his bed,' Joe told him. 'The same goes for Pierro. The doctors have made it clear that they do not want her receiving any more shocks until she has regained more of her strength.'

When they arrived at the hospital car park, Joe told the four backpackers that he had several errands of his own to attend to and arranged to meet them back at the car for two o'clock. This, he explained, would give them ample time to visit the girl and then grab a more substantial lunch than the processed cheese sandwiches to which they had grown accustomed. Once they were past the front entrance and Joe was out of sight, Colin took the opportunity to make his excuses.

'We'll catch up with you guys in a moment,' he told Niall and Jonas. 'We have something else that we need to attend to first.'

'What else could you possibly need to do here?' asked Niall.

'The doctors want to do some follow up checks on my x-ray,' replied Colin. 'It shouldn't take too long and Matt is coming with me so that we can still see Celeste together.'

The lie was obvious, but Colin had told it with such casual ease that it was not questioned. He and Matt slipped away from their friends and followed the signs to the psychiatric ward, which was located in the southern wing of the hospital.

'Do you have any idea what you are going to say to her; assuming of course that she is even here?' asked Matt. 'Thirty years is a long time, you know.'

'Don't worry; I have it all under control,' insisted the Irishman.

Matt thought back to the first time that Colin had asked for his trust. Back then he had been completely lost amidst the sand and spinifex of the desert and considered himself fortunate to have found the company of one so experienced and worldly wise. Now he wondered if his friend was nothing but a fantasist, who was always at home within his own thoughts, but had no real grasp of the wider world around him. Here they were, chasing the shadow of a dead man, whilst there was a cold-blooded killer on the loose. Should the unthinkable happen, Matt wondered if Colin would really be someone to whom he could trust his life.

'This is it,' said Colin, as they came to the desired wing. 'Let me do the talking.'

A large lady in her late forties to early fifties staffed the reception. She was seated at a desk covered by a Perspex shield and a heftily built security guard stood sentinel by her station. This was not quite how either of the visitors had expected minimum security to be. Colin stepped up to the desk. The receptionist ignored him, keeping her attention on the computer screen in front of her. He coughed. She glanced first towards the security guard and then sighed before finally asking 'may I take your name, please?'

'Colin,' he simply answered, not wishing to give his full identity away.

'Colin, eh; would there happen to be any more to that?'

He considered lying, but then thought better of it.

'Colin O'Meara,' he said.

She picked up a clipboard and briefly scanned the information that it held.

'You're not on the list. Do you have an appointment?'

She used the mouse to open a new window on her desktop and then began typing.

'I didn't know that we needed an appointment. The sign said that visiting hours were between ten and twelve and I assumed that we could just turn up.'

She paused with her fingers hovering over the keys and looked up at him without moving her head.

'Have you ever been here before?' she asked.

'Er, no I haven't. This is my first time.'

Matt was cringing behind his friend and doing his best to look invisible. It was not working as the woman looked first to him and then back to Colin.

'In the best interests of the residents, we prefer for visitors to make an appointment in advance,' she said. 'This is so as not to cause any undue surprises that could unsettle or distress those residents.'

Colin was visibly lost for words. The receptionist let out another sigh.

'Who are you here to see?' she asked.

'Miss Naomi Green.'

'Ms Green? Wait here, please.'

The receptionist's surprised reaction suggested to the boys that she had not been expecting a request to see that particular patient. She rose from her seat and exited via a door, which was located just behind her desk. She was not gone long before she returned accompanied by a nurse.

'How can I be of assistance?' the nurse asked.

'Like I said to the receptionist here, we want to see Naomi Green, please.'

The nurse looked confused and when Matt glanced down at her name badge he realised why.

'You're Naomi Green?' he asked.

'Yes, that's me. I must say that you two boys are acting most oddly. Exactly what can I do for you?'

'We're from Birribandi,' said Matt.

'I should have guessed. Your accent is such a giveaway.'

She had such a warm and relaxed demeanour that her sarcasm seemed more of an invitation than a rebuke.

'We're backpackers working the harvest trail,' added Colin. 'Up until last week we were working under a man named Rhett Butler.'

Hiro was lain belly down on his bed sketching when he heard a knock at the door. He had been sketching a lot lately. The desert offered little stimulus and his fellow backpackers even less. Recently, however, he felt inspired and spent every waking hour working on his drawings. He put down his pencil before rising to answer the door.

'Hi, we thought that you may like some company.'

It was the two English girls. If he concentrated, he could understand these two quite well. He glanced back at his journal, which lay open on the bed and then back to the girls.

'We go outside?' he offered. 'Is sunny day.'

The pair exchanged a look of amusement, but did not pass comment. They had decided that it was time that they both got to know their Asian colleague a bit better. It was not fair on the Japanese man that he should have to spend his time on the peripherals of the group simply because he was not as well versed in the English language as everybody else. Hiro, they thought, had remained an enigma for far too long.

The hospital had a small cafeteria for use by visitors and that is where Matt and Colin took up seats with freshly poured cups of coffee in front of them. Joining them at their table was Naomi Green. One time resident and now a nurse at the hospital; there were many questions that the pair hoped she would be able to answer. She was just one year younger than Rhett, but she could have passed for his daughter. In spite of her troubled past, the years had been kind. Her blonde locks were yet to give way to the greying of age and she still had a trim, healthy figure.

'I knew when I read the article in the paper that there would be people keen to hear my story again. I thought that they would be reporters or maybe even the police. I never expected a pair of backpackers.'

'Do you mind speaking to us, because we could leave if you would prefer,' offered Matt.

The Englishman was still uneasy with putting a complete stranger on the spot in this way and hoped that she would pull the plug then and there to end Colin's morbid quest before it had the chance to get out of hand.

'Not at all,' she replied. 'I have had thirty years to come to terms with what happened to me. Three of those years I spent as a patient in this very hospital and when I left, I trained as a nurse so that I was able to come back.'

'Is that allowed?' asked Colin, receiving a disapproving glance from Matt in return.

'My record was expunged. Suffice to say, mistakes were made around that time. I was suffering from post-traumatic stress, but I was far from crazy. The killing was an accident and the conviction was deleted from the records.'

Colin raised his cup to take a sip, but the liquid was still scalding hot and burned the tip of his tongue. He quickly returned it to the table top.

'What made you want to come back here?' he asked.

'The one thing that human suffering teaches us is the importance of hope. By returning, I am able to pass on that hope to others.'

'Are you aware of a patient named Celeste? She's a Canadian girl that was admitted recently. Given the nature of her injuries, she is likely to require some psychiatric support as well as medical.'

The nurse raised her cup and delicately blew on it before taking a sip. Both Colin and Matt were keenly analysing her every move, hoping to garner as much information as possible from her body language. Thus far, she had given nothing away.

'For reasons of confidentiality, I cannot discuss details of any of the patients here, but I am aware of the young lady in question. I am guessing that you worked with her in Birribandi.'

'That's right,' said Colin. 'And so did Rhett.'

Matt gave another disapproving look to his friend, whom

he thought was perilously close to overstepping the mark, but the he carried on undeterred.

'We understand that our late foreman was with you the night that you were assaulted,' he said. 'He was even questioned by the police, I believe.'

'What's your point?' the nurse asked, calmly.

'Having worked alongside the man, I could easily believe that he was capable of assaulting a woman. Just before he died he even threatened to do just that to our friend and we all know what happened to her.'

'You think that Rhett had something to do with the attack on your friend?' she asked. 'I thought that the assault took place after he died.'

Colin took another sip from his mug, which had now cooled to a more palatable level.

'That's right,' he confirmed. 'Rhett was already dead, but the attack could have been carried out by a friend or an associate of his. It's happened before.'

The nurse ignored Colin's backhanded comment.

'So what exactly are you hoping to gain from speaking to me?' she asked.

'I want to find out the extent of Rhett's involvement in your attack. He was with both you and the other man that night. Did he play a part in the assault?'

The nurse took a deep and prolonged breath.

'I suppose that now he is dead, I can finally tell the truth,' she said. 'Rhett was involved in both the assault and the...' she faltered briefly, '...and the events that followed.'

Matt shifted awkwardly in his seat, but Colin remained calm and focused. The revelation did not surprise him as it merely confirmed his suspicions. He never had any doubt that the old man was capable of murder.

'Why didn't you bring any charges against him?' Colin

asked.

She pushed her cup away from her as if she no longer had a thirst for it.

'Enough suffering had gone on. A man died because of what happened that night. I was in a position to end it and that is what I did. There was no way that I could have endured a lengthy court case. To have been made to dredge up the sordid details of that night on a witness stand in front of all those people would have been too much to bear. Especially at so young an age, I simply could not have done it.'

'So Rhett did rape you?'

Matt coughed under his breath. He did not agree with the forthrightness of Colin's choice of words and he was showing it. Their interviewee, however, was still comfortably at ease with the tone of the questions.

'Both men had an equal measure of the crime that was committed that night. Like I said earlier; one of them lost his life because of it. I did not want any more suffering to take place.'

'What about your suffering, surely you would have been better off seeing him brought to justice?'

'I couldn't.' She paused briefly and swallowed heavily. For the first time cracks were starting to appear in her confident visage. 'After all that had happened, coming to this place was the best thing for me. I made a deal with the state prosecutors and by pleading insanity they spared me the stress and indignation of a lengthy trial.'

'So you did kill the other guy?'

'Colin!' exclaimed Matt, who now had no doubt that his friend had gone too far.

The nurse silenced the Englishman by raising her hand.

'My hands were on the knife when it delivered the mortal injuries,' she said.

Her choice of words seemed unusual. Colin sensed that the nurse was holding back the truth.

'What do you mean "your hands were on the knife"?' he asked. 'Surely you either stabbed him or you didn't.'

'All I am saying is that I have accepted responsibility for what happened. That man died by my hand.'

Although Matt had earlier wanted to stop the interrogation, he was drawn in by the nurse's admissions and was now just as absorbed in her answers as his friend was, so he allowed Colin to go on.

'What are your thoughts on the stabbing in Birribandi?' the Irishman asked.

This sudden shift in the conversation caught the nurse off guard and her stunned reaction made it obvious that she was yet to hear of Pierro's murder.

'You haven't heard, have you?' asked Colin.

'Heard what?' she replied, her complexion beginning to pale.

'The chief suspect in the assault on Celeste was murdered on Tuesday night. He was stabbed to death, except that this time we can safely rule out the previous victim as a suspect. It all sounds a little familiar, doesn't it?'

She placed her head in her hands as she attempted to come to terms with the news. Looking up, she said 'you still think that the crimes are somehow connected, don't you? After thirty years, it isn't possible.'

'Like I said, in the recent killing the rapist could not have been killed by his victim. The motives are completely different, unless of course there is something that you are not telling us.'

She began to tremble. It was only a slight movement, but she was trembling nonetheless. She took a large gulp of coffee to settle her nerves.

'All we need is the truth,' said Colin. 'There is no need for you to become involved in this case. Just tell us what happened thirty years ago. How did the man who attacked you die?'

He reached across the table and placed his hands over hers. It would have been a most inappropriate gesture if done just moments earlier, but it now seemed like the most natural thing in the world. After three decades of keeping her peace she was about to confide in a pair of strangers from the other side of the world.

'About a week after the attack, I received a message through one of Rhett's friends that both he and Jonno; that was the other man, wanted to meet up with me. Although I hadn't named either of them, the fact that the police had been in contact got them scared. They were both claiming to have been too drunk to remember what happened and were said to be devastated when they heard about it.'

'You didn't seriously consider going along, did you?' asked Matt.

'I was very young at the time and a part of me hoped that they were telling the truth. Rhett was quite charming back then. I'd met him several times at the bar and I longed to turn back the clock to when it was fun with him. He had a real swagger to him as everyone in the town thought that he was going to make it as a footballer. All the girls used to call him Retro.'

For a brief moment, she smiled as her thoughts returned to a time before her life had turned sour. Both Colin and Matt shook their heads with pity for the tortured woman.

'Whether they felt guilty or not; rape is rape,' said Colin.

She snapped out of her trance-like reminiscence.

'I know that now, but back then I was a very confused and distressed young girl. It probably sounds crazy, but I actually hoped that if I could talk it through with the two men then maybe it would be like it never happened.'

'Pretend it was all just a misunderstanding,' offered Colin.

'Like I said; it sounds crazy now. Anyway, I went to the house that the two of them shared, where they were both waiting. I could see straight away that neither man had been coping well since the incident, but this was more through fear for themselves than any feelings of actual guilt. I knew instantly that I had made a mistake in agreeing to see them. They both knew full well what they had done to me.'

'Did they attack you?' asked Colin.

'Not at first. At first they just begged and pleaded with me to keep quiet. They said that prison would destroy them, but if I named no names then the police would be powerless to arrest them. I was offered favours, money, anything to buy my silence and when I refused, it made them angry. I tried to leave, but Jonno blocked my way and struck me across the cheek when I tried to pass. I was scared. I thought that this time they were going to kill me for certain.'

'And that is when you picked up the knife,' said Colin.

Naomi nodded, solemnly.

'It was lying on the kitchen worktop. I never intended to use it on him. I just hoped that it would be enough to scare him off. Then Rhett grabbed me from behind. He wrapped his left arm around my body keeping me from moving and enclosed his right hand over mine.'

Colin and Matt straightened in their chairs. They were both acutely aware of how many times and how close Rhett had come to Rose and Jenny. The terrifying ordeal they were having described to them could so easily have happened to their own girlfriends. The story that Naomi Green had to tell no longer felt so distant.

'He began to whisper things in my ear,' she continued. 'Sick things. He told me that I wanted to use the knife and that the thought of taking my revenge was making me wet. He said that he could tell that the bloodlust was turning me on. As he spoke, Jonno moved in closer and then I felt my arm begin to move, but not of my own volition. Rhett was forcing it. He guided my hands as they plunged the knife into Jonno's stomach in three short, sharp stabs.

After the third strike Rhett left go, but the knife was still inside Jonno's stomach with my hand on it. I was frozen rigid with fear and I simply could not let go. As he slumped forward and his weight pressed down on the blade, I could feel it slide deeper into his body. I could see the very life drain from his eyes as he died by my hand.'

'You didn't kill him at all,' interrupted Matt. 'Rhett did.'

She ignored his assessment of the situation.

'Afterwards, he told me that I had deserved my revenge and that I was now the same as him. He then said that I should tell the police that Jonno was the only one who had attacked me and that the more blame I apportioned to the dead man, the more it would justify my actions.'

She spoke with regret, but she did not shed a tear. That well had dried up long ago.

'Why did you never tell anybody this?' asked Colin. 'Surely after time, when you had come to terms with what had happened to you, you could have exposed him for what he was.'

'I...I couldn't.'

She turned away from the two men.

'What if he had attacked someone else? What if he has attacked someone else?'

'Colin don't,' said Matt. 'This hasn't been easy for her, you know.'

The Irishman paid no attention to his friend's attempts to deter him from getting to the truth. His questions increased in pace and frequency.

'Is there anything that you could tell us? These crimes have to be related. What if there is a copycat out there? Did he have any friends? This could be an old buddy of his paying some sort of sick homage.'

'I've already said enough.'

She had a faraway, spaced out expression and Matt for one knew that it was time for them to leave.

'I'm sorry if we have brought up some unpleasant memories, but you have been a help to us. Hopefully, after today you will never have to hear the name of Rhett Butler ever again.'

She wished them luck and promised to include them and their friends in her prayers. They both thanked her again and then left to go and meet up with Niall and Jonas. Matt had been left shocked by the encounter, so much so that he was even beginning to share in his friend's paranoia.

'Do you really think there could be a copycat killer; someone recreating those crimes of thirty years ago?' he asked Colin.

'It seems plausible, but I'm not actually buying into that idea myself,' the other man replied. 'I just suggested it to see her reaction.'

'So who do you think is doing this; surely not Stephen?'

'Stephen's innocence is the only thing in all of this that I am certain of. There is only one man who could have done this, but he's avoiding suspicion because right now he has the perfect alibi; the whole town is convinced that he's dead.'

'You're crazy,' said Matt.

'There is a part of me that actually wishes that were the case. The fact is that Rhett is the only person who is capable of carrying out such sick crimes. If you remember this all started the night after you convinced me to put that stupid picture up.'

'Do not start with the superstition thing again. I've already told you that people don't go coming back to life.'

Colin sighed with frustration.

'I'm not saying that Rhett's returned from the dead as such. Naomi said that he guided her hands and made her kill the other rapist. What if he is doing the same again? What if Rhett is somehow influencing people into acting out sick crimes from beyond the grave?'

Matt did not like what he was hearing and refused to play host to his friend's supernatural conspiracy theory.

'If you are talking about possession, it is just as crazy a suggestion as your one about Rhett being raised from the dead and equally impossible. I knew that it was a bad idea coming here today and this proves it. Once we get back to the caravan park I don't want to hear any more stories about Rhett, okay?'

They were careful not to mention the meeting with Naomi Green when they got back to the bus. Joe was talking on his mobile phone when they caught up with him, so they had to wait. Once he had terminated his call, he beckoned for their attention.

'That was the sheriff on the phone. He has advised me that Stephen is going to be moved to a secure remand facility further up state. The sheriff said that they are no longer looking for any other suspects and it is now likely that Stephen will be passed over to await trial. I know that he is your friend, but it is looking increasingly like he is going to go to prison for this. I'm sorry.'

The four backpackers were left shocked and deflated. Until that moment they had all felt as if they were in a nightmare and would soon wake up. It was now all too apparent that this was not going to happen. They now realised that the tragedies unfolding around them were real and even if they got through them unscathed things would never be the same again. Never before did they all have so much at stake; their future, their freedom and their lives.

Chapter 31

When the group returned to work on the Friday following Rhett's death, they numbered just six. Niall had joined the forced absences of Celeste and Stephen, as he was at the police station visiting his friend. The sheriff permitted just one of them to see the incarcerated before he was to be transferred to a more secure facility out of town and Niall was the obvious choice. For everyone else, it was business as usual.

Jonas and Hiro took the flanks, which left the two couples to occupy the space immediately around and behind the trailer, with Paul giving them a helping hand. The two boys were eager to keep their clandestine visit of the previous day to themselves and so made sure to keep the conversation focused on their respective partners.

'So what did you two ladies get up to while we were away?' asked Colin.

The two girls shared a knowing smile.

'We managed to stay busy,' answered Rose, 'Hiro kept us entertained, didn't he, Jen?'

Her sister giggled.

'He certainly did,' she confirmed.

'Did he get his guitar out again?' asked Matt.

'It was even better than that. He did impersonations for us.'

'Impersonations; I can't imagine that they could have been much good.'

'Actually, they were very good,' said Rose. 'I especially liked the one that he did of Colin.'

The Irishman's ears pricked up at the mention of his name.

'Don't go telling me that sushi boy has been mocking the way that I speak. He cannot even complete a cohesive sentence in his own accent let alone mine.'

'I didn't say that it was cohesive,' said Rose. 'Just that it sounded like you.'

'Exactly like you,' added Jenny.

Colin weighed the small chunk of wood in his hands. He tried to calculate whether he could hit Hiro with it from the distance that he was at. Although he was taking his mocking in good spirits, something about the story troubled his friend. Matt was getting a sense of déjà-vu, the source of which he could not quite put his finger on. Before he was able to trace this elusive memory, Paul came up with a distracting idea.

'How about we have a little music?' the Aboriginal suggested. 'Dad has an old transistor radio on the back of the tractor; I could see if we can pick up any reception out here.'

'Do we have to?' asked Colin. 'I've heard Australian rural radio before. It's like the signal has taken thirty years to reach its destination. Listening to AC/DC or Cold Chisel is not going to motivate me into picking any more sticks than I am doing already.'

'Don't be such a spoilsport,' Rose scalded him before turning to Paul, 'put it on. We could do with a few tunes to loosen us all up a bit.'

The young Aboriginal walked around to the rear of the tractor. The vehicle was moving slowly and he was easily able to climb aboard without risk of accident or injury. He rummaged through a box on the back before retrieving the small radio from it. Surprisingly, a clear signal was easy to come upon, but as the first few notes resonated from the tinny speakers, Colin shook his head with the bittersweet knowledge of being proven right. It was, of course, a song by Cold Chisel.

Without the shadow of Rhett overseeing proceedings the atmosphere was certainly more relaxed and thoughts of the recent tragedies were quickly put to the backs of minds. Two of the young backpackers, however, were about to receive an unpleasant surprise.

As the last few chords of the song faded, the music gave way to the morning news bulletin. The leading story concerned the surprise death of a nurse at a local hospital. There were only scant details at that time, but the presenter announced that the police were treating it as a suicide. They were yet to release a name, but said that they were keen to speak to two men who may have spoken to the deceased earlier in the day.

'How depressing,' said Jenny.

Rose agreed with her younger sister.

'Does anybody in this place die of natural causes?' she asked.

'At least this time it does not concern any of us. We are already being treated like prisoners as it is. Not being allowed to leave and having to come here to work as part of the chain gang each day.'

As the two girls spoke, Matt and Colin tried not to let their anxiety show. They each felt hollow in the pit of their stomachs. No matter how they looked at it; they were responsible. Like Naomi Green had been thirty years earlier, the pair of them had now become unwitting killers.

The police car parked by the entrance to the caravan park did not come as a surprise to either Matt or Colin, but it did raise questions from the rest of the group.

'Surely not more bad news?' asked Rose.

'We have all been together,' replied Jenny. 'Whatever reasons they have come back for can only relate to the previous tragedies and not be anything new.'

'Niall has not been with us,' Jonas pointed out. 'Maybe he broke Stephen out and they go on the run.'

'I wish that could be true,' answered Colin. As they all stood to exit the bus, he pulled the German to one side. 'Can you take my bag for me and put it in your van? I have a feeling that the sheriff will want to speak to me and I'd prefer not to meet him with a shit load of weed about my person.'

'No problem,' replied the German, 'but what if he wants to look in my van?'

'Trust me, he won't. Besides, if the weed was discovered, I would own up to it. I wouldn't let a friend take the fall for me.'

The two men quickly exchanged rucksacks. As they all left the bus the sheriff called over to Colin, just like he had expected.

'What's the problem today, officer?'

The sheriff did not like Colin's flippant attitude and let the Irishman know it with a slight scowl. As before, the deputy was by his superior's side and just itching to put the force into law enforcement.

'Mr Wilson has told me that he took some of you kids into Cooper's Creek to visit Ms Espuche yesterday,' said the sheriff.

'She's our friend and she's in hospital. There isn't anything unusual about wanting to visit a sick friend, is there?'

'Not at all. Did you pay a visit to anybody else while you were there?'

'Actually, I did. Shortly after we arrived, a nurse approached me and asked if I was one of the backpackers from Birribandi. When I told her that I was, she asked if I could drop by and see her after I'd visited Celeste. She said she wanted to ask me some questions.'

The lie would not be difficult to expose if the policeman had spoken to the receptionist at the hospital. The sheriff's countenance did not indicate whether or not he bought the story.

'What sort of questions did the nurse want to ask you?'

'You know, the usual stuff; where am I from, how am I liking Australia, where did I plan on heading next?'

The sheriff was not amused. He had gone out of his way during the past week to make the investigation easy on the backpackers and did not expect to be repaid with such a blatant lack of respect.

'Do not play games with me or I will have you charged with wasting police time,' he warned.

The deputy sneered at Colin from over the sheriff's shoulder. It was like the younger lawman wanted Colin to dig himself deeper into trouble. The Irishman put his hands up defensively.

'Okay, okay, I'm sorry. She asked me a load of questions about Rhett, that's all. None of them really made any sense. I assumed she was a friend of the family or maybe even an old girlfriend of his and that she had only just heard of his death.'

'And what did you tell her?' asked the sheriff.

'I told her that I only worked with him and didn't really know him that well. She didn't seem too cut up by his death, just a little bit shocked, that's all. I gave her Joe's number and told her to contact him if she wanted to find out the funeral arrangements.'

The Sheriff took a moment to pause and contemplate what action, if any, to take. Now that they knew that he was watching them they were unlikely to go stirring up any more trouble. He also had both men's passports and could therefore ensure that they were going nowhere in the immediate future.

'Very well, but if you remember anything unusual about the way that she acted, let me know immediately. That's all that we need from you for now, but remember that this investigation is far from over.'

Colin had almost gotten away with it, but as he walked away, the sheriff called out to him again. He turned around and this time it was the deputy who was leading the questioning. The junior officer had clearly been whispering in his superior's ear.

'Before we go, I want to take a look in that bag of yours,' said the younger lawman. 'You don't mind, do you?'

'Not at all, officer,' replied Colin.

He handed over the satchel, which he had earlier borrowed from Jonas. The policeman rummaged through the bag with a complete disregard for its owner's rights, but Colin knew that he would find nothing incriminating inside. Once the search was completed, the deputy handed the bag back to him.

'Now I want to take a look in your van,' he said.

'Do you have a warrant?' asked Colin.

'I don't need one; the owner is standing right over there. Do you want me to go and ask his permission?'

Colin knew that it would be futile arguing with the policeman, besides which, he had nothing illegal in the van that he had to worry about. His drugs were still inside his bag, which was stored safely inside Jonas's van. He led the deputy to his caravan and opened the door for them both to enter.

'What exactly are you looking for, officer?' queried Colin. 'That is, if you don't mind me asking.'

Sarcasm was the only weapon he could use against the lawman and he wielded it liberally.

'You can ask all of the questions that you want,' replied the deputy. 'Some kids in town have said that a stranger matching your description has been dealing drugs. I'm sure that the allegations are unfounded, but we have to follow up every lead, you understand.'

Colin could feel his sweat glands starting to heat up, but so long as the deputy limited the search to just his van, he would be okay.

'It's nothing to do with me, officer,' he said. 'I've never touched drugs. We Irish are happy enough with our Guinness.'

The policeman ignored the backpacker's comments as he began his search. First he checked the wardrobe and then went through drawers, before finally reaching his hands under the bed's flimsy mattress.

'Too easy,' he said, whilst retrieving a small, clear plastic bag from the bed, which he then held up for Colin's inspection.

The bag contained at least a dozen small tablets.

'Let me guess,' said the deputy. 'You've never seen these before in your life.'

It was now Colin's turn to be on the receiving end of the sarcasm.

Chapter 32

Rose was desperate to get to the station to see Colin. Just like Stephen before him, her boyfriend had been bundled into the back of the sheriff's car and forcefully removed from the camp. And just like Stephen before him, Colin fiercely protested his innocence the whole time.

'How can they do this?'

'It's their town. It's their country. Maybe if we could contact the nearest embassy they could help, but for the time being we have no choice but to go along with what the police tell us.'

'It is not right though, is it? Tell me that this is not right.'

Rose searched Matt's eyes, but he had no answer for her. She pushed past him and into the caravan. Colin had been given no time to collect any of his personal belongings to take with him, so she was gathering stuff that she thought he may find of use.

'Where did those pills come from' she asked. 'They cannot have belonged to Colin. This just does not make any sense.'

'I think the pills were planted there to set him up.'

She looked at him, undisguised scepticism in her eyes.

'Somebody planted the pills under Colin's mattress? Do you realise how ridiculous that sounds? I mean, who would want to do such a thing?'

'You could ask who would want to rape Celeste or kill Pierro. The fact is that somebody out there is getting their kicks from seeing all of us suffer.'

'Why us though? We have not hurt anybody.'

Matt did not want to tell her any more than he had to. Just forty eight hours earlier he thought Colin's theory to be insane and he was certain that Rose would think the same if he was to mention the possibility of Rhett somehow possessing people.

'Maybe it is someone who just doesn't like backpackers.'

She picked up on the insincerity in his voice immediately.

'What are you not telling me? Who was this nurse that killed herself and what has she got to do with Colin?'

'It's just like Colin said to the sheriff; we were in the hospital and she approached him with a bunch of questions about Rhett.'

She let out a sigh.

'Maybe Colin will be more forthcoming. Where did he put his bag?'

'He gave it to Jonas.'

'I'd better go get it and have a look to see if there is anything inside that he may need. I have already got his toothbrush, but I cannot seem to find his wallet. I know that he doesn't keep it on him when we work, so it must be in the bag.'

She quickly popped into the adjacent van and when she came back she held a rucksack, which she threw down onto the bed.

'I'll let you do the honours, Matt. I hate to think what nasty surprises he may have in there. If it's more drugs, I'm going to burn them.'

Matt undid the zip and emptied the bag out onto the bed. There was no wallet among the contents or even a bag of weed, just a thickly bound black journal. Matt recognised it instantly.

'This isn't Colin's bag. You must have picked up Hiro's by mistake. I've often seen him updating that journal.'

Rose lifted the tome from the bed and began to leaf through the pages.

'I wouldn't do that if I were you,' warned Matt. 'Hiro is very protective of his possessions and particularly that book.'

She did not respond. She just continued to flick through the pages as if mesmerized. Matt could see the colour drain from her face.

'Rose, what's wrong?' he asked.

She looked up from the pages with the knowledge of impending dread in her eyes.

'Matt, where is Jenny?'

'She's with Hiro, trying to explain to him what is happening in this place. I certainly don't envy her that task. What do you need her for?'

'We have to go and get her, right now.' She spoke with forthrightness, but her tone was unable to disguise an undercurrent of urgency, which bordered on panic. 'I know who killed Pierro.'

Hiro was taking the news well. Jenny noticed that he seemed to react to whatever she told him with a certain degree of detachment. It was almost as if she was recounting the plot of a movie or a news story from lands far away. The Japanese man did not seem remotely shocked or worried by the events unfolding around him.

'Hiro, do you understand what I am telling you?' she asked.

'We may be in serious danger; all of us.'

'Yes, yes danger,' he replied.

She may as well have been asking him what topping he would like on his pizza.

'I need a strong cup of coffee. Would you like one too?' she offered.

'Yes, yes coffee,' he replied.

She may as well have been telling him that they were all about to die.

She got up from her seat and walked over to the coffee machine. Picking up an overturned mug from its saucer, she placed it under the funnel and then selected an extra strong cappuccino. Her back was turned to the seated Asian. She heard the high-pitched screech of the chair legs on the cold tiled floor, which indicated that her companion had risen from his seat, but she was not braced for the spontaneous and violent attack that was about to follow his rising.

Although the deputy had been the arresting officer, it was the sheriff who was to lead the questioning of Colin. The policeman wasted no time in getting straight to the point.

'How long have you been dealing drugs?' he asked.

Colin was caught up in a state of shock and bewilderment. He had always known that there was a risk of him getting caught with the weed, but these pills had seemingly come from nowhere. The whole scenario reeked of a set up.

'I want a lawyer,' he demanded.

'You can have full access to legal representation in the morning,' replied the sheriff. 'It is too late to organise anything for this evening and it would be better for all concerned if you chose to co-operate with us now.'

'I am not saying a thing until I speak to a lawyer. This

whole interview is a sham and you know it. I have never seen those pills before in my life. If you don't believe me; take fingerprints. You pigs have nothing on me.'

The sheriff glanced over his shoulder towards his deputy, who was standing menacingly at the back of the room, like an attack dog just itching to be let off its leash.

'If the drugs do not belong to you,' said the sheriff. 'Am I to assume that they are the property of your roommate? Would you like us to bring him in for questioning?'

Colin slammed his fists down onto the table top.

'You leave Matt out of this,' he shouted. 'You people really are pathetic. It's like you don't even care which one of us that you hurt. First Stephen, then me and now Matt. Will you not stop until you see every backpacker in this town behind bars?'

The sheriff was in no mood for such wild accusations. He had heard it all before. Niall had been extremely vocal following his visit to his incarcerated friend earlier in the day. In the end, the sheriff had to issue a verbal warning to the Irishman before taking him back to the caravan park.

'We have witnesses willing to come forward who will testify that you were dealing marijuana in the Tavern last Friday evening.'

'They're lying,' replied Colin, who was able to compose himself now that the sheriff was getting closer to a crime of which he was guilty.

The sheriff reached into a manila file and retrieved a photograph, which he then placed on the table.

'Do you know this man?' he asked.

Colin glanced down at the picture. It was of the youth to whom he sold the weed. He was careful not to give anything away.

'I've never seen him before,' he replied.

'His name is Scott Donovan,' the sheriff added.

Colin shrugged. This time he could at least say that the name meant nothing to him.

'Mr Donovan was in the Tavern last Friday night,' continued the sheriff. 'He never returned home and has been missing ever since. We believe that his disappearance is drug related. Witnesses have confirmed that you were one of the last people to be seen with him before he went missing.'

Colin was completely taken aback. First the Police accuse him of owning the pills and now what; kidnapping, murder? He was completely out of his depth and did not know what to say.

'I don't understand,' he pleaded. 'Are you now accusing me of abduction?'

'This is a waste of time,' interrupted the deputy. 'He knows something; he's just not telling us. Maybe he will be more cooperative after a night in the cells.'

Colin looked to the sheriff, but he was too afraid to say anything. The sheriff put the photograph back in the folder and stood up.

'My deputy is right. We will continue this interview in the morning.'

The sheriff left his subordinate to deal with taking Colin to his cell. The junior officer responded with a gleeful smile.

Matt entered the dining hall brandishing the journal in his arms and Hiro's eyes immediately widened when they focused on the incriminating tome. The Japanese man quickly rose from his seat to offer protestations, but Matt was in no mood to listen. As the Asian reached out to grab the book, Matt thrust it up into its author's face, ramming the hard edge into Hiro's chin.

With his opponent temporarily stunned, Matt threw the

book down onto the table top and followed up his initial offensive with a firm punch to Hiro's gut, before shoving the Asian to the ground, sending chairs clattering across the floor. By the time that he heard Jenny's screams he had already neutralised what he perceived to be any possible threat.

'Matt, what are you doing?' cried Jenny, as she made to help the stricken man, but was restrained from doing so by her sister.

'Leave them to it,' said Rose. 'Matt knows what he is doing.'

Hiro was seated on the floor with blood running from his bottom lip and confused terror in his eyes. He clumsily tried to push himself backwards, away from Matt, but he was under no immediate threat from the Englishman. All that Matt intended was to stop him from escaping.

'I should have figured this out sooner,' said Matt. 'I knew something was not quite right this morning when Jenny told me about the impressions. Colin is not the only person who you have been mimicking, is he, Hiro?'

The fallen man did not answer. Matt loomed over him, although he had no intention of striking a defenceless opponent.

'There is one other impression that you like to do, isn't there?' he asked. 'I think that there is one impression that you like to do more than any other.'

Jenny struggled against her sister's restrictive embrace.

'Matt, stop this right now,' she pleaded. 'Have you gone mad?'

Her words had no effect on Matt. He had all the proof he needed and now sought only the confirmation.

'Do your impression of Rhett,' he ordered. 'Do Rhett for us all to hear.'

Hiro was confused.

'Wha…' he began.

'Do Rhett now!' Matt yelled. The anger in his voice was enough to unnerve even Rose.

Hiro attempted to push himself away on the floor, but Matt was determined to settle things then and there. He reached down and picked up the Japanese man by the scruff of his shirt and then pushed him up against the wall. All of the pent-up tensions and anger from the previous week were surfacing and Matt now had an outlet for them.

'Do your impression of Rhett,' he repeated. 'I want to hear you speak like that murdering bastard did.'

Hiro tried to pull himself free, but the more he struggled, the more Matt tightened his grip.

'Do it!' he screamed.

'Facking cant! Facking cant!' Hiro shouted back.

The intonation was not as clear as Matt had heard previously, but it unmistakably matched the voice of his late foreman. He released his grip and Hiro ran to the corner of the room to get out of his way.

'That is the voice that Celeste heard as she was being tortured and abused,' said Matt, turning back to face the sisters. 'Not Rhett, not Pierro, but this sick bastard doing one of his impersonations.'

Jenny did not believe it.

'Matt, this is crazy. I don't know how you came up with this idea, but it is not right. Do you realize what you have done?'

'Show her the journal,' advised Rose, as she loosened the grip that she had on her younger sibling.

Jenny shook herself free of her sister's arms and crossed the room to where she took the book from Matt. As she turned the pages and digested what they held, her confusion turned first to disgust and then anger. Finally, as she collapsed into a chair, she felt only despair. Tears streamed down her cheeks.

Hiro tried to speak to her, but his speech was garbled and incoherent. Seeing that he was not getting through to her, he attempted to make a run for it. He was stopped in the doorway by Niall, who had come to see what the commotion had been about.

'Don't let him go,' barked Matt.

The Irishman held Hiro firmly, but did not apply too much pressure. He was still completely in the dark over what had just happened and had no desire to hurt the clearly distressed man.

'What's going on?' Niall asked.

Rose and Jenny both avoided his gaze and turned instead to Matt. They themselves were not entirely sure what was happening and hoped that he could shed some light on it for them too.

'I don't know how or why,' Matt began, 'but Hiro is behind all of the awful things that have been inflicted upon us this past week. It was Hiro who attacked Celeste. It was Hiro who murdered Pierro and it was Hiro who planted the pills in Colin's van.'

Niall did not believe it.

'What are you talking about; do you have proof that he could have done any of those things?'

Matt glanced over to the journal that Jenny still clutched in her arms and then back to Niall.

'It all started with something that Colin said to me yesterday. He had gotten it into his head that Rhett was behind all of the crimes.'

'That's impossible,' said Niall. 'Rhett's dead.'

'I said the same thing to Colin, but he was adamant. He thought that somehow the old man had come back and was doing all of this from beyond the grave. He thought that maybe Rhett had possessed Stephen and acted out the crimes through him. I didn't believe it, but it did get me thinking. Rhett could not possess someone, but somebody could choose to copy him.'

'Copy him how?' asked Niall. 'Rhett wasn't a murderer.'

'Actually, he was.' The revelation came as a surprise not just to Niall, but also to Rose and Jenny. 'Thirty years ago, Rhett got away with committing both rape and murder. Those two crimes have sadly been repeated this week, but this time not by the old man. This time it was Hiro acting out a sick fantasy.'

'I still don't understand,' said Niall. 'What do you have to connect Hiro to Rhett?'

Matt took the journal from Jenny.

'It is all right here in this book,' he said. 'Now I am going to call the sheriff and put an end to this madness once and for all.'

Chapter 33

Jenny sat in stunned silence trying to come to terms with the events of the previous hour. First Colin had been taken away and then Hiro; on suspicion of murder. Just when she thought that things had been restored to some semblance of normality, the nightmare had returned even stronger than ever.

She had never felt more lonely or afraid. Seeing Matt attack Hiro the way he did had shown a side to him she had not known he possessed and it terrified her. Her boyfriend had left with the sheriff to give a formal statement when Hiro was taken away and she had no idea what she would say to him when he returned.

'Are you okay, sis?' asked Rose.

Jenny shook her head, but did not respond verbally.

'I know that you are struggling to come to terms with all of this,' said Rose, 'but at least now it is over we will finally be able to leave this place.'

This time Jenny nodded. She so desperately wanted to believe that something positive had come from the evening, but was struggling.

'Why don't you go and freshen up,' suggested Rose. 'The

boys and I can clean up here and then we will get dinner on.'

Jenny stood and put her arm around her sister.

'Thank you,' she said. 'I just feel like...'

Rose stopped her.

'We cannot allow ourselves to dwell on what has happened; not now. It is too late to change anything, so the best thing to do is to just try and move on. At least allow some time to pass before you try and make any sense of what has happened.'

'Okay,' Jenny promised.

She then went back to her caravan to prepare for her shower. At least now she had no need to fear anymore. The one consolation that she could take from the evening was that the worst had now passed. Finally, the threat that had hung over the camp for the past week had been removed.

'What happens now?' asked Matt.

'Now we have to get him to confess, which may not be easy given his level of English,' replied the sheriff.

'Why do you need a confession? The evidence is right there in that journal.'

'I would not go getting carried away with yourself. I admit that the journal does add a promising new angle to our investigation, but it is far from being conclusive.'

Sheriff Lee sat back in his chair. In his hands was the journal kept by Hiro throughout the Japanese man's stay in Birribandi. As the policeman flicked through the pages his lifetime in law enforcement prevented him from reacting in the way that the others had. He was desensitized to such images, but that is not to say that he was not disgusted. There were many incriminating drawings and each had a common theme.

There were multiple depictions of the assault on Celeste; all pencil sketches displaying exceptional detail. These were followed by drawings of Rhett standing over the blood spattered body of Pierro with the still dripping knife in his hand. After that, they began to take on a more surreal theme. In one drawing the Australian was a marble giant with a mighty sword in one hand and scales in the other. Impaled on the sword was the lifeless form of Pierro, contorted in hideous agony whilst a helpless Stephen sat bound and gagged on top of the scales. Another picture showed what could only be described as the resurrection of Rhett. Here the Australian was drawn as half man, half phoenix as he ascended from the inferno of his exploding truck.

Hiro's talent was evident throughout the series of pictures with his most extravagant work being the most telling. Dozens of simplified drawings of Rhett appeared to be spread throughout the page at random. However, when the observer pulled back and held the page at arm's length, they could see that all the tiny points joined to make one coherent whole. That whole was a self-portrait of Hiro himself.

'Why do you think he did it?' asked Matt.

The sheriff put down the book.

'It looks like a classic case of schizophrenia. If what we suspect is true, then I would say that our young Japanese friend has been acting out his delusions under an assumed personality.'

'Why Rhett, though? In fact, why any of this? What could have made him flip like that?'

'The trigger could have been any number of things. He's spent the last couple of months isolated in a strange place and unable to bond with anyone around him. I guess the loneliness finally got to him. Perhaps, he saw some of that loneliness in Rhett before he died and felt some sort of connection.'

The sheriff's theory made sense to Matt. He thought back to Colin's fixation with the idea that they had placed a curse on Rhett, pulling the deceased man back into this world. He wondered if maybe Hiro really had been possessed, but thought better than to voice such an outlandish thought to the sheriff.

'What will happen to Stephen now?' he asked.

'I'll make a call in the morning and he should be released by lunchtime. There won't be a problem in him making bail now that we have a more promising suspect in custody.'

'Make bail? Surely you can just let him go now that you've caught the killer.'

The sheriff straightened in his chair.

'It isn't that simple, kid. The only evidence we have is purely circumstantial and the means by which we acquired it is dubious to say the least. We certainly need something more solid if we are going to get a conviction and there is still the possibility that Hiro didn't do it.'

'Of course he did it.'

'I hope for your sake that you are right. If he is innocent then I won't be able to turn a blind eye to the fact that you assaulted him tonight.'

Matt had not even considered that his earlier treatment of Hiro might have been unlawful.

'I was protecting my friend,' he explained. 'Hiro was alone with Jenny and who knows what he could have done had I not intervened.'

'Like I said; I hope that you are right.'

Matt was starting to worry. He now realised that although the journal had convinced himself of Hiro's guilt, the sheriff needed much more concrete evidence to build a credible case.

'What about the drugs that were found in Colin's van?' he suggested. 'Have you taken fingerprints? Maybe we can prove that Hiro planted them.'

The policeman shook his head.

'Sorry, but I don't see any connection there.'

He then reached into his drawer and pulled out a photograph, which he placed on the table. It was the same one he had shown to Colin earlier.

'Do you recognise this man?' the sheriff asked.

Matt looked at the Polaroid. He had no idea how the policeman had found out about Colin's misjudged drug deal, but he was careful not to give anything away. As he looked back up at the sheriff he shook his head.

'His name is Scott Donovan,' said the sheriff. 'He's not a bad kid, but we do know that he sometimes dabbles with drugs.'

'What does that have to do with Colin or Hiro?' Matt asked.

'Scott went missing a week ago. His friends have told us that they saw him talking to Mr O'Meara and they think that he may have bought marijuana from him. If you can come up with anything that may link Hiro to this man's disappearance then I may take your accusations seriously. Otherwise your friend is staying where he is.'

Matt could not even remember if Hiro had been with them that night at the bar. There was certainly no connection he could think of that would link the two men.

'Sorry, officer, but I've never seen that man before in my life.'

The sheriff smiled.

'Somehow, I thought you would say that.' He stood up and took his hat and jacket from a coat stand. 'Come on, I'll give you a lift back to the caravan park. It's already dark and this town is no longer safe at night like it used to be.'

As they were leaving they were joined by the deputy.

'Do you mind if I tag along?' the younger policeman asked. 'The two prisoners are safely locked away and I want to take a look at the Jap's van. If he kept a record of his crimes he may have taken some souvenirs as well.'

The sheriff nodded and the three of them climbed into the patrol car. The two policemen took the front seats and Matt was placed in the back where the criminals would normally sit. With no handles on the inside of the doors and a mesh screen between him and the men in front, he was given a unique insight into how Colin and Stephen must have felt on their respective journeys to the station.

J enny turned off the shower and wrapped a towel around her body. She did not feel the cold as she was still part numb with the shock of the evenings developments. Could Hiro really have perpetrated those vile crimes? At least now there was no doubt in her mind that she would be leaving at the first opportunity. Birribandi held far too many unpleasant memories for her to stay for one moment longer than was necessary.

The night air was still and the sky clear as she walked from the shower block to her caravan. All above her the stars shone with the intensity of fires that had raged for millennia. It was as if God had taken the roof from the doll's house and was peering in, but for once she did not feel like looking back. She got dressed and then stepped out to find her sister. The park was unusually quiet for this time, but she assumed that was because everyone was still in shock from the latest revelations. Hiro had always been so quiet that nobody could quite believe what he had done. A light was on in the dining hall and she guessed that was where they all must be.

'Hello?' she offered, inquisitively, as she stepped into the eerily quiet room.

The chairs had all been put back in their places so that there was no longer any sign of the earlier scuffle, but where was everybody? She could detect the scent of marijuana in the air, but it was unlike any of the boys to smoke in the dining hall. As she crossed the room to open a window and clear the smell, she noticed something unusual in the corner of her eye. There was an ashtray on the bench, but that is not what was unusual. It was the object inside the ashtray that had caught her attention. It was the smallest, most tightly rolled cigarette that she had ever seen and it was still smouldering.

'Looks like you folks got a visitor,' said the sheriff, as he turned onto the dusty driveway leading up to the caravan park.

A car was parked by the side of the road. It had been strategically positioned to be out of view and earshot of the park's inhabitants.

'Have you any idea who may be calling at this time of night?'

'Nobody that I can think of,' answered Matt

'Perhaps I better take a look first. You two wait here.'

The sheriff parked up just behind the other vehicle. He got out of the car and closed his door behind him. Matt watched the lawman walk slowly through the front gate and then disappear, leaving him alone with the deputy.

'You did really well tonight, kid,' said the deputy. He was only about five or six years older than Matt and his tone seemed condescending. 'It takes a lot of guts to confront a man that you think is a killer.'

'I didn't really think about it like that,' replied Matt. 'I just wanted to make sure that I got that psychopath as far away from the girls as possible.'

The deputy smirked to himself before turning to Matt.

'You're absolutely convinced that the Jap did it, aren't you?'

'Of course,' replied Matt. 'I've always known that Stephen is no killer and who else could it have been?'

The policeman smirked again, but this time he did it so that Matt could see.

'There is one part of your theory that doesn't quite add up,' he said.

'What do you mean?' asked Matt, starting to feel concerned by the policeman's tone.

'Well, you said that Hiro was acting under an assumed personality; repeating those infamous crimes of thirty years ago.'

'It seems the only logical motive,' explained Matt. 'I mean, you saw the journal that he kept.'

'Don't get me wrong, I know where you're coming from, but where the story falls apart is the means by which Hiro learned of Rhett's past. Nobody knew about the old man's guilt apart from Naomi Green and she's dead. You see, it isn't possible that Hiro could have known those things that you say he did.'

Matt was visibly lost for words and he knew that the deputy could read the doubt that was now forming on his face.

'There is, however, one other explanation for all of this,' added the deputy, 'but I don't think that you're going to like it.'

'Tell me,' pleaded Matt, a tad desperately.

The thought that he had been wrong and attacked Hiro falsely was making him feel sick. He noticed the deputy raise his arm and pull open a small hatch that was built into the dividing barrier.

'If you come closer there is something that I'd like to show you,' the deputy said.

Matt could see that the lawman was fumbling with something just out of sight. He shifted his weight forward, putting his face to the gap in the barrier. As he did so, there was a swift movement of the deputy's arms and then Matt's face exploded in pain as the policeman rammed the butt of his shotgun into it, sending the Englishman recoiling back into his seat. Matt could feel the blood running from his nose and lips as the world around him slowly faded into blackness.

Jenny did not struggle whilst Pierro's killer bound her hands and feet. She knew that she had no hope of overpowering the man and wisely chose to avoid risking any unnecessary injury to herself. Rose lay opposite, with similar bindings and a gag over her mouth. Jenny had at least escaped the gag. She assumed that Jonas and Niall had already been caught and subjected to the same fate, so there would be nobody left to hear her if she did scream. She did not scream.

'You kids have made this too easy,' her captor said. 'I had a plan for removing the Jap from the equation, but your idiot boyfriend did it for me. He then goes and leaves you girls all alone with just the fatty and the baby for protection. Too fuckin' easy by far.'

Jenny said nothing. She was desperate to learn where Niall and Jonas were, but worried that asking after them would only place them in greater danger. The man who now had her completely in his power had already killed at least once and she feared that he intended to do so again.

'You cannot keep this silence up forever,' her captor warned. 'When I've finished with your sister, I'll be coming back for you.'

'The only place you are going is jail,' said a voice from

behind.

The sheriff had managed to sneak up undetected to within just a few yards of the hostage taker and had his gun cocked and ready to use. Like many officers of his generation he carried a Smith & Wesson revolver as opposed to the .40 calibre Glock semi-automatics favoured by the younger recruits.

'It's over, Rhett. I don't know how you managed it, but your reign of terror ends now.'

'Is that so, sheriff?'

Rhett was neither surprised nor troubled by the appearance of the lawman.

'This stunt you've pulled right here will be enough to send you down for life and that is before we even factor in the rape and two counts of murder.'

The sheriff wisely kept his distance and did not take his eyes off the old man once. Not even to check on the two girls.

'Two counts of murder? I appreciate the flattery, but you over estimate me. That Italian grease ball is the only stiff that I can take the credit for.' He smiled viciously before adding; 'well, recently anyway.'

'What about Scott Donovan?' asked the sheriff. 'The body we pulled from your ute. I'm assuming that's who it was.'

'You guessed right, but I didn't kill the little prick. When I found out that he'd been buying weed from that foreign scum, I decided he needed to be taught a lesson in loyalty. I tied him up and locked him under cover in the back of my ute. He was still alive when I flipped her. I only intended to scare Scotty, but his death has proved most fortuitous, don't you think?'

The sheriff gritted his teeth, barely able to suppress his anger. He was sorely tempted to pull the trigger, but he had a duty to uphold the law and he would not compromise that duty even for a vicious killer like Rhett. His deputy had now entered the scene and with their combined might they had a good chance of apprehending the killer without any more blood being shed. The second policeman was brandishing a shotgun, which he also had trained on the fugitive.

'I see that backup has arrived,' Rhett observed.

'Then you can also see that it is pointless trying to resist arrest,' said the sheriff. 'Now move away from the girls and put the knife down.'

'That ain't gonna happen, Norman.' Rhett knew that it incensed the sheriff when he addressed him by his Christian name. 'There's still more blood to be shed before this night's over.' He paused a moment whilst calculating his next move. 'So what are you waiting for? – Shoot!'

The sheriff was taken aback by the boldness of his foe.

'I'm not going to gun you down in cold blood,' he said. 'Now I repeat; put the knife down.'

Rhett laughed. It was a cruel, sadistic laugh that was familiar to all who knew him.

'I wasn't talking to you, Norman.'

The sheriff's eyes narrowed as he tried to gauge the old man's intentions. Then it all clicked into place; there was only one way that Rhett could have altered the results of the coroner's report. He began to turn towards his colleague, but he was too slow. The burst from the shotgun echoed around the desert night like thunder and propelled its target off his feet before gravity dumped him back down dead against the side of a caravan.

'Nice shot,' said Rhett, 'but it could have come a little sooner. I never could stand having to listen to that self-righteous prick.'

'You seemed to be enjoying the moment,' the deputy replied. 'I didn't want to interrupt.'

The two men walked toward each other and embraced

warmly.

'Where's the pommie kid?' asked Rhett.

The old man had quickly returned to a more business like attitude. They were both now fully exposed and well past the point of no return. The situation needed to be dealt with swiftly.

'He's in the car sleeping off a hangover,' the deputy said.

Rhett smiled, proudly.

'And the other two?'

'Safely locked in their cells; they aren't going anywhere.'

Jenny struggled to her knees, which was not easy given that her hands were tied behind her back, leaving her with little room for manoeuvre. She shuffled around until she was facing the deputy.

'Why are you doing this?' she asked. 'You're a policeman; you're supposed to protect us.'

Rhett stepped between the two of them and squatted down until his eyes were at the same level as the girl's. She could feel his breath on her face. It was putrid and rotten; like how she would expect the inside of an abattoir to smell.

'Let's just say that blood is thicker than water.' He glanced across towards Rose, making sure that Jenny caught the gesture. 'You of all people should know that.'

'You're his…father?'

The idea of Rhett being carnally intimate with anybody could not have been anymore vulgar, but she knew that he told the truth. Having seen the deputy murder his superior in cold blood, she had no trouble believing that he was the offspring of Rhett Butler. Her thoughts drifted towards Celeste and what horrors may lay in store for Rose and herself.

'I'm the only family he has.' This time he took a prolonged glance back at his son for his audience's benefit. 'Since your sister's boyfriend and his accomplice killed his mother that is.'

She tried her hardest to resist giving in to his taunts. It was clearly madness that he was talking, but she could not help but feel that there was a hint of bitter sincerity in his voice. Could Colin and Matt really have known about this? Surely not, but she did not have time to waste thinking about it. She had to try and reason with the deputy. It was her only hope.

'Help us, please,' she pleaded to the young lawman, but he looked back at her with vacant eyes, the only person he was prepared to listen to was his father.

'What now, Dad?' he asked.

Rhett stood and walked away from Jenny. He grabbed Rose and lifted her onto her feet. The elder girl struggled under his touch and managed to shake herself free. With her ankles tied, she did not make it far and soon found herself back on the floor, provoking raucous laughter from both men.

'I can tell I'm gonna have a lot of fun with you,' Rhett said, as he once more lifted the helpless girl from the floor. This time he did not allow her to wriggle free. 'I'll take this one back to the house. You can bring the other with you when you are finished here.'

Jenny had no doubt that she was going to die. The casual way with which the two killers acted in front of her was evidence enough that they were happy in the knowledge that she would not live to testify against either of them. They had no intention of leaving any witnesses behind.

Rhett hauled Rose over his shoulder and began to make his exit. As he passed the still twitching corpse of the sheriff he stopped walking. Jenny at first thought that he was taking one last moment to appreciate his son's handiwork, but in reality he was merely being thorough. He reached down and picked up the policeman's revolver, before stuffing it into his belt. Then he was gone.

With his father departed, the junior member of what would

shortly be the state's most notorious criminal family did not seem so cocksure of himself. He avoided looking Jenny in the eye as he set about bringing his father's plan to fruition. There were some petrol canisters that Rhett had brought with him and the deputy began to douse the caravans. He used up a full canister outside and then picked up another, along with his shotgun, and headed into the dining block.

This was the opportunity that Jenny was waiting for. Obviously, the policeman turned killer did not expect her to be able to escape after witnessing Rose's clumsy attempts to move with her ankle's tied, but he was not aware that his father had made a crucial mistake when fastening the girl's binds.

As soon as she was sure that the deputy was out of sight she once again raised herself onto her knees. The ties around her wrists were tight, but they allowed just enough give for her to slide one hand out. It caused her considerable effort and pain as she stretched her limbs to their limits, but nevertheless she succeeded. Once she had regained full use of her arms and hands, removing the foot bindings was not a problem.

The deputy had said that Matt was sleeping off a hangover. She guessed that this meant that he was merely unconscious and hopefully she would be able wake him. She crept as quietly as possible towards the body of the fallen sheriff and reached down to unclip the keys from his belt. She then ran as fast as she could out of the park.

Matt had been roused to consciousness when he heard the sound of a car engine pulling away. He did not get a look at the driver as his vision was still a little blurry. His nose and jaw stung, but he had no trouble recollecting how he had picked up his injuries. A policeman had assaulted him without reason or provocation. What had the deputy been thinking?

It was pointless wasting time trying to establish the cause given his current predicament. The air around him felt colder than before, but he did not think that he had been passed out for long. There was no telling when the deputy would be back, so he had to act quickly. His number one priority was to get out of the car.

He lay down on his back and drew his legs in so that his knees were almost touching his chin. After exhaling deeply to compose himself, he kicked out at the handle-less door as hard as he could.

Nothing.

He repeated the process, but again nothing. After a third attempt, he managed only to dent the interior panelling. It was clear that he needed to take a different approach to the situation. He closed his eyes to better focus his thoughts and it was whilst in this almost meditative state that he heard the sound of approaching footsteps. The frequency of the beats of shoe against the ground indicated that whoever was approaching was doing so in a hurry. He pushed himself up off his elbows to take a look. When he saw that it was Jenny, he beat against the inside of the glass window to get her attention.

His girlfriend looked weary, yet frightened. When she saw him, relief spread across her face. The patrol car was not locked and she opened the rear door for him. As soon as he stepped out she flung her arms around his shoulders and embraced him tightly.

'Thank God you are okay,' she said. 'I was terrified that he would have hurt you.'

'Are you talking about the deputy?' asked Matt. 'He hit me with the butt of his shotgun. What's happened; has he gone crazy?'

'There's no time for that now. We have to go and help Rose.'

Matt could not make any sense of what she was telling him.

'What's happened to Rose? You are going to have to slow down and tell me what is going on.'

She took a deep breath.

'Rhett's back. He's the one that murdered Pierro and the deputy is helping him. They already killed the sheriff and now they have Rose.'

'Rhett, but that's impossible; he's dead.'

Although her words did not make any sense to him, he could see in her eyes that she was telling the truth.

'I told you that we don't have time,' she said. 'Rhett took Rose and the deputy is still in there attempting to set fire to the caravan park. He's in the dining hall, so he didn't see me sneak away, but we have to go quickly. If he catches us he will kill us.'

'What about Niall and Jonas; where are they?'

She began to tremble with panic.

'Oh my God; they're still inside. He's going to burn them alive.'

Matt knew that they could not leave their friends to die. As much as it pained him to say it, Rose would have to wait a little longer for their help. If the pair of them acted quickly, they could take the deputy by surprise. They would only get one chance to stop him. He hoped that Jenny had the strength and understanding to see this.

'We have to go back.' He put his hands on her shoulders and looked her squarely in the eyes. 'Are you able to do this?'

She nodded, gravely.

'Good, because I have an idea. I want you to wait until I am in position and then you'll need to try and draw the deputy out of the dining room. We'll only get one shot at this, so we have to make it count.'

Matt peered around the first caravan to make sure that the coast was clear and then he and Jenny both crept quietly back into the centre of the park. Whilst the girl got back into the position in which the deputy had left her, Matt crouched down low behind the door to the dining block. He then picked up a log from the timber pile and readied himself for the diversion.

He gave Jenny the signal and she began to scream as loudly as she could. She knew that this alone may not draw the deputy out, but she thought she knew what would.

'He's alive!' she shouted. 'The sheriff's still alive. You have to come help him. Please, he's still alive.'

As she had hoped, it was not long before the deputy came to the doorway to see what the commotion was about.

'What's gotten into you, bitch?' he cruelly demanded.

Careful not to let him see that she had escaped her bindings, she remained on her knees with her hands behind her back.

'The sheriff is still breathing. You have to help him. It's not too late; you can still make this right. Help him, please.'

The deputy was unmoved, but all Jenny needed was to get him to take just a couple of steps forward. She knew that he did not have an adequate enough view of the stricken sheriff to determine for certain that the man was dead. If he wanted to confirm the girl's claims for himself, he would have to move closer.

Sure enough, the lawman took a few, short steps toward his former commanding officer. This was the opportunity that Matt had been waiting for. He quickly leapt to his feet and brought his crude weapon to bear above his head, ready to swing down towards the corrupt lawman. Unfortunately for him, the deputy was standing directly between him and one of the caravans. As soon as the Englishman had taken to his feet his reflection appeared on the window in front of the deputy, as the moonlight transformed the glass into a mirror.

Before Matt could complete his intended swinging arc the deputy turned and parried the blow with the stock of his shotgun. The policeman had at least 20lbs weight advantage over the younger man, which he quickly put to good use. After blocking the initial attack, the deputy retaliated by using his firearm as a club and caught Matt with a fierce blow to his forearm. The pain was crippling and caused him to loosen his grip on the log, which slipped from his grasp.

Matt had no time to gather himself before he was brought to his knees by a second swing of the shotgun, which the deputy now wielded like a baseball bat. Battered and bruised into submission, the young backpacker was completely at the mercy of one of the cold blooded killers whom had helped tear this small traveller community apart.

'I was going to let you burn along with your two friends in there,' the deputy said. 'But now you are not going to be let off quite so lightly.'

Matt barely had the strength left to face his attacker. If getting burned alive was what the man considered to be getting off lightly, he knew that his death was not going to be quick. As he tried to crawl away on his hands and knees, all he could think about was how he had let Jenny and Rose down. His greatest regret was that their deaths would involve much more suffering because of his own failure.

The rogue lawman threw down his shotgun and unclasped a small knife from his belt.

'My old man always said that a blade is the best way to kill a man. He told me that it allows you to get in close and look your foe square in the eye as you take their life from them. I guess that I'm going to get to find out for myself now.'

As the deputy slowly stalked his intended victim, delaying

the inevitable to extend his own depraved pleasure, he had left the shotgun unguarded on the ground behind him. This gave Jenny her only chance to save her boyfriend.

'Leave him alone or I'll shoot,' she said.

Jenny had never handled a weapon before, but at the range she was at, simply pulling the trigger would be enough. The deputy was surprised, but not worried as he turned and took a step towards her.

'You haven't got what it takes,' he sneered.

She could feel her finger begin to shake on the trigger and knew instantly that the deputy was right. There was no way that she was capable of killing. The deputy took another step toward her.

Matt was still on the ground and his head was groggy from the beating he had taken. As he crawled away from his attacker, he moved closer to one of the caravans. It was the same van that had alerted the deputy to his earlier assault, but the van was also notable for another reason. Underneath it was where Colin had hidden the elicit stash of beer and spirits that he had stolen from Pierro's storeroom on the night of the party.

With the killer's full attention planted firmly on the barrel of the shotgun that was pointed at him, he was not giving any thought to Matt. The Englishman knew that Jenny could not hold off the corrupt policeman for long, but she could delay her attacker long enough for him to creep up behind him. He was not about to make the same mistake twice and this time it was not a log he had in his hands, but a bottle of vodka.

Unlike in the movies, the bottle did not shatter as Matt forcefully brought it down onto the back of the deputy's skull. Instead, there was merely a chilling thud and then the policeman's eyes rolled back and he slumped to his knees, before falling face down onto the ground. Blood began to pool around his head.

There had been a crack after all, just not in the bottle.

Matt offered an exploratory kick to the man's side. There was no movement, but the slight give of flesh against his foot. He crouched down and extended his index and middle fingers to feel for a pulse. He detected none.

'Be careful,' Jenny warned.

'I hit him hard. I think I killed him.'

He did not feel remorse, but he did have a heavy, sickly feeling in the pit of his stomach. Somehow, he knew that something inside him had changed irreparably.

'Are you certain?' Jenny asked, careful to keep her distance.

Matt placed his hands under the man's chest and rolled over the body. The deputy's eyes and mouth were both open. They were forever frozen, providing a lasting snapshot of the moment that his life left the corporeal realm. Matt looked up towards Jenny and his eyes said all that was needed. She turned away in distress.

'It wasn't our fault. He brought it on himself.'

'I know.' She nodded, sadly.

'Come on, we have to find Niall and Jonas,' he said, hoping to take her mind off the dead man. 'Hopefully, they are okay.'

Their two friends were found bound and gagged in the kitchen. Jonas was conscious, yet unharmed, whereas Niall had a nasty wound on the back of his head, but was thankfully still breathing. They untied them both and Jonas helped the pair carry Niall to the police car.

'What now?' asked Jenny.

Matt checked that everyone was in the car and then he started the ignition.

'First we go to the station and get Colin. Rose is going to need all of the help that she can get and I want him by my side when I catch up with Rhett.'

'What about outside help?' asked Jenny. 'There must be somebody that can help us.'

Matt glanced at his reflection in the rear-view mirror. He had a deep cut on his bottom lip and his whole face was bloodied and bruised. This had become about more than just stopping Rhett and rescuing Rose. It was personal.

'We cannot afford to take any more risks,' he told her. 'I just killed a policeman and another one is lying dead not six feet away from the body. By the time that we manage to convince anybody of our story, Rose will be dead. It's down to us now and nobody else.'

He shifted the police car into gear and pulled out of the caravan park. The night was far from over and he knew that the lives of several people now depended on him. He was determined not to let any of those people down.

Chapter 34

Once they got to the station, Jenny went straight for the first aid kit in order to tend to Niall's wounds. She remembered where it was stored from her previous visit following the mugging.

Matt, meanwhile, headed directly to the cells, but when he got there he did not unlock the one that held Hiro. One of the others could do that after he had left. He did not yet feel up to facing the man he had wrongly accused of murder. Colin was the prisoner that he had come to set free and his friend was lying on his mattress, but not sleeping when Matt found him.

'Isn't it a little late for visiting hours,' said the Irishman.

There was little light in the small cell and Colin was unable to make out the cuts and bruises on Matt's face.

'This isn't a visit; we're getting you out of here.'

Colin swivelled around so that he was seated on the edge of the bed.

'A jail break, are you crazy?'

'It's a long story, but you were right about Rhett; he's back.'

Colin was not as surprised as the others had been. He

always suspected that they had not seen the last of their old foreman. The news, however, did bring one thought instantly to his mind.

'He's killed again, hasn't he?'

Matt confirmed his friend's fears with a nod.

'The two cops are dead and Rhett has taken Rose,' he said.

'He has Rose?' Colin asked, this time allowing stress to show in his voice.

'That's why I'm here. We stand a much better chance of getting her back if we do it together.'

As they left the cell and stepped out into the lit corridor, Colin saw Matt's injuries for the first time.

'Jesus Christ, what happened to your face? Are you hurt?'

'I'll be fine, but Niall has not been quite so lucky. He took a nasty knock to the back of his head. Jenny and Jonas are with him now, administering first aid.'

'What about Hiro?' Colin asked.

'He's fine too.' Matt did not feel the need to elaborate further. 'Right now we have to figure out where the old man has taken Rose. Any other questions can wait.'

They quickly retrieved the killer's police file and tore down a street plan from the wall of the sheriff's office. Rhett's house was no more than a five minute drive away and would not be difficult to locate. They both prayed that was where Rose would be, as it was the only lead they had. Before leaving they went to check on Jenny and the others to make sure that everybody knew what was expected of them.

'We do not know when Rhett will be expecting the deputy to turn up, so he may already know that something is wrong when we get there,' said Matt. 'We need you to contact the police stations in the surrounding towns. Try and get them to send officers out as quickly as possible. If we can't stop Rhett, maybe they can.'

Jenny reluctantly agreed to his plan. She did not like the idea of Matt and Colin taking on a killer by themselves, but she knew that they were the only ones who could save her sister.

'Before you go, there is something that you should know,' she said. 'The deputy was Rhett's son. That is why he helped him. The two of them have been in this together the whole time. He must have faked the autopsy results to make us believe that Rhett was dead and planted the drugs under Colin's mattress. We cannot let Rhett know that his son has been killed.'

Matt became unsteady as the news sunk in, but Colin was still too far behind on events to make the connection to the death of Naomi Green.

'That was why she killed herself,' Matt said, more to himself than those with him.

'Are you talking about his mother?' asked Jenny.

Matt avoided looking her in the eye.

'Her name was Naomi Green. She was a nurse at the hospital in Cooper's Creek. Rhett raped her thirty years ago and the deputy was obviously a result of that ungodly tryst. We told her about the murder and the idea of a copycat killer came up in our discussion. She must have thought that the copycat was her son. That is why she killed herself and it is our fault.'

'There is no time for regret now,' said Jenny. 'Rhett is to blame for all of this; not you. You cannot allow yourself to think like that if you want to help Rose.'

Matt knew that what Jenny said made sense, but with two deaths now on his conscience, he feared as to where the path he was on would lead him. Even if he survived the night, he would have to live with the consequences of his actions for the rest of his life. He gave the car keys to Colin and the two of them reluctantly set off to face Rhett for the final time.

Chapter 35

'Have you got a plan or are we just going in blind?' asked Colin, as he steered the commandeered patrol car through the deserted streets.

'I haven't had time to think about any of this,' replied Matt. 'I guess that we will just break into the house, overpower Rhett and then get Rose out.'

Colin indicated his approval with a nod. The simpler the plan; the more he liked it.

'Do we have any weapons?' he asked. 'We should have looked for a gun cabinet back at the station, but once I heard about Rose, I stopped thinking straight.'

'There are guns in the back of the car,' replied Matt. 'We brought them from the caravan park. There is a shotgun and a pistol; both of which had belonged to the deputy.'

'What about Rhett; do we know if he's packing?'

Matt tried to remember what Jenny had told him.

'I think that he took the sheriff's gun, but I can't be sure.'

'In that case, we'll have to assume that he did. I clocked the sheriff's gun each time he turned up at the park and he carried an old six shooter. This means that we have more firepower than Rhett, which gives us the advantage.'

'If we can make it count,' Matt replied, sceptically.

'Have you ever fired a gun before?' asked Colin.

'No, have you?'

'I tried a bit of clay pigeon shooting at a ranch I stayed at in New South Wales. It wasn't much; I only got five shots, but it's still something, so I'll take the shotgun. That leaves you with the pistol and we're going to have to figure out how to use it before we go in there.'

Colin slowed the car and pulled over at the corner of a deserted street. It seemed as good a place as any to indulge in a spot of target practice. Before getting out of the car he took the Glock from the back seat. The weapons were all that the pair had to use to their advantage and if they wanted to make them effective, they had to familiarize themselves with them first.

'Here,' he said, offering the gun to Matt. 'Take a practice shot at that brick wall over there. Do you see the chipped brick in the centre? Try aiming for that.'

Matt extended his right arm, which was holding the gun, and placed his left hand under his right elbow to provide extra support. He then closed one eye and brought the sights into line with his target. As he pulled the trigger, he felt a slight upward pull from the handgun. Though the recoil was not great, it did take him by surprise and lifted his arm as he fired. The shot blew a small hole into the wall a good two feet above the chip that he had been aiming for.

'Now you know what it feels like, do you think that you can correct your aim for the next time?'

Colin assumed that the gun had a full magazine, but he did not want to waste one bullet more than necessary.

'I should be able to,' replied Matt. 'I think that I missed because I pulled rather than squeezed the trigger. That's what they always say in the movies, right? I cannot believe that I made such a stupid mistake.'

'We'll be fine,' Colin assured him. 'Now get back in the car. You probably woke half the neighbourhood with that shot.'

One practice shot was not ideal training to take into a hostage situation, but it was all that they could afford. The next shot to be fired would be at a live target and that would be a different proposition altogether. The only consolation was that both men now knew what it felt like to pull a trigger. That experience, though slight, could save their lives.

As they drove away, a dog began to bark and several house lights were turned on. Fortunately for the two backpackers, nobody had managed to see the cause of the disturbance.

It did not take them long to reach Rhett's street and as the pair approached, Colin turned off the car's headlights and slowly brought it to a standstill. He did not want the vehicle's engine to alert the Australian of their presence and decided that they would complete the rest of the journey on foot.

'Check the glove compartment for any spare ammo,' advised Colin. 'I would prefer to have more than two shots when we go in there.'

Matt opened the small hatch and found a box of shotgun cartridges. There were no extra magazines for the pistol, but that was of little consequence as he did not know how to reload the weapon anyway. He passed the cartridges to Colin.

'Here you go,' he said. 'Jenny told me that the deputy shot the sheriff with the shotgun, so it'll probably need reloading before we go in.'

'Thanks,' replied Colin. He placed a hand on the door handle ready to exit, but briefly paused. 'Are you ready for this?'

'Not really,' replied Matt, 'but do either of us have a choice?'

Colin slowly shook his head.

'Not if we want to save Rose.'

Both men were scared, but the fear that they felt could be much more easily overcome than the guilt that would replace it should they back out at this late stage. They attempted to fortify their minds against self-doubt as they stepped out of the car, ready for the deadly showdown with their former supervisor.

The neighbourhood was run down, even by Birribandi standards and neither of them was sure which house was the one that they wanted, because there was no street lighting to illuminate the door numbers. As he scanned the avenue for clues, Matt spotted something that he recognised.

'It's that one there,' he said. 'That car parked outside is the same one that was outside the caravan park earlier.'

Colin took a deep breath.

'This is it,' he said. 'Once we go through that door, there is no turning back.'

'I already killed one man tonight,' replied Matt. 'If I have to kill a second, then so be it.'

Colin nodded. He did not want to ask his friend about the earlier killing at such a critical time, but he knew that after the ordeal that Matt had already been through, he would not let him down. It was not only the lives of the two men at stake, but also that of Rose and mistakes were unthinkable.

The two men approached the house with their weapons at the ready. Both of them were equally excited as they were terrified. The adrenaline gave them a sense of invulnerability as it coursed through their veins. It was as if they were each ensconced within an invisible sphere of hypersensitivity. Every sight, sound and smell within a ten foot radius was intensified, but beyond the sphere the world had faded into nothing more than an insubstantial shadow.

As they neared the house, they could see that it resembled something out of a bad horror movie. The ground floor windows were boarded up and slats were missing from the porch floor. Despite the old man's strong determination not to let a termite infestation take a hold of the caravan park, he had let the little critters get more than a foothold on his own property. Like an outward projection of its occupier, the house was a twisted and dilapidated mess.

Colin crossed the driveway first, before crouching down low by the front door, ready to force his way in. He then beckoned for Matt to take a peek through the gaps in the window coverings.

There was only a small opening, but it was enough to give him an unrestricted view directly into the killer's living room. He saw Rhett standing by a torn and tatty sofa stuffing some belongings into an equally scruffy holdall. The Australian seemed composed and Matt surmised that the old killer was as yet oblivious that his scheme was not going to plan. Rose was nowhere in sight and Matt assumed that Rhett had her held captive on the upper floor.

'He's in the living room,' Matt whispered. 'It's open plan so once we're through the door, we will have him in our sights.'

'Is Rose there?'

'No. I'm guessing that he must have her in the bedroom.'

Colin clenched his jaw at the mention of his girlfriend being held prisoner in the bedroom of such a vile pervert. He knew exactly how he wanted to handle the situation and did not intend to show the old man any mercy.

'On the count of three, I'm going through that door and as soon as I see that bastard, he's getting both rounds in the chest,' he said. 'You follow me in straight after and start shooting as soon as you are inside. I'm taking no chances with this.'

Matt nodded his agreement and then quietly took his place behind his friend. Colin double checked that his shotgun was ready and then began to mouth a silent countdown. As soon as he reached one, he violently kicked the door open and brought the gun down to bear on the area where Matt had told him that Rhett would be standing.

The Australian was caught completely by surprise and Colin did not bother with any words of warning as he quickly let off two quick-fire shots, which shook the very foundations of the building. The first missed its target by just inches, hitting the sofa behind where Rhett was standing, but the second was affected by the recoil of the powerful firearm and blew apart a small lamp a good few metres from the target.

Matt followed his friend through the door while the earlier shots continued to reverberate around the room, but amidst the smoke from the shotgun barrels and exploding fragments of sofa and lamp, he was not as quick to get a fix on the old man as his friend had been. Rhett had leapt behind the sofa when the shooting started and this cover bought him a brief moment to think.

His own gun had been tucked into the belt of his trousers and easy to reach. It was in his hands before his feet even touched the ground. He heard the second man enter and knew that both of them were standing in the vicinity of the doorway. Without looking, he quickly let off three shots and then ducked out of the room and ran up the staircase.

When Matt saw Rhett rise from behind the sofa with a gun in his hand, his first instinct was to dive for cover rather than to fire his own weapon. He safely made it behind the shelter of the kitchen counter, but his friend was not so lucky.

As Matt looked back, he saw two of the shots impact into the wall of the house in an explosion of plasterboard, but there was no third impact against the structure. Instead, he saw Colin slump to the ground with a swiftly expanding patch of crimson on his shirt. Matt got back on his feet and ran towards his fallen friend, whilst all the time keeping his gun trained in the direction that Rhett had been, but the space behind the sofa was now empty.

'He made a run for it,' said Colin, who was in considerable pain and struggled with his words. 'He's gone up the stairs. You have to get to him before he hurts Rose.'

Matt crouched down to inspect his friend's injury. The bullet had hit Colin on his left shoulder. It was an extremely messy wound, but he was unable to tell if it was life threatening. Matt then reached across to the battered couch and tore a strip of material from the damaged covering. He wrapped it around his friend's shoulder and under his arm twice, before tying it tightly to stem the flow of blood.

'This should help for the time being, just don't try and move,' he said. 'I'm not having that bastard add you to his list of victims.'

'Don't worry about me,' replied Colin. 'It'll take more than a bullet to finish me off.'

The Irishman was sweating profusely as if he had a fever. Matt did not want to leave him in such a precarious position, but they were almost out of time. Rhett had gone upstairs to where Rose was and if Matt did not follow immediately, she would surely die.

'I've got to go,' he said.

'I know,' replied Colin. 'Just promise me that you'll get Rose out of there.'

Matt nodded.

'If you can reload - do it,' he said, 'and keep your gun pointed at the bottom of the stairwell. If I don't make it down, you have to take that bastard out.'

Colin reluctantly agreed to let his friend go it alone. As

long as he was able to remain conscious and pull a trigger, he could still make sure that Rhett did not escape via the staircase.

After leaving his friend, Matt double checked his weapon and then crossed over to the other side of the room. As he approached the stairwell he made sure to keep his back to the wall, before peering around the corner to take a look. Rhett was crouched on the top step waiting and quickly let off two rounds. Both shots missed him, but Matt could actually feel the heat of the bullets as they passed just inches from his face.

Being on the higher ground undoubtedly put Rhett in a stronger position than Matt. However, the Englishman had now counted five shots that his enemy had fired. If Colin was correct and the sheriff's gun was a six shooter, this would mean that Rhett was down to his final shot. Whilst Matt had already lost the element of surprise, he could certainly still outgun his foe. He quickly swung his arm around the corner and started to fire upwards. After three shots, he moved into the stairwell hoping to see the bloodied corpse of the kidnapper. The staircase was now empty.

Matt slowly ascended the stairs with his gun raised high, ready to fire at the slightest provocation. Each step creaked under his weight and acted as a signal to his adversary, who could return to deliver a potentially fatal shot at any moment. He let out a sigh of relief when he made it all the way to the top of the staircase without encountering his murderous foe. The upper floor opened onto a narrow corridor with three doors leading off from it. Only one of these doors was open and it beckoned Matt to approach. He cautiously walked down the corridor, wondering all the while if his next step would be his last.

As he approached the doorway, he could hear Rose crying. She did not sound panicked or hysterical, just afraid and alone.

Each whimper was like a screw turning into his heart, but he had to block out his feelings and detach himself from all emotion if he was going to get her out of there alive.

He pointed the gun squarely in front of him and readied his finger on the trigger as he stepped in front of the doorway. He then took the final step into the bedroom, where for the final time he found himself face to face with Rhett Butler; drug dealer, rapist, hostage taker and murderer.

Matt had never been more afraid in his entire life.

Colin concentrated on taking long, deep breaths. He loudly sucked the air in through his mouth in the vain hope that the sound would drown out his pain. How could he have been so careless as to find himself in this position? Rose was counting on him and he had let her down once again.

He thought back to the day of the mugging. If he had been more alert and reacted quicker, he could have spared her a lot of pain and punished those bastards who hurt her. His thoughts then drifted to when Rhett had beaten him in the field. Why had he not fought back? He could feel the anger growing in the pit of his stomach and then spreading outwards through his body. He was tired of being a victim.

Using the shotgun as a crutch, he levered himself up onto his feet. He continued to concentrate on his breathing and he swallowed hard. Everything seemed to be working. At least it did not feel like any of his organs were failing. He could even move his left arm at the elbow, although his shoulder was still giving him considerable pain. Even the slightest movement caused the most excruciating agony that he had ever experienced. It felt like it was being chewed on by a bear. If he was to carry on; he could not afford to let it distract him any longer.

Rhett's holdall was still on the couch, where it had been left when the shooting started. Colin thought he could guess what the old man would consider to be among his essential items when packing. He slowly moved towards the couch and took a look inside the bag. He reached in with his right hand and rummaged through the clothes until his fingers touched upon the chill of a metal container. It was Rhett's tobacco tin. Colin opened it and found three pre-rolled cigarettes inside. He raised one up to his nose and took a sniff. There was nothing better than the familiar aroma of marijuana.

He spotted a box of matches on the kitchen counter next to the gas cooker. After taking one of these and lighting up, he took a deep, satisfying puff on the spliff. He followed this with a second and then a third, all the while making sure to inhale as much of the intoxicating smoke as his lungs would allow. Within moments, the pain in his shoulder was reduced to nothing more than a dull ache and he felt calm and at peace. He then reached into his pocket and extracted some shot gun cartridges, which he used to reload the weapon. Now he was ready and this time he would not fail. This time he would either kill or he would be killed.

The Australian had Rose locked in a firm grip with the nub of his revolver pressed squarely against her temple.

'Drop the gun or the slut dies,' he snarled.

Matt retained a strong grip on his firearm and lined up the sight with the forehead of his former boss even though he knew that he had little hope of making such a difficult shot. If he lowered the weapon as he had been told, Rhett would shoot him dead for sure. His only chance was to try and bluff his foe into giving up.

'Don't listen to him,' said Rose. 'If you lower the gun he'll kill us both.'

'I know,' said Matt. 'And if he kills you, he will be left with no bullets and I'll have a clear shot. So the way that I see it, Rhett is the one who should lower his gun.'

'You've got balls coming here; I'll give you that,' said Rhett. 'If you want to walk out of here with them both intact, you will drop the gun, right now.'

Matt did not flinch. If he was to get through this ordeal, he would have to play Rhett at his own game.

'The police are already on their way,' he said. 'Now the word is out that you are alive, every cop in this state is going to be looking for you. In fact, it would surprise me if a marksman was not lining up his shot as we speak.'

For the first time, the old killer looked to doubt himself. He was standing directly in front of the window and the curtains were not drawn. If he attempted even the subtlest glance over his shoulder, he would surrender his advantage.

'You're bluffing,' Rhett said.

'Try me,' retorted Matt. 'If the cops are not prepared to shoot a man in the back, then I'll just have to shoot you myself.'

The Australian looked deep into Matt's eyes and beyond, as if attempting to read the younger man's very soul.

'You haven't got it in you,' he sneered.

'Don't be too sure,' replied Matt. 'I already killed one man tonight. Where did you think that I got this gun?'

He could hear movement from downstairs and knew that Colin was making his way to him. He just needed to buy some more time.

'You killed my son?' asked Rhett.

Matt braced himself to fire. There was no telling how the old man would react and he needed to be prepared for the worst.

'Any man pathetic enough to die by your feeble hand has no right calling himself my kin,' said Rhett. 'You've done me a service; I should be thanking you.'

Matt sensed that his adversary was lying. There had been a definite shift in the old man's eyes and his voice sounded more resigned to defeat. As if to confirm this assumption, Rhett roughly shoved Rose away from him and brought his gun down to bear on Matt instead.

'If you pull the trigger now, we both die. You will save the girl, but at the cost of your own life. Are you seriously prepared to sacrifice yourself for that little bitch?'

Sweat dripped from Matt's forehead. It was now obvious that the old man no longer cared whether he lived or died.

'What are you waiting for?' asked Rhett. 'You would be smart to pull the trigger first. If you are lucky, I may only maim you with the return shot.'

The reason behind the killer's procrastination suddenly dawned on Matt. Rhett wanted him to make the first move and in doing so become a murderer himself. Matt could feel his finger tightening on the trigger. He desperately wanted to give in to the taunts, but he knew that if he did, he too would become a cold blooded killer. Once he walked down that path there would be no return for him.

'I'm guessing that when you killed my boy it was in self-defence,' continued Rhett. 'It's a lot harder when you have to make the first move, isn't it?'

Matt did not reply. He desperately wanted to pull the trigger, but the only thing worse than the old man firing back at him would be if Rhett did nothing at all. Matt did not wish to execute a man in cold blood; even one as cruel and savage as the killer stood before him now.

'Come on,' urged Rhett. 'What are you waiting for; shoot!'

'Does the same offer apply to me?'

Colin entered the doorway and brought the sights of his weapon into line with the Australian. He was weak from losing a lot of blood and had to prop himself against the doorframe to stay on his feet, but he was still perfectly capable of pulling a trigger.

'You can't win this one Rhett; let it go,' said Matt.

The young backpacker had a new sense of conviction and his confidence had been renewed by his friend's arrival.

The old man sniggered.

'I'm actually starting to like you two,' he said. 'If you'd shown this kind of spirit sooner the three of us might have gotten along.'

Rhett slowly lowered his gun until it was by his side, pointed at the floor. Matt breathed a sigh of relief, but the old man had not yet offered his last word.

'Tonight's been fun, hasn't it,' he mused. 'Which makes it such a shame, that in the end, we all lose.'

With those final words still hanging in the air, Rhett quickly raised his gun to his right and fired. As Rose fell to the floor clutching her stomach, the two backpackers unleashed their remaining arsenal onto their now defenceless foe. This outback killer's reign of terror had finally come to an end, but not without a price.

Chapter 36

Rhett had nobody to mourn his passing. Rose, however, could rely on both Matt and Colin to ensure that she would not face the same fate as the man who tried to take her life. Colin did his best to stem the bleeding and keep the wounded girl conscious, whilst Matt ran down the stairs to call for help. Thanks to Jenny's efforts back at the police station, help was already on its way and an air ambulance arrived within half an hour.

Rose was airlifted by helicopter to the hospital at Cooper's Creek, where she was assigned a private room on the same ward as Celeste. The doctors worked through the night to save her life, but it came at a cost. Such was the damage caused by Rhett's final act of malice that an emergency hysterectomy had to be performed, meaning that she would never be able to have children of her own.

Colin also required surgery, but in his case the bullet had made a clean passage through his shoulder leaving no permanent damage. With time, he would be left with only the scars as a reminder of the ordeal that he had endured. Despite his injuries, Colin insisted on keeping a bedside vigil around his girlfriend until she regained consciousness.

Matt and Jenny relocated to a local hostel in Cooper's Creek, where they could more easily visit their friend and sibling in the hospital. The events of the previous week had brought the four closer together than they could have thought possible and created an unbreakable bond that they would always share, but they knew that their time together was running out. Although they had helped each other survive the greatest trial of their lives, what they all needed more than anything was to go home.

Back in Birribandi, the caravan park was closed down and marked for demolition. It had borne witness to some of the most brutal crimes in the state's history and as such, none of the town's residents wanted to keep it as a reminder. Birribandi was home to a small community and none had been left unaffected by the tragedy that had unfolded around them.

Each of the backpackers was granted a visa extension without having to see out the duration of their three months, but for some they could not put the country behind them soon enough. Hiro had been the first to go and he flew back to Japan as soon as he had fulfilled all the legal requirements surrounding his status as a witness to the tragedies. For obvious reasons, he did not bother to say goodbye.

Niall had also made a swift exit from the town. He went to Brisbane to meet up with Stephen after his friend's belated release from custody. He promised the others that they would all enjoy a reunion one day, but it would likely require some time before the group would be able to get together without having to relive the horrors that they all had shared.

Jonas was the most reluctant of all to leave. He looked upon Matt as a saviour and felt a sense of camaraderie and pride with his fellow backpackers. In his idealized view of the world they were all triumphant heroes. Sadly, the sentiment carried little enthusiasm with his friends and the young German left shortly after Niall, to fulfil his dream of going to Cairns.

'Do you think that you will ever return?' Jenny asked.

Matt took time to consider the question.

'I don't know,' he replied. 'Just a few weeks ago I could not have even imagined that I would ever want to leave. After what has happened, I feel like I finally need some stability in my life. Returning to England and joining the real world no longer seems like such an unattractive prospect. What about you?'

Jenny shrugged.

'I may come back one day, but not like this,' she replied. 'My backpacking days are over.'

Matt did not want their last few days together to be tinged with sadness and decided to try to lighten the mood.

'This last week has been like Hell, but I am going to miss everyone,' he said. 'I've learned a lot staying in Birribandi. Did you know, for instance, that the city of Melbourne was founded by Batman?'

'As a matter of fact, I did,' Jenny replied. 'What makes you mention that?'

He looked back at her, slightly puzzled.

'It was something that Jonas said to me shortly after I arrived and I found it quite funny at the time. To be honest, I assumed that he was just talking nonsense. I mean, Batman; really?'

She laughed.

'Jonas was telling the truth. If you don't believe me - look it up. Batman founded the city of Melbourne.'

Despite how ridiculous the idea sounded, he felt that anything Jenny believed had to be true. He took her hands in his and pulled her close to him. They held each other tightly and for the briefest of moments, all of their problems slipped away. If their fateful encounter with Rhett Butler had taught them one lesson, it was that life could change in a heartbeat. From that day forward, they would be grateful for each and every one.

The End

Thank you for reading. If you could take a moment to return to where you purchased this book and leave a review, it would be much appreciated. Independent authors rely on reviews for readers to find their work and decide if it is for them.

Stealing Asia
By
David Clarkson

Ben is a backpacker struggling with life on the road. That is until a chance encounter brings him together with the enigmatic Asia. She is smart, beautiful and everything else that he could possibly desire in a woman. She also has an uncanny habit of attracting danger.

When events conspire to keep the pair apart, Ben begins to question if it is coincidence or a conspiracy. He learns that Asia's life may be in danger, but is unsure of exactly where the threat is coming from and who to trust. Only one thing is certain; unless he acts fast, it will be too late. In order to protect his new love, Ben is forced into making a drastic decision...

Diamond Sky
By
David Clarkson

A group of scientists led by Dr Emmy Rayne has made the scientific breakthrough of the century. Their research into astral travelling has opened up the universe for exploration like never before. Unfortunately, not everyone on the team has the same agenda. The next phase testing is outsourced to the military and Emmy begins to fear that all her work to help mankind could be used to destroy it.

As the experiments begin to produce unexpected side effects, Emmy's only hope lies with a passing traveller, whose car has broken down, stranding her at the nearby town of Jackson's Hill. Lucy Skye is in mourning for her recently deceased father and their strong connection could provide the link that Emmy needs to reverse the damage done by her out-of-control technology.

Together, the two women must overcome a deadly combination of science and superstition in order to defeat a growing evil, which threatens not only this small outback town, but the fate of humanity itself…

Made in the USA
Monee, IL
25 May 2021